SNOW GHOST

*Other Five Star Titles
by Al Lacy:*

Legacy
Silent Abduction
Blizzard
Tears of the Sun
Circle of Fire
Quiet Thunder

JOURNEYS OF THE STRANGER

BOOK SEVEN

SNOW GHOST

AL LACY

Five Star
Unity, Maine

Five Star Christian Fiction Series.
Published in 2001 by arrangement with Multnomah Publishers, Inc.

Set in 11 pt. Plantin by Al Chase.

Printed in the United States on permanent paper.

Library of Congress Cataloging-in-Publication Data
Lacy, Al.
    Snow ghost / Al Lacy.
      p.   cm. — (Journeys of the stranger ; bk. 7)
    ISBN 0-7862-2949-7 (hc : alk. paper)
    1. Montana — Fiction. 2. Revenge — Fiction.
    3. Large type books. I. Title.
    PS3562.A256 S66 2001
    813'.54–dc21   00-049063

For Danae Jacobson, a very special young lady,
who reads all my novels.
We both share a deep admiration for horses . . .
especially for the magnificent black stallion
who appears in this book.
God bless you, Danae. I love you.
PHILIPPIANS 1:3

Cute Group 4/01

PROLOGUE

The last part of the nineteenth century in the Old West, with its furious broth of fur trappers, hardy pioneers, foul-smelling buffalo hunters, rugged lawmen, outlaws, avaricious prospectors, evil-eyed gamblers, trail-driving cowboys, and enigmatic Indians, has left behind countless legends and tales that never cease to fascinate us.

Ghost stories make up a large part of the Old West folklore. Today there are still places, remote from the bustle of city life, where old timers gather audiences around campfires at night and tell chilling tales of the Old West.

The landscape itself, with boundless panoramas of wilderness and open country—pocked by dead trees and weird rock formations, along with dark, stormy nights and howling blizzards—creates its own illusions and has spawned ghostly tales of every form.

The vibrant and violent times of the Old West have left behind a rich legacy of eerie stories and unsolved mysteries. The stories of outlaws killing innocent men, women, and children who came to the West seeking a better life; Indians massacring travelers in the wagon trains; lawmen and soldiers losing their lives while attempting to keep peace on a brawling frontier; gunfighters killing each other on dusty streets; and oftentimes innocent men hanged by angry or panic-driven lynch mobs laid the groundwork for chilling tales that live on in our day.

The myth and mystery of those wild days have it all: phantom herds that gallop across the endless western skies on hooves of fire; murdered men rising from the grave to exact justice on their killers; the specters of hanged men destined to stalk the plains, mountains, and deserts forever; and in Indian folklore, the snow ghosts—shadowy semblance of slain enemies back from the dead for vengeance.

Come, let us follow John Stranger, the mysterious man of the Old West, who carries a Bible in his saddlebags and a Colt .45 Peacemaker on his hip, as he encounters the snow ghost of Silver Bow County, Montana.

CHAPTER

ONE

The Montana sky hung low, its gunmetal gray clouds spitting tiny snowflakes stirred by a slight icy wind. It was colder than usual for November; sub-zero weather didn't usually hug the land until late December or early January. But in spite of the 18-below temperature, the citizens of Butte City moved busily about town.

Neighboring ranchers Dan Cogan and Clay Madison trotted their mounts into Butte City in early afternoon, turned onto Main Street, and headed north. They angled their horses to the hitch rail outside Kevane's Barber Shop and dismounted. The horses' nostrils sent plumes of vapor into the frigid air.

The hard snow crunched beneath the ranchers' boots as they rounded the hitch rail and mounted the steps to the boardwalk. Each breath of cold air was like a thin blade biting into their lungs.

Clay reached the door first. He turned the knob, pushed open the door, then bowed and swung his arm toward the interior, saying, "After you, pal. Age before beauty."

Dan laughed as they stepped into the welcome warmth. "Age before beauty, eh? You turned forty-six three weeks ago, and I won't be that old until March!"

Clay chuckled. "Well, you just look so much older than I do!"

Barber Eugene Kevane finished wrapping a hot towel around the face of the man in the barber chair. A white tonsorial cape covered the rest of him. Two other men sat in straight-backed chairs against the wall.

Eugene looked at the ranchers and smiled. "Don't you two ever stop jabbing at each other?"

Dan elbowed Clay, who was slipping out of his sheepskin coat. "If we quit pickin' on each other," he said, "we'd probably both get sick!"

The men on the straight-backed chairs grinned.

Clay and Dan greeted the seated men—Frank Cosgrove and Jackson DeLong. Cosgrove was owner of the Silver Bow Hotel, and DeLong was president of the Butte City Bank and chairman of the town council.

While Dan hung his coat and hat on a peg above the row of chairs, Clay Madison set his glance on the man in the barber's chair. "So who you got under the towel, Eugene? I don't recognize him by his boots."

"Young fella calls himself Herb Guthridge," Kevane said. "Just moved into town. He's now chief cook at the Meadowlark Café."

"Oh, yeah," Clay said, and nodded, heading for the warmth of the potbellied stove at the rear of the shop. "I did hear that ol' Mack Duffy was gonna retire and move south somewhere." Madison held his hands, palms down, over the top of the stove and addressed the man under the towel, "Welcome to Butte City, Herb. I'm Clay Madison. Own a ranch 'bout five miles east of town."

Dan passed the barber's chair on his way to the stove and said, "Let me say welcome too, Herb. I'm Dan Cogan. My ranch is three miles east of town."

Herb made a humming noise beneath the hot towel and waved a hand.

"Cold enough for you fellas?" Jackson DeLong said.

"Plenty," Dan said. "I had to use an ax to break the ice on my stock tank this mornin'."

Eugene spoke up. "Dan, Clay, you boys wantin' haircuts or shaves or both?"

"Just haircuts," Clay said for both of them.

"Shouldn't be too long then."

"No hurry," Dan said. "We've got time."

Jackson set his gaze on Dan and grinned. "Somebody told me Elaine got all of you she could take and up and left."

Dan chuckled, still holding his palms over the stove's heat.

"Yeah," Clay said. "I figured she'd do that one day. Must be miserable livin' with the likes of him!"

Dan and Clay looked at the newcomer as Eugene removed the towel and used a shaving brush to lather him for the razor.

"Well, Eugene," Clay said, "you didn't tell us this young fella was so handsome! You married, Herb?"

"Yes," he replied, giving them an uncertain look.

"Well, that'll probably disappoint the young single women in this town."

Herb blushed, and then grinned sheepishly.

No one spoke for several moments. Then Jackson said, "Speaking of Elaine, Dan, I heard she went somewhere about two weeks ago, but I never did hear why."

Dan turned around to warm his backside. "She's in Billings with our son and daughter-in-law. They're expecting their third child. Elaine is there to help out until the baby's born and Marie is back on her feet."

"Oh. Well, congratulations! The baby's due anytime, then?"

"According to her doctor's calculations . . . December fifth."

"Early Christmas present, eh?"

"Yeah. And what could be better? Best invention the Lord ever made is grandchildren!"

"Amen to that!" Eugene said. "Like the fella says, 'If I'd known grandchildren were so much fun, I'd have had them first'!"

"So, Dan, you doing your own cooking?" Frank Cosgrove asked.

"Most of the time. Isn't anything like Elaine's, but it beats starvin' to death."

When Eugene paused to strop the straight-edged razor again before finishing the shave, Herb said, "Come on over to the café this evening; I guarantee you'll like my cooking."

"Well, it just so happens that my pal Clay, here, has offered to buy me an early supper at the . . . ah . . . the *other* café, before we head home."

Herb sat up, a sly grin on his half-lathered face, eyes wide in mock surprise. "The *other* café? There is no other café in this town! Oh, I know what you're talking about. You mean you're going to eat at that hash house they call the Big Sky Café."

Herb eased back into the chair so that Eugene could finish shaving him, and said, "The only *real* café in Butte City is the Meadowlark, and you gentlemen must never forget that."

Dan moved close to the barber's chair. "How long have you been in town, Herb?" he asked.

"Don't move your mouth or I might cut you," Eugene said quickly. "I'll answer for you." The barber spoke over his shoulder to the other men. "He arrived here a week ago today. I know that because he came in on the stage that morning and went right to the Meadowlark. Merlin Loberg took one look at his shaggy hair and sent him over here to me. Merlin was afraid some of that long mop might fall into the soup!"

Herb waited till Eugene made the last stroke with the

razor, then said in his own defense, grinning all the while, "I wore my hair that way so people would think I was one of those fancy long-haired composers like Beethoven, Mozart, or Bach."

Frank laughed. "If you were one of them you'd have to be a ghost!"

"Yeah," Eugene said, as he wiped Herb's face with a damp towel, "but whoever heard of a ghost getting a shave?"

The sound of laughter in the barber shop grew even louder.

Before Eugene could lift the cape, Herb stood up and draped it over his head, saying, "No! I'm not the ghost of a composer . . . I'm the ghost of Payton Sturgis!"

The laughter died instantly and the barber shop seemed to echo with the sudden silence. Herb pulled the cape off his head and saw that his new acquaintances were not smiling. Their hard eyes and stony features made him stammer, "Did I . . . say something wrong?"

Jackson riveted Herb with piercing eyes. His voice sounded harsh as he said, "Where did you hear that name?"

"Why . . . ah . . . it was the stagecoach driver. When I was getting on the stage at Billings he told me that some guy named Payton Sturgis was hanged for murder here a couple of years ago, and that before they hanged him he promised to come back and kill everybody who was responsible for hanging him. I . . . I didn't know his name would upset you men. Everybody knows dead men don't come back to life. I . . . I thought it would be something you'd laugh at."

Eugene laid a hand on the man's shoulder. "Well, Herb, now you know. Even mentioning the name *Payton Sturgis* is something you don't want to do. Everybody in this town would just as soon forget they ever heard of him."

Herb took a deep breath and let it out slowly. "Yes, sir,"

he said, "I see that. And believe me, it won't happen again."

"You didn't know, Herb," Dan said. "No hard feelings."

Herb quickly donned his hat, put on his coat and gloves, and hurried out the door.

The five men stood in silence for a moment, then Frank cleared his throat nervously and said, "Poor kid. How was he to know? I wish that stage driver would keep his mouth shut."

There was another moment of uncomfortable silence, then Eugene said, "Well, Frank, you're next. Let's get your hair cut."

The snow was coming down harder now, and a stiff breeze blew as Clay Madison and Dan Cogan trotted their mounts east in the fading light of day.

Payton Sturgis's name hadn't crossed their lips since leaving the Meadowlark Café where they'd eaten supper to show Herb Guthridge they were his friends.

The Cogan ranch, with its two-story house, barn, and out-buildings, seemed to huddle together in the storm. As they drew near the gate, Dan eyed his cattle and horses in the corral and said, "Feeding time, and they know it. Thanks for the meal, Clay. My turn next time."

"And I won't forget it."

"You never do!" Dan veered his animal toward the gate. "See you soon."

"You bet," Clay said, then pulled rein. "Dan—" he called after his friend.

Dan halted and turned in the saddle, waiting for Clay to speak.

"You're not gonna let the reminder of the Sturgis thing bother you, are you?"

"Nah. I'll be fine."

"You sure?"

Dan forced a grin. "Payton is dead and buried, Clay."

"Okay. See you in a day or two." Madison put his horse to a fast trot home.

When Dan hauled up at the back porch of his house and dismounted, he could see winking lantern lights starting to appear in windows on the east edge of Butte City. They flickered at him through the falling, swirling snow.

He went inside and lit a lantern, then built a fire in the potbellied stove in the parlor. In the kitchen, at the rear of the house, he set the lighted lantern on the cupboard. It was almost dark when he went outside and led his horse toward the barn. The other four horses in the corral nickered, their long faces hanging over the split-rail fence. The cattle huddled silently behind them.

As he got near the barn, his attention was drawn to the dense woods. He wiped snow from his eyelashes and studied the movement of the falling snow against the dark backdrop of shadows in the wind-whipped trees.

Were his eyes playing tricks on him, or did he see the silhouetted figure of a man move from behind one tree to another? He kept his gaze trained on the trees until it seemed there were numerous figures moving among them.

Dan shook his head and chided himself. "C'mon, Cogan," he said aloud. "There's no one out there. It's just your imagination."

Dan knew that to stare into the wind-stirred snow against the shadows of the forest could create the illusion of human figures moving among the trees. Like just now. It sure seemed the first figure he had seen was the real thing. He grinned to himself and said, "Snow ghosts."

He led his horse toward the barn and told himself that some old Crow medicine man probably came up with the snow ghost idea centuries ago. To actually believe that those

15

illusory figures—ducking and darting between the trees—were the ghosts of vengeful enemies was nothing more than an overactive imagination.

"Come on, boy," Dan said to his gelding, "let's get you and your pals inside the barn for supper."

When his hand touched the latch of the barn door, he caught movement to his left. He jerked his head that way, and there at the edge of the woods, amid the whirlpool of falling snow in the last light of day, he was sure he saw a man dart from one tree to another.

Dan swallowed hard, riveting his gaze on the second tree. There was no more movement at that spot, but again he saw the shifting figures amid the other trees.

Why did Herb Guthridge have to bring up Payton Sturgis! In the past few months, Dan had been able to go sometimes a week or more without the thought of that heartless killer entering his mind. And now Payton's memory was there to haunt him again. For an instant the scene at the gallows when Payton stood with the rope around his neck, threatening to return from the grave, captured his mind.

"No!" he said, shaking his head. "No! When a man dies, he *stays* dead! Get a grip on yourself, Dan! You're letting your imagination run away with you!"

He forced himself to stand there and study the images among the trees as the wind continued to whip the falling snow.

He thought about how the Crow had been controlled by fear of the supernatural. He knew that sometimes the Crow warriors, eager to rid themselves of the eerie enemy stalkers, had pursued them deep into the forests during snowstorms, only to be found frozen to death days later. Those who found them blamed the snow ghosts.

Dan led the horse inside the barn. He lit a lantern, removed the saddle and bridle from the gelding, and brought the other animals in. He left the door to the corral open so they could come and go as they pleased after feeding time. He filled the troughs with oats and hay, then doused the lantern and left the barn.

It was completely dark now, so he used the glow of the lantern in the kitchen window to guide him through the whirling snow. The wind slashing across the fields and hills in powerful gusts sent stinging ice pellets into his face, and the night's cold embrace chilled him to the bone.

Dan held his hat against the wind and slogged through the drifts along the path to the house, his mind on Elaine and the new grandchild Marie would soon bring into the world, until he reached the back porch. Suddenly he felt a presence that sent tingles through him and made the hair on the back of his neck stand up.

A second later he saw something move at the corner of the house. He squinted at the spot. All he saw was the whirling snow in the glow of the lantern. Okay, he thought, just a trick. I've had Payton on my mind, and it's spooking me.

He started up the porch steps and caught a flash of movement at the edge of the house again. He sucked in a sharp breath, his heart beginning to pound. It took him a few seconds to find his voice. "Hey! Who's there? Make yourself known!"

The wind whined and the snow whirled. Then the dark form of a hatless man eased around the edge of the house, keeping to the shadows, and halted.

Dan's voice trembled as he peered into the darkness and called out, "Come out into the light where I can see you! Who are you? What do you want?"

The figure remained in the shadows but spoke above the whine of the wind in a silky, sibilant voice. "You know who I am, Dan! I told you and the others I would come back!"

"I don't know who you are! Come out here into the light and state your business!"

"You *do* know who I am, and you know my business is to take you into the dark regions of death, where you sent me, Dan! I told you I would come back to get you! I'll eventually get every man responsible for my death!"

"No! I saw Payton Sturgis die at the end of that rope! I saw him buried! Now who are you, and what do you want?"

"It's time, Dan," the man said, emerging from the shadows and halting in the lantern light from the kitchen window. He angled his face toward the light, and Dan could see the wind pluck at the man's blond hair.

Dan Cogan's blood turned to ice. A sharp pain lanced through his chest.

CHAPTER

TWO

Butte City, which lay west of the Continental Divide, was surrounded by gold, silver, and zinc mines. Its mile-high altitude always brought plenty of snow and arctic air in the winter. This winter would be no different, Clay Madison told himself as he drove toward town.

Clay scanned the hills and fields. He squinted against the brilliance of the midmorning sun reflected off the thickly carpeted snow. Except for the whisper of a biting wind, he found himself gazing into a silent world of mounded whiteness.

The fields and hills were frozen into eerie stillness. Naked trees, frostbitten and coated with a crust of ice, reached up toward the sun with their skeletal fingers, begging for warmth.

Clay could tell that no one had been along the road since the three-day snowstorm had passed forty-eight hours before. His horses broke trail through the sixteen-inch drifts, their muscular chests and shoulders pressed into the harness and their heads bent low as they pulled the wagon.

The temperature must be way below zero, Clay thought, as he listened to the crunch of snow beneath the wheels and the horses' hooves, and the pistol-like popping sound of frozen tree limbs in the wind. Every so often the wind gusted over the white landscape, making snow-devils around the wagon and tossing ice crystals into his face.

On his way to town, Madison planned to stop and check on Dan Cogan to see if he'd heard anything from Elaine. As he drew near the Cogan place, he was puzzled to see no sign of smoke rising from either chimney. His wonder increased as he drew near the gate and saw no tracks in the snow. Neither were there tracks leading from the house to the barn or any of the other outbuildings.

Strange.

He guided his puffing team of horses through the gate and aimed their noses toward the back side of the house. The area around the house was unbroken by any footprints or animal tracks. Clay drew rein at the back porch and saw that the snow on the porch floor hadn't been disturbed. He looked toward the corral. He could see Dan's horses standing together, heads protruding over the top rungs of the split-rail fence. They whinnied at him, and the cattle beyond them bawled.

Clay eased down from the wagon seat, his boots sinking deep into the snow. He mounted the snow-covered porch steps and knocked on the door. When no one responded, he knocked harder and called, "Dan! Hey, Dan! It's Clay! You in there?"

Silence.

Madison turned the knob and entered the kitchen. It was as cold inside the house as it was outside. His breath hung heavy in the air. "Dan! It's Clay! You in here?"

He closed the kitchen door and noticed that the water in the drinking pail was frozen solid. He moved toward the lantern on a small table by the window and picked it up. The lantern had burned until it ran out of fuel.

He glanced at the pegs where Dan always hung his coat and hat near the back door. The hat hung in place, but the coat wasn't there.

Clay set down the lantern and walked toward the parlor. When he reached Elaine's sewing room, he paused and looked inside, but it was unoccupied. The formal dining room and the parlor were just as empty.

Clay lifted his hat and ran shaky fingers through his graying hair, then headed toward the stairs to the second floor. The frozen steps creaked under his weight as he climbed, calling, "Dan! Can you hear me? It's Clay!"

Quiet as a tomb, he thought, then shook his head impatiently at his choice of words.

He moved slowly down the hall past the spare bedrooms and paused at each door to look inside. No one there. He looked toward the last door on the right, Dan and Elaine's bedroom. As with the other rooms, the door stood open. Better check there too, he thought.

Clay's heart seemed to freeze in his chest at the sight before him. His scalp prickled and tiny stinging needles ran down his spine.

Dan Cogan lay on the bed, still in his coat. His skin—a cold bleached white—was startling in its brittle, frozen appearance. His eyes bulged, glassy and vacant, and his mouth was locked in an open silent scream.

Clay's eyes misted, and his voice was a rasp deep in his throat as he half-whispered, "Oh, Dan! What was it you saw?"

Without touching his friend's body, Clay looked it over for signs of any wounds. He couldn't see any, and there was no blood anywhere. He dashed to the bedroom across the hall, jerked the spread off the bed, and hurried back to place it over the body. His last glimpse of Dan's eyes sent a shiver through him.

He looked around the room. No sign of a struggle. Had Dan died elsewhere and been carried to the bedroom and

21

placed on the bed? No wounds. No blood. No marks or bruises on his neck.

When Clay swung his gaze around the room the second time he saw a sheet of paper lying on the dresser with a pencil beside it, its lead tip broken. He picked up the paper, and as he read, his face turned ghostly pale:

Dan Cogan is only the first to die. I will get even with the others as I swore I would before they hanged me. None shall escape. I will take every one into the dark regions of death with me.

Payton Sturgis

Doomed men:
Dan Cogan
Darrell Amick
Eugene Kevane
George Walz
Jackson DeLong
Frank Cosgrove
Les Osborne
Tom McVicker
T. J. Pederson
Darwin Smith
Milo Wilson
Lawton Haymes
Judge Virgil Reed
Sheriff Lake Johnson
John Stranger

The letters spelling the name *John Stranger* were darker than the others and almost illegible. Madison noticed that the last *r* was not quite finished. Then he realized that's when the pencil lead had broken.

Sheriff Lake Johnson, a beefy man in his mid-fifties, added wood to the stove in his office as he talked with his new deputy, Monte Dixon. Dixon had been deputy sheriff of Silver Bow County for exactly one week now. The twenty-five-year-old lawman had grown up in Scottsbluff and served as deputy marshal there until coming to Butte City.

Dixon stood close to the stove with a steaming cup of coffee in his hand. "I thought Nebraska was cold, Sheriff," he said. "That was nothing compared to this. Will it stay this cold for the rest of the winter?"

Johnson chuckled as he dropped the last piece of wood into the stove and replaced the cast-iron lid. "Oh, no. It'll get worse come January."

Dixon grinned and shook his head. "You're just full of good news, boss. I should've taken that job down in Tucson."

Johnson poured himself a cup of coffee and rubbed a hand over his thick mustache, and smiled. "Well, you'd probably be facin' more hungry gun muzzles and chasin' more outlaws right now. Our crime rate stays real low in winter. Even the bad guys stay in where it's warm."

"All of 'em?"

Johnson cleared his throat. "Well, no. Not all of 'em. We get a bad dude now and then who isn't deterred by ice, snow, and cold. But in Tucson they don't get any breaks at all."

Dixon drained his cup. "Well, I think I like it here best. In Scottsbluff we had a lot of bank and stagecoach robbers and gunfighters comin' through twelve months of the year. It'll be a nice change for me to just settle back and—"

Dixon's words were interrupted by a rider sliding and skidding to a stop in front of the office. Sheriff Johnson set his coffee cup on the desk and peered through the condensation

23

on the window. "Looks like Clay Madison—and he looks upset."

The sheriff moved to the door and opened it just as Clay crossed the snow-crusted boardwalk. Inside, Clay glanced toward Dixon and pulled a folded sheet of paper from inside his coat with shaky fingers. "Sheriff," he said, "something awful has happened! Dan Cogan's dead! I found this slip of paper next to his body!"

"Hold on, Clay," Johnson said, laying a hand on the man's arm. "Get a grip on yourself. You're tellin' me you found Dan dead?"

Clay took a ragged breath and scrubbed a hand over his face. "I found him dead on his bed. No sign of a struggle, but Payton found a way to kill him, anyway. He—"

"*Payton?* What are you talkin' about?" Johnson gripped the frightened rancher's arm. "Now just hold on a second. Come over here and sit down."

"I don't want to sit down, Sheriff. You've got to come with me and see for yourself! Payton Sturgis has done exactly what he said he would do! He's back, and—"

"Hold on, I said! What's this Payton Sturgis stuff?"

"Read the paper, will you?" urged the frightened rancher.

"All right. But I wish you'd sit down. By the way, Clay, this is my new deputy, Monte Dixon."

"Mr. Madison," Dixon said, and nodded.

Clay Madison returned the nod but didn't say anything.

Lake Johnson's eyes widened as he read the message and Dixon looked at him expectantly.

It was the sheriff's turn to go pale. He turned puzzled eyes to Clay and said, "This . . . this is preposterous! You and I both saw Payton Sturgis die at the end of a rope! We were there when Ivan Charles nailed the lid on the coffin, and we watched it lowered into the ground and saw the grave filled in. Dead men don't climb out of their graves!"

"Excuse me, Sheriff," Dixon said, "just who was Payton Sturgis?"

"I'll explain it later, Monte," Lake said. He folded the paper and placed it in the top drawer of his desk. "Right now we need to get out to the Cogan place." He shook his head and added, "This is gonna be rough on Elaine."

"Can you at least tell me what's on that paper, Sheriff?" Monte asked.

"Yes, but it'll make more sense to you when you know the whole story. Payton Sturgis was a cold-blooded killer in this town. We hanged him. Just before I dropped the trapdoor from under his feet, he swore to come back from the grave and kill every man responsible for his arrest and hanging. I'll let you see the paper later, but it's a message that says he's back to fulfill his threat. Dan Cogan was the first to die. The list of 'doomed men,' as the writer put it, is on that paper, and it's signed, *Payton Sturgis.*"

"Are you on that list, Sheriff?"

"Yeah . . . let's go, Monte." As they stepped outside, Lake turned to Clay. "I want to take Doc Bristow with us if he can go. He needs to take a look at the body."

Clay nodded.

The sheriff laid a hand on his shoulder. "Listen to me, Clay. This *isn't* Payton. I know you're upset and all, but get it out of your mind that Payton is back."

Clay pulled his lips into a thin line and nodded again.

Lake Johnson and his deputy mounted their horses, which stood at the hitch rail, and rode alongside Clay's wagon as they headed down the street. The sun was shining brightly from a cobalt blue sky, but it seemed to withhold its heat, for the air was crisp and frigid.

As they drew up in front of the doctor's office, Lake slid

from his saddle and said, "I'll run in and see if Doc can go with us. I'd rather you boys kept Dan's death to yourselves for now. You haven't told anyone else about it, have you, Clay?"

"No, sir. I took time to feed Dan's stock, then rode hard for town. Nobody else knows."

Lake gave a quick nod and disappeared into the doctor's office.

While they waited in the freezing cold, Monte asked, "Did this Sturgis kill a lot of people, Mr. Madison?"

"Yeah. If you consider nine a lot."

"Nine? He murdered *nine* people?"

"Yep."

"He some kind of maniac?"

"Might say that."

A buggy drew near with a short, pudgy man at the reins. He smiled, lifted a hand, and said, "Howdy, Clay . . . Monte."

"Mornin', Judge," both men said in unison.

When Judge Virgil Reed had passed from earshot, Monte said, "I assume his name's on the list, too."

"Just above the sheriff's."

"You . . . ah . . . don't really believe this Sturgis is back, do you?"

Madison paused for a long moment, then said, "No, it's impossible."

The door of the office opened, and the sheriff emerged with Dr. Paul Bristow on his heels, carrying his little black medical bag. Both men were almost the same age, but the doctor's hair was totally silver, whereas Lake still had some "pepper" in his thinning hair.

The doctor walked to the side of Madison's wagon and climbed up. "This is awful, Clay," he said. "You're sure Dan's dead?"

"You'll see. I guarantee you won't need that bag!"

As the horses plodded through the deep snow, Dr. Bristow turned to Lake, who rode beside him, and said, "You mentioned a piece of paper left with Dan's body. What was on it?"

When Lake had quoted the message verbatim, the doctor thought for a long moment, then turned to Madison. "Clay, Lake said you told him there was no sign of a struggle."

"That's right."

The doctor tugged the collar of his coat a little tighter. "No sign in or around the house?"

"Nowhere. The only tracks outside the house are mine. The house is in order and as clean and orderly as Elaine always keeps it."

"Did you examine the body for a wound?"

"I didn't roll him over, but from what I could see he had no wounds and no bruises or marks of any kind. There was no blood anywhere. I'm no doctor, but it sure looks to me like he died of fright."

"Fright?"

"Yes, sir. When you see him you'll understand."

The tracks in the snow at the Cogan place were exactly as Clay Madison had said. The horses and cattle looked on from the corral as the four men alighted and made their way to the back porch of the house.

"The body's upstairs," Clay said, as he opened the kitchen door and led the way to the staircase.

The frozen stairs popped and complained as the four men climbed to the second floor. They moved down the hall with Clay in the lead. "Bedroom's the last door on the right," he said. "I covered the body, Doc. Didn't think I should leave it exposed."

"Fine," Bristow said as he set his medical bag on the bedstead.

The lawmen rounded the bed and stood on the far side. Their breath hung in small clouds in the cold room.

Dr. Bristow reached inside his overcoat and put on his wire-rimmed half-moon spectacles before slowly pulling back the cover from the body. The men gasped at the sight of Cogan's face.

Monte Dixon had seen dead men before, but nothing like this. Lake Johnson wanted to turn away but kept his eyes focused on the body. He felt a keen sense of shock and horror.

The men stood around the bed without saying a word as Dr. Bristow examined the corpse. "Frozen stiff," he said. He tried to close the wide-open mouth, but it wouldn't budge. The open eyelids too were frozen in place.

The doctor looked the body over carefully, seeking any sign of a rip or tear in the clothing to indicate a wound. When he found none, he said, "Will you men help me turn him over?"

They all three gingerly grasped the frozen corpse and turned it over. When Bristow was satisfied there were no punctures, he had the men return the body to its former position.

"Well, gentlemen," the doctor said, "there's no indication of any violence at all. Another possibility is some kind of poison, but—"

"That's not stomach pain showing on his face, Doc," Lake said.

"Exactly what I was going to say," Bristow said. "That leaves only one possibility."

"Heart failure," Clay said.

The physician nodded in agreement. "I can come to no

other conclusion but that Dan's heart simply stopped beating."

"But why?" Monte asked.

Bristow looked at him over the top of his half-moon spectacles. "Just as Clay said on the way out here—fright. Something Dan saw scared him so much that it stopped his heart."

"But what could do that?"

The doctor's features were grim as he said, "The face of the man who wrote what's on that paper and signed it Payton Sturgis."

"Then he's an impostor!" Lake said in a choked voice. "Somebody's made himself up to look like Payton. And for some unknown reason he's wantin' to kill every one of us who brought about Payton's execution."

"Looks like we've got our bad dude, Sheriff," Monte said.

Lake gave the deputy a blank look.

"You were telling me at the office that we get a bad dude now and then who isn't deterred by the snow and cold."

"Well, we've got one now, that's for sure."

"I'd like to hear about this Payton Sturgis. You said you'd tell me about him later . . ."

Lake rubbed the back of his neck and released some tension in a gusty breath. "Okay," he said. "You ever heard of a mysterious man who rides the West, called John Stranger?"

"Sure. Who hasn't?"

"Well, it was Stranger who caught Payton Sturgis after he'd taken the lives of nine people. Stranger brought Sturgis to me, and I put him under arrest and jailed him. The twelve-man jury convicted him, and Judge Reed sentenced him to hang. I put the noose around his neck and pulled the lever that dropped him to his death. So whoever's impersonatin' him seems to want revenge."

Clay shook his head in confusion. "But it's been two years,

Sheriff. Whoever this impersonator is, why would he wait so long to get revenge?"

Lake shook his head as if to say he hadn't a clue.

"And another thing," Clay said. "Dan knew what Payton looked like. How could any man make himself up to look exactly like Payton? Dan is dead because he thought he was looking into the face of the man who said he would come back from the grave and kill him!"

"I won't argue that point," Lake said. "But I'm tellin' you, Clay, our deadly visitor isn't Payton come back from the dead."

"So why try to make us think he's Payton?"

"Scare tactic," the doctor said. "What else could it be? He sure scared poor Dan."

Lake Johnson sighed. "Let's put the body in your wagon and take it to Ivan. Then I'll send a wire to Elaine in Billings. I'm glad she'll have her son and daughter-in-law with her when she gets the news."

"When do we let the rest of the town know about Dan, Sheriff?" Dixon asked.

Lake thought for a moment, then said, "The thing I'm concerned about is panic. Once this is out, the people will be scared out of their wits. Especially those men whose names are on the list—and their families."

"You can't keep it a secret for long, Sheriff," the doctor said. "Say, for instance, when Elaine gets the telegram, she wires Pastor Walker to make funeral arrangements."

"I was plannin' on tellin' the pastor about it today," Lake said. "I know we can't keep the lid on it long, but I'd like to let the men on the list know first. Ivan can keep it under his hat till then."

The four men carried Dan Cogan's body down the stairs and out the back door. They placed it in Clay's wagon and headed back to town.

CHAPTER

THREE

The bone-chilling wind knifed through the men's coats as they escorted Dan Cogan's body to town. It flapped their hat brims and snatched at their upturned collars with icy fingers, then eased off, as if not quite ready to release its full fury across the land.

Doc Bristow glanced at the cold sun in the southern sky, then back to the approaching storm and announced, "Looks like more snow on the way, boys."

"Just what we need," Lake Johnson said, pulling down his hat more tightly.

The doctor had been studying Clay Madison, who was seated beside him, all the way from the Cogan ranch. Clay remained lost in his own disturbing thoughts. Although he had seemed to agree with the sheriff that this was not the work of the ghost of Payton Sturgis, Bristow could see the man was filled with fear. The doctor couldn't help feeling a pang of dread himself, for Clay was right when he'd said no man could make himself look enough like Sturgis to have fooled Dan Cogan.

As they entered town the doctor said, "Fellas, I'll just have you leave me off at my office. No reason for me to go with you to Ivan's place."

Clay came back to the present with an effort and glanced at the doctor. "All right, Doc," he said.

Lake Johnson reminded Clay they would need to stop at the office, after dropping off the doctor, to pick up the note. He wanted to show it to Ivan.

Just the mention of the note chilled Clay's blood. He nodded, but didn't reply.

Ivan Charles's place of business was a single two-story building at the north end of Main Street. It was divided into two sections on the ground floor. One side was a carpentry shop and the other was an undertaking parlor. There was a door between the two sections, which provided easy access for Ivan and his hired man, Bill Pollard.

Ivan was a tall rawboned man of forty-five. He was quite slender, with a head of thick coal-black hair. He had protruding cheekbones above sunken cheeks and deep-set eyes that were hooded with heavy black eyebrows. He had a jutting, pointed chin and big ears. People had often told him he reminded them of Abraham Lincoln.

Ivan and his assistant were in the carpentry shop, making a kitchen table, when they looked up to see Sheriff Johnson enter the open doorway between the shops.

"Good afternoon, Sheriff," Ivan said in his deep voice.

"Afternoon, Ivan . . . Bill."

"What can I do for you, Sheriff?" Ivan asked.

"I need to talk to you in private, if I may."

"Certainly. My office all right?"

"Yes," Lake said, running his gaze to the stack of coffins in a back corner. The scent of fresh-cut wood filled the air.

Lake followed Ivan into the funeral parlor. As Ivan headed for his office, Lake said in a low voice, "No need to go any farther, Ivan. I didn't want Bill to hear my business with you just yet."

"What kind of business, Sheriff?"

"Something very strange. Clay Madison's wagon is out back with a body in it. I decided the back door would be best. You'll see why in a moment."

"Who's the dead person?"

"Dan Cogan."

Ivan, who had been heading for the back door, stopped abruptly, his eyes widening in shock. "*Dan?* What happened?"

"Complicated story. Clay and my deputy are out here with the body. Let's bring it in, then I'll tell you about it."

"Is Elaine still in Billings?" Ivan asked.

"Yes. I'm sending her a wire when I leave here."

"Poor woman. It's going to be tough on her."

Ivan stopped beside the door long enough to shoulder into his heavy coat and don his hat. He flipped the latch and pushed the door open, allowing Johnson to exit first.

Clay and Monte stood in the deep snow next to the wagon, stomping their feet and working their arms to keep warm. Ivan leaned over the side of the wagon and reached for the edge of the bedspread.

Lake quickly looked up and down the alley before saying, "I don't want anybody to see his face, Ivan. Gotta keep this under wraps for a little while. I don't even want Bill Pollard to know yet."

"Okay. Let's get the body inside."

The four men carried the body through the back door, and as Ivan instructed, they placed it on an embalming table in the back room. There was a potbellied stove in the room, which gave off welcome heat.

Ivan took hold of the spread and pulled it off the corpse. When he saw the bulging eyes and open mouth, his head bobbed and his body stiffened. Then he leaned close over the head and touched his thumb to an eyelid. "Frozen," he said.

"Once the body thaws, if the eyes won't close, I'll stitch them shut. I may have to do the same with the mouth." Abruptly he turned to the sheriff. "Now, tell me what happened."

Lake asked Clay to tell the story up to the point when he entered the sheriff's office to report Cogan's death, then he took over.

When Lake had finished, Ivan asked, "Do you have the note with you? I'd like to see the handwriting."

Johnson pulled the folded sheet of paper from an inside pocket. "I'll tell you right now, it can't possibly be Payton's handwriting."

Charles took the paper and unfolded it. As he studied the script, he looked more shaken than when he'd looked on the corpse. He touched a trembling palm to his forehead. "Gentlemen, it *is* Payton's handwriting!"

"Impossible!" Lake said.

"Oh, but it is Payton's, Sheriff. I have work orders in my file in the storage room that he wrote up when he worked for me. I remember exactly what his handwriting looks like."

"I want to see those work orders!"

"All right," Ivan said. "I'll be back in a few minutes."

When the undertaker was gone, Lake said, "Fellas, he's got to be mistaken."

No one responded for a moment, then Monte said, "So Ivan came here after Payton did? Is that right?"

"Yes," Clay said. "Probably about six months later, wouldn't you say, Sheriff?"

"Yep. Just about that."

"But didn't the town already have an undertaker?"

"It did," Lake said. "Ivan came here and opened up the carpentry shop. Our undertaker, Walton Beemer, died shortly after that. Because Ivan had once worked for an undertaker back East and knew the business, he took over as undertaker, then bought this building and set it up the way it is."

"Since Payton was around town doing odd jobs," Clay added, "and Ivan needed an assistant, he hired Payton to work full time in both businesses. He taught Payton how to embalm and prepare a body for burial, and he taught him carpentry."

Ivan entered the room, carrying a small box. He set it on the table next to the dead man's feet and opened the lid. "The work orders are right here, Sheriff," he said, riffling through the papers. "It was a real jolt to me, Monte, when I learned that Payton had murdered all those people."

"You never suspected him at all?"

"Not in the least. He seemed to be such a nice young man. Hard worker. Always did well at whatever task I gave him."

"Payton always got along good with everyone in Butte City," Clay said. "None of us would have believed he was the murderer if John Stranger hadn't come up with the proof."

"Here they are," Ivan said, pulling a small stack of work orders from the box. He spread them out on the table. "You'll note the dates on these are 1868 and 1869." Then he picked up the note found on Dan Cogan's dresser and placed it next to the orders.

Lake drew in a sharp breath. "This can't be! It just can't be!"

"Well, it *is*, Sheriff," Ivan said. "The handwriting is exactly the same, including the signature, which is unique. Be mighty hard to forge that."

A chill filled the room in spite of the warmth from the stove.

Ivan spoke with a quiver in his voice. "Sheriff, you said Doc Bristow concluded that Dan died of heart failure brought on by fright."

"That's what he said."

Clay sucked in a shaky breath and looked at Ivan. "What do you think? Is it possible for a man to make himself look like Payton? I mean—enough to fool Dan?"

Ivan didn't answer immediately. Instead he looked down at the papers.

Clay persisted. "And is it possible for some living man to duplicate the handwriting of a dead man and to perfectly forge his signature? Especially one as unique as Payton's?"

Ivan rubbed his bony forehead. "Clay, I . . . I want to say that the answer to both of your questions is no. But I can't. I don't understand this at all. It has me mystified. I have to say it would be very unlikely for a man who looked like Payton to fool Dan. He had been face-to-face with Payton dozens of times. It's even more impossible—if such an adjective is allowed—for anyone to so perfectly duplicate Payton's handwriting—and even *more* so, to duplicate his signature."

"Are you saying, Ivan, that Payton's ghost has returned?" Clay said.

The undertaker ran splayed fingers through his thick, black hair. "I don't know how to answer you. My common sense tells me there has to be a rational explanation. But something deeper—something inside me that I can't describe—tells me that Payton, or his ghost, is among us."

Monte looked baffled. "But Ivan, does a ghost have a physical body? I mean, how does a ghost pick up pencil and paper and write a message?"

"I'm an undertaker, Monte. I've never even believed in ghosts. I can't answer your question. I'm plenty confused right now, myself. These papers—the handwriting, the signatures—what other conclusion is there? What do you think, Sheriff?"

Lake Johnson's craggy features reflected the perplexity that showed in his voice as he replied, "I . . . I have to say that no matter what it looks like, there is no ghost among us. I can't explain what we've seen here, but when a man dies, he stays dead. The soul goes to heaven if he knows Christ, and it goes to hell if he doesn't. There's no coming back from either place."

Ivan's hands trembled. His face twisted with fear. "I'm going out to the graveyard."

"What for?" Lake asked.

"I want to look at Payton's grave—make sure it's intact."

"I'll go with you, Ivan," Monte said.

Clay nodded. "Me, too."

The sheriff said flatly, "You're not gonna find anything wrong at the grave. Payton's body is still six feet under. Dead men don't come back. I'm tellin' you boys, this handwritin' thing has to have a rational explanation."

"Is it all right if I go with them, Sheriff?" Monte asked.

"Sure, if it will satisfy your curiosity. I'm going to the telegraph office and send the wire to Elaine. You head on back to the office when you've found the undisturbed grave, Monte. I'll see you there after I tell my pastor about Dan."

"Yes, sir."

As Lake Johnson rode down Main Street toward the Western Union office, a shudder racked his body unrelated to the icy wind. His mind replayed the terrified look on Dan Cogan's face. He shook the vision from his mind, and it was replaced with the note and the handwriting evidence Ivan Charles had produced.

A worm of doubt wriggled its way through his mind, leaving a trail of terror and uncertainty. Not since John Stranger had led him to Christ two years ago, and he had become a member of the church in Butte City, had he experienced such anxiety and confusion. He needed to talk to his pastor. There had to be an answer to this horrid situation.

Lake dismounted in front of the Western Union office and spoke to a couple walking by before entering. Telegrapher Wally Simms looked up from his desk behind the counter as Johnson entered. Wally was in his late sixties, and wore the traditional green visor and arm garters. His upper front teeth were missing, which caused him to speak with a lisp. He rose from the desk to meet Lake at the counter and grinned his toothless smile. "Howdy, Sheriff. Gonna get us another snowstorm, looks like."

"Feels like it's already in my bones," Lake said.

"Sendin' a message, Sheriff, or expectin' one?"

"I'm sendin' one I don't want to send, Wally," Lake said, as he picked up a pencil and started writing on the pad provided. When he finished the message, he turned the pad toward the telegrapher.

Wally smiled and picked it up. "Okay," he said, letting his eyes take in the message. "I'll get this right on the wi—" His head came up, eyes blinking. "Dan Cogan dead! What happened?"

"Long story. You'll get all the details once I go public with it. Right now, all Elaine needs to know is there in the message. I know you're sworn never to reveal anything you wire, but I want to make sure you understand: Keep Dan's death to yourself till I tell you different. Got it?"

"Yes, sir. Mum's the word, Sheriff. Man, I sure am sorry about Dan."

"Me, too. Just put it on my office bill as usual, Wally. See you later."

Pastor Bob Walker had come to Butte City five years before, at the age of thirty-one, and founded the only church. This tough mining town proved to be somewhat antagonistic toward the gospel, but Walker and his wife, Phyllis, prayed hard and put feet to their prayers by going from house to house. Their sweet spirits shone through when they were turned away, sometimes in anger, and little by little the Spirit of God did a work in hearts and drew many people to the Lord Jesus Christ. Now the church was flourishing, and new converts were added regularly.

The parsonage was on the same property as the church at the south end of Main Street. Phyllis answered Lake Johnson's knock and smiled at her visitor. "Hello, Sheriff. Come in out of that wind."

The four Walker children were playing a game on the parlor floor, and paused to greet Johnson.

The sheriff returned the greeting, then said, "Is the preacher here?"

"He's over at the church—in his office."

"Is it all right if I go knock on his door?"

"Certainly. He's studying, but he'll be glad to see you."

Moments later Pastor Walker was welcoming Lake into his office. Lake could see an open Bible on the desk, along with some papers and a couple of letters.

"Pastor, I'm sorry to bother you, but I have somethin' very important to tell you, and to talk about."

"Hey, my friend, I'm your pastor. When one of my members needs to talk to me, they *get* to talk to me. Take off your coat and sit down."

Johnson hung his hat and coat on a clothes tree near the door and took a chair in front of the desk. Walker opened the door of the small stove in the corner, tossed in a log, and returned to his chair behind the desk. "Now, what do you want to talk to me about, Lake? You look troubled."

"I *am* troubled, Pastor. It's in regard to Dan Cogan."

"Something happen? It's not Marie's baby, is it?"

"No, sir. It's Dan. He's dead."

Walker's face blanched. "Dead? What do you mean? What happened?"

Lake Johnson told the preacher every detail of Dan Cogan's death, how they had compared the note signed *Payton Sturgis* with the handwriting on the work orders, and that Doc Bristow's professional opinion was that Dan had died of fright.

Walker's face was grim as Lake finished the story and eased back in his chair. "Pastor, I need some answers. Ivan and Clay seem convinced that Payton has come back from the dead. Monte is on the edge of it. I told them I couldn't explain it, but I knew that when a man dies, he stays dead. He goes to heaven if he knows the Lord, and he goes to hell if he doesn't. There's no coming back from either place."

"That's right," Walker said.

"Even before I was saved, Pastor, I didn't believe in ghosts. But this has me baffled. I saw the handwriting. And I saw Dan's face frozen in a mask of terror. You heard Payton promise to come back from the dead and get every one of us who had anything to do with his execution. Tell me, is this possible?"

Pastor Walker shook his head slowly and said, "No, it's not possible. According to Scripture, dead men don't raise themselves from the grave.

"In Bible days, people were raised from the dead, by the power of God, through a prophet or an apostle—or by Jesus Himself. But since the Scriptures were completed, those kind of miracles ceased. Through effectual, fervent prayer we see sick people made well as promised in James 5:13–15, but God's written Word is His only manifestation today."

Pastor Walker picked up his Bible and flipped pages until he came to John 10. "Look at what it says, here, Lake." He turned the Bible so Johnson could see it. "Read me what Jesus said of Himself in verses 17 and 18."

Lake read,

> Therefore doth my Father love me, because I lay down my life, that I might take it again. No man taketh it from me, but I lay it down of myself. I have power to lay it down, and I have power to take it again. This commandment have I received of my Father.

Lake raised his eyes and met his pastor's gaze. "Says here, not only did Jesus say He had power to lay His life down, but He had power to raise Himself from the dead."

"That's it, Lake. The only Person who ever had the power to come back from the dead is the Lord Jesus Christ, and that's because He's the Giver of life. So, in the face of what seems to be credible evidence that Payton Sturgis has come back, God's Word makes it clear that no man can bring himself back from the dead. No matter what anyone says to the contrary, or how circumstances seem to prove different, we must always believe God's Word."

Lake rubbed his temples. "I've got a lot to learn yet, don't I, Pastor?"

"We all do. And the better hold we get on this Bible, the better hold it will have on us." Walker picked up his Bible and flipped pages again, stopping at Psalm 119. "This psalm, Lake, is all about the Word of God. There are other words within it to describe the Word—*law, testimonies, precepts, statutes*. Now, look at what David wrote in verse 80. 'Let my heart be sound in thy statutes; that I be not ashamed.' If we have our hearts soundly based in the Word of God, we'll never have to be ashamed before God *or* men."

"Takes real faith, doesn't it?" Lake said.

"Yes. The Bible says we are saved by faith. So as we live our Christian lives, we also live by faith and walk by faith."

The sheriff pulled at his ear nervously. "So even though there's no rational explanation to this Payton Sturgis thing, if I hold to the Bible, I'll always be right."

"No matter what subject God addresses in His Word, He knows what He's talking about. Let your heart be sound in what God has said, and you'll never have to hang your head in shame."

Johnson nodded. "Okay, but as sheriff of this county, people are going to expect me to come up with the man who scared Dan to death. The circumstances say it's Payton. Most people are going to believe I'm chasin' a ghost, but they're still going to expect me to stop him."

"But *you* know you're not chasing a ghost, Sheriff. Keep that in mind and believe me, when you catch the killer it will all come out with a reasonable explanation. And since you've let your heart be sound in the Word, you'll not be ashamed."

The lawman took a deep breath and let it out. "Yeah. You pray for me, won't you?"

"Sure will. And, ah, Lake . . ."

"Yes, Pastor?"

"I have a suggestion on what to do to catch this ghost."

CHAPTER

FOUR

Butte City's cemetery was just north of town. Payton Sturgis's grave lay at the extreme east edge of the cemetery, away from all the other graves.

Clay Madison, Ivan Charles, and Deputy Monte Dixon had left town together in Madison's wagon. They huddled deeper into their coat collars, their faces aching from the wind that buffeted them mercilessly. The massive cloud bank to the north would soon cover the sun. Already, tiny ice crystals were beginning to fall.

When Clay had guided the horses through the gate and turned due east on a narrow road that wound through the cemetery, he looked at Ivan and said, "Exactly what are you expecting to find at Payton's grave? You don't think we'll find a hole where he's climbed out, do you?"

"Clay, I don't know what to expect. I just want to see if there's any sign of disturbance."

As the wagon moved beneath double rows of naked cottonwoods and aspens, the three men scanned the even rows of grave markers on both sides of the road. The cemetery was situated on a hill, where the winds had swept the snow to lower ground. Here and there were obvious mounds of more recent graves, where the earth had not yet settled.

Clay and Ivan knew what to look for. Payton Sturgis's grave had been dug on the far side of a huge old cottonwood

43

to separate it as much as possible from the final resting place of decent folk. Soon the centuries old solitary tree came into view. Its trunk, thick and gnarled, stood firm as the branches twisted in the wind.

What they saw when they came to Sturgis's grave made them stare with numb disbelief.

"What on earth—?" Clay said.

In front of them was a long line of identical grave markers in the form of crosses. Clay pulled back on the reins and the wagon rolled to a halt. The three men climbed down and stood in the shallow depth of snow, gaping at the sight.

At the extreme north end of the row was Payton Sturgis's grave, the marker bearing minimal information:

Payton Sturgis
Born: March 18, 1841
Hanged: December 12, 1868

The other grave markers were to the left of the Sturgis grave. There were fifteen of them driven into the snow-covered sod where no graves had yet been dug. Each marker bore a name—the same names listed on the sheet of paper left near Dan Cogan's body. Cogan's marker was in the middle of them all.

The trio stood in silence for a long moment before Monte said, "I think this guy means business."

"Yeah," Clay said. "You suppose there's some kind of significance to placing Dan's marker in the middle of the others?"

"Maybe it indicates that the order of the markers is not necessarily the order in which they are intended to die," Ivan said. "But there's no question that these markers are a solemn warning that Payton—er, the man who frightened

Dan Cogan to death—means to put the other fourteen in their graves as well!"

The entire sky had turned a leaden gray and was spitting snow and ice pellets against the window of the church office. Sheriff Lake Johnson glanced out the window and said, "I like your suggestion, Pastor. You're absolutely right. Don't know why I didn't think of it. I'll contact John Stranger and get him to come back to Butte City as quickly as possible."

"Good," Walker said. "I just figured that since it was Stranger who solved the murders before and caught Payton, he'd be a good one to figure out how our mystery man caused Dan's death, and bring him to justice."

Lake rose from his chair. "I've got to round up the other men on that list and let them know what's happened. They need to be prepared. Whoever this maniac is, he'll strike again before long."

The preacher rounded the desk and grasped Lake's shoulder. "Remember that you're on that list too, my friend. Keep a sharp eye."

"I'll do that," Lake said, as he put on his hat and slipped into his heavy sheepskin coat.

"Really has me puzzled how this guy could make himself up to look exactly like Payton. I wonder if he made himself sound like Payton, too."

"If he did either or both, Sheriff, the man is most likely a resident of Butte City . . . or at least the area. How else would he know what Payton looked like?"

"He wouldn't. Unless he knew Payton *before* somewhere and just recently learned that this town hanged him two years ago."

"Unless . . ."

"Unless what?"

Walker scratched his forehead. "Unless Payton had an identical twin. And the twin somehow went two years without knowing Payton had been hanged, but as soon as he found out, he came here, frightened Dan to death, and wrote the note. I know . . . it's a little far-fetched. I'm just trying to figure this thing out."

"There's a real hitch in your identical twin theory, Pastor. The note. Even identical twins don't have the same handwriting. How would this twin manage to perfectly duplicate Payton's handwriting? Especially if he had to do it on short notice?"

The preacher grinned. "Forget that I even brought it up, Sheriff. Best thing for us to do is let our friend Mr. Stranger figure it all out. I'm sure he'll do a better job of it than the two of us could do together."

Lake was about to put his hand on the door knob when footsteps sounded in the hallway outside and a rapid knock rattled the door.

The sheriff stepped aside to let the pastor answer the knock. When he opened the door, a wide-eyed Monte Dixon looked past him and gasped, "Sheriff, you've got to come and see what's happened at the cemetery! Grave markers . . . next to Sturgis's grave! Fifteen of 'em! And one of 'em has your name on it!"

Ten minutes later, the pastor and the sheriff stood with the other three men in the cemetery.

Lake shook his head, brushing snow from his eyelashes. "This dude has a vivid imagination, I'll say that for him!"

"You called him a maniac, Sheriff," Pastor Walker said. "Maybe a closer description is 'cunning psychopath.' "

"I'm afraid you're right. The problem with psychopaths is that they assume various guises—serial killer, mass murderer, sadist, revenge seeker. The scary part of the threat is that it

46

could happen to any one of us on that list."

Johnson's words sank deep into the minds of the hearers.

"What we've got here, Sheriff," Ivan said, "is a vengeful ghost, not a madman. Even the most cunning madman couldn't make himself a perfect enough equivalent of Payton to frighten Dan to death. And certainly such a madman couldn't perfectly duplicate Payton's handwriting."

Pastor Walker opened his mouth to speak, but Ivan cut him off. "I know what you're going to say, Preacher. No disrespect meant, but you must realize that the Bible isn't always right."

"That's where you're wrong, Ivan," Walker said. "God authored that Bible, and He's always right. I don't care how much it looks like we're dealing with the ghost of Payton Sturgis. You'll find out when it's all over that we're dealing with a real flesh-and-blood human being. Mark my word on it!"

Ivan looked fearful, but said no more.

Lake Johnson's mind went to Psalm 119:80. *Let my heart be sound in thy statutes; that I be not ashamed.*

"Sheriff," Monte said, "should I take the markers down?"

"No. Let's leave them for now. We've got to round up every man whose name is on these markers. They have a right to know what happened to Dan before it leaks out and they hear it from someone else. I'll tell them about the note with the list of names and these grave markers. If any of them want to come out and see the markers for themselves, I want them to do it."

"I'll help you and Monte round them up, Sheriff," Clay said.

Pastor Walker and Ivan volunteered as well.

Lake nodded his appreciation and headed back toward Clay's wagon. "With this much help, we'll get the job done in a hurry," he said. "Let's decide which men each of you will contact. I'll tell Eugene, since his barber shop is next door to my office, then I'll head for Western Union to send a wire to Denver. Tell the men to meet at my office."

"Sheriff, I'm sure it would be an encouragement to these men if you tell them about the wire," Pastor Walker said.

"Oh, of course. I'm gonna contact John Stranger and get him here as soon as possible. He brought Sturgis to justice, and he can crack this case, too. Besides, his name's on the list and on one of those markers. He needs to know about it."

Ivan suddenly walked back to Payton's grave and just stood there, looking at the marker.

"Just a minute, fellas," Lake said.

The other men watched as Lake walked up to the undertaker. "Look, Ivan, you put his body in the coffin, lowered it into the ground, and covered it, didn't you?"

Ivan nodded.

"Then it's still down there. This psychopath is an impostor. You're an undertaker. Certainly you know dead men don't come back."

Without a word Ivan Charles turned and headed for the wagon.

In late 1870 there were eleven gold, silver, and zinc mines surrounding Butte City. Three of those mines were run by the McVicker Mining Company which was owned by Tom McVicker, who lived with his wife, Nadine, in a large home in the town's affluent section.

The McVicker gold mine was on the north side of town, the zinc mine on the west, and the silver mine on the south. As the storm moved in on Butte City, McVicker was at his main office at the silver mine.

Two miners stood in his office, their faces coated with dust.

"I can't answer your question, men," McVicker said. "Les is the only one who knows how to handle that problem. He's working over at the gold mine all day today, and I was about to ride over there and talk to him about a couple of things. I'll ask him and let you know what he says when I get back in an hour or so. You can go ahead with your work, can't you?"

The miners assured him they could, and left the office.

McVicker stuffed as many logs as possible in the potbellied stove to keep the office warm for his return, then put on coat, hat, and gloves and stepped out into the storm.

McVicker entered a shed where the horses were kept, led his bay mare out into the snowy air, and swung into the saddle. It took less than twenty minutes to ride to his gold mine. The stove in the office there would be a welcome sight.

In the office cabin at the gold mine, McVicker Mining Company foreman Les Osborne donned his hat and shouldered into his heavy coat. "I'm getting too old for this kind of weather," he said with a chuckle. "One of these autumns I'm going to take Martha and head south with the birds."

Miner Henry Pate, who was warming his hands at the potbellied stove, said, "Sure, I can just see that. You won't ever leave Tom, and you know it."

"You're right. I've been with Tom for a mighty long time. Guess I'll just stick it out till *both* of us get so old we have to go south."

Pate laughed. "Well, that'll be another hundred years, at least."

"I hope not," Les said. "One of these days my bones will get too brittle for this Montana deep-freeze. Anyway, Henry, I'll ride on over to the main office and talk to Tom about it.

He'll be willing to replace those old carts with new ones when I tell him they're falling apart one by one. I should've talked to him about it sooner."

"We can still get them in Billings, can't we?" Pate asked.

"I'm sure we can."

"Good. Soon as Tom gives you the okay, you oughtta send a wire to the supplier in Billings and get 'em started over here. We need 'em bad."

"Will do. See you later."

Les Osborne pulled his collar tight around his neck and leaned against the ruthless wind and driving snow. Moments later he mounted his piebald gelding and settled into the saddle.

The foreman trotted south along the edge of the forest that lined three sides of the town. As he rode close to the dense timber, the wind set up a longing wail, and he felt a prickle slither down his spine.

He was reminded of the many times he had been in snow-storms in this high country and seen the snow ghosts, or so they were called by the Crow. Even as the haunting wail met his ears, the familiar illusion was there in the wind-stirred snow against the dark backdrop of the forest.

He smiled to himself. *There they are, you superstitious Indians,* he thought. *Your ever-lovin' snow ghosts.*

A wide creek wended its way across the rugged terrain, coming down snakelike from the Rockies to the east and flowing into the valley far to the west. Several years ago, Tom McVicker had built a bridge over the creek between his silver and gold mines to make it convenient for his heavy-laden ore wagons to traverse the rugged terrain. The miners used the bridge as well.

As Osborne neared the stream, it was running slowly at a depth of about two feet. Winter's ice was pushed against the banks like a border of white piping on the cold, dark water, and small chunks of ice floated downstream, bobbing on the surface.

The haunting wail of the wind in the timber met his ears again. He guided his horse toward the bridge and glanced toward the source of the wail. Once again he saw snow ghosts sprinting from tree to tree.

"Hey, Les, ol' boy," he said. "What's the matter with you? A Crow you're not. Why should those imaginary figures scare you? Maybe it's that spooky wind in the trees."

Osborne was about fifty feet from the edge of the snow-covered bridge when he saw the form of a man sprawled face-down in the middle of the bridge. He had been there only a short time, for his coat, pants, and boots were barely flecked with snow.

The piebald nickered nervously as his hooves touched the wood of the bridge, giving off a hollow sound. Osborne looked around for a riderless horse, but could see none.

As he drew close to the figure, Osborne was relieved to see the rise and fall of the man's back. He looked to be tall and slender, but Les couldn't yet identify him. He dismounted and hunkered down beside the man. He could see blond hair, and the man appeared to be on the young side, but his face was partly covered with his hat.

Before Osborne's fingers could touch the brim, the man suddenly jerked the hat away from his face and sprang to his feet, glaring at the startled mine foreman with burning, hate-filled eyes. His head was tilted to one side, as if there was something wrong with his neck and he couldn't straighten it.

Les Osborne's jaw slacked as he stood up and gasped, "Payton! Wh—wh—how—"

Osborne's horse neighed and wheeled about. The fiery-eyed man slapped the animal on the rump, sending it galloping away. Then to Osborne he said in a silky, slithery voice, "I told you I would come back, Les!"

A terror unlike any he had ever experienced overwhelmed the mine foreman. For a split second, his mind played back that final moment at the hanging, when Payton Sturgis plummeted through the trapdoor of the gallows. He could still hear the snap of his neck.

"Now it's your time to die, Les!" the man hissed.

"No! You're dead! You can't be—"

A rock-hard fist lashed out, chopping Osborne on the jaw. His feet went out from under him, and he fell on the snow-laden bridge.

Tom McVicker tugged at his hat brim as he trotted his mount north. Soon he topped a gentle rise and started down the snow-mantled slope before him. The bridge over the creek came into view, and the mine owner blinked to make sure his eyes weren't playing a trick on him in the driving snow.

Yes, there were two men and a horse on the bridge, and one of the men had to be Les Osborne. His horse's black-and-white blotches stood out against the falling snow. McVicker then saw the piebald wheel about and gallop away. The mine owner was still forty yards from the bridge when he saw the other man punch Les and knock him down.

"Hey!" McVicker shouted, putting his horse to a gallop. "What do you think you're doing?"

As he drew closer, he focused on the man's familiar features. His heart seemed to stop beating as he drew rein. "Payton!"

The blond man bent over, drew Les's revolver from its holster, and trained the gun on McVicker.

Tom jerked back on the reins and pivoted his horse,

gouging her sides with his heels. He put her to a gallop back up the slope, expecting to hear the gun fire and feel a bullet strike his back.

When he reached the crest of the slope and knew he was out of pistol range, he pulled rein and ventured a backward look. The bridge was obscured by the wind-driven snow. It was as if it didn't exist.

Was he really sitting on his horse, peering through a wild snowstorm toward the bridge? Or was he about to wake up from the most macabre nightmare of his life?

For a moment, McVicker's mind teetered between nightmare and reality. There was no Payton Sturgis on the bridge, and there was no Les Osborne there either. Les was at the gold mine.

Then he heard a bloodcurdling scream from the direction of the bridge. Then dead silence. Except for the banshee-like wail of the wind.

CHAPTER

FIVE

The snowfall had eased off and the wind died down some when Tom McVicker skidded his bay mare to a halt in front of the Silver Bow County Sheriff's Office. Lake Johnson's office was on the southeast corner of Butte City's main intersection.

At the barber shop next door, Eugene Kevane had no customers at the moment and was sweeping the floor near the big front window. From the corner of his eye, Kevane saw a rider skid to a halt at the hitch rail. He leaned the broom against the wall and went to the door.

When McVicker found the sheriff's door locked and a sign in the window announcing that both the sheriff and his deputy were temporarily out of the office, he breathed an oath and swung a gloved fist through the air.

At that instant, McVicker heard the barber shop door opening and turned in that direction.

Kevane saw who it was and said, "Hello, Tom. The meeting won't start for a little while yet. Come on in and wait with me."

"Eugene . . . I need to speak to the sheriff right now!"

"Can it wait until the meeting?"

"What meeting?"

"Come on in. I might as well explain it to you, 'cause the sheriff won't be back until everyone's been contacted."

Eugene motioned Tom to enter the shop ahead of him,

then he closed the door and stuck the CLOSED sign in the window. "Let's go to the rear of the shop, Tom, so no one can see us."

"Eugene, what's going on?"

"Okay, let me explain. Right now, the sheriff's at the Western Union office waiting for a reply to a telegram he sent earlier. Monte, Ivan Charles, Pastor Walker, and Clay Madison are out collecting all the men who sat on the jury at Payton Sturgis's trial two years ago."

"Payton Sturgis's trial?"

"Yeah. Grab a chair and let's sit down. I'll tell you what I know. The sheriff said he'd tell us plenty more at the meeting."

When Tom McVicker heard the story of Dan Cogan's death, and that Doc Bristow said he had died of heart failure, an icy horror seeped through him.

Eugene concluded, "The sheriff wants every man who was on the jury at the Sturgis trial, plus Judge Reed, to be here. And he wants us to keep the information about Dan's death, and whatever else he tells us, to ourselves for the time being."

"He . . . he didn't say what all of this has to do with Sturgis's trial?"

"No. I can't even imagine. The trial was two years ago. But we'll find out at the meeting." Eugene paused. "You looked like you were in a hurry to see Lake when you rode up. Is anything wrong?"

Tom's hands trembled and his eyes fluttered. "Eugene . . . I—" He rubbed his eyes with shaky fingers. "I just had a horrible experience out at the bridge. And I believe I know what this is all about."

"You do?"

"I don't have to remind you of what Payton said just

before he went through the trapdoor . . ."

"Course not."

"If I don't miss my guess, Dan's heart failure was brought on by Payton Sturgis. He's back from the dead to get us, just like he said."

"*What?*"

"I just saw him at the bridge."

"You saw Payton? You were close enough to be sure it was him?"

Tom nodded, swallowing with difficulty. "It was him. He had Les."

"Had Les? On the bridge?"

"Yeah. As I was riding toward the creek, I could make out two men and a horse on the bridge. It was still snowing pretty hard. As I got closer, I recognized Les's piebald. Seconds later the horse whirled around, and the tall man slapped it on the rump, making it gallop away. Then he punched Les with his fist and knocked him down.

"I shouted at him as I rode toward the bridge. Then I recognized him. It was *Payton!* His head was bent to one side as if something was wrong with his neck. He bent down, yanked Les's revolver from its holster and pointed it at me. I spun my horse around and put her to a gallop as fast as she could go. I thought Payton would shoot me out of the saddle, but he didn't fire at all. That's where I was coming from when you saw me pull up outside.

"Payton's got Les. I heard Les scream while I was riding away. I . . . I didn't want to face Payton all by myself. I rode for town so I could tell the sheriff what I'd seen, and get him to round up a bunch of men and go back out there. Les is probably dead by now."

Eugene stared blankly at the floor. His voice was little more than a whisper. "I have no reason to doubt your word,

Tom, but are you sure it was Payton? With the wind blowing the snow, maybe it just looked like him."

"It *was* Payton, Eugene! I saw him with these two eyes! Les was on the jury. Payton said he would come back and kill every one of us. It was *him*, I tell you!"

"But nobody comes back from the grave, Tom."

McVicker shook his head. "If this tall man who knocked Les down wasn't Payton, then tell me, who would he be, and why would he do that to Les? And tell me this: Why does the sheriff want to meet with all of us who sent Payton to the gallows? Coincidence, Eugene?"

The barber had no answer.

"I've never believed in ghosts before," Tom said, "but I believe in them now. And he's back to kill us, just like he said. Oh, poor Elaine Cogan! How horrible for her! And if Payton has killed Les by now, Martha's a widow. And my poor Nadine! She's going to fall to pieces when she hears that Payton's back to carry out his threat."

Eugene's voice quivered as he said, "I can't argue with you, Tom. I've never believed in ghosts either, but I have to agree with you. Oh-h-h! Althea's going to come apart, too, when she hears this!"

Sudden activity in the street drew Eugene to the front window. "It's Monte and some of our fellow jurymen, Tom."

McVicker rose from his chair by the stove. "We'd better go on over to the sheriff's office and join them," he said. "This town's going to panic when the word gets out."

"Tom . . ." the barber said, as they started toward the front of the shop. "I think it would be best if you hold off telling what happened at the bridge until everybody's together, including the sheriff. Save you having to tell it three or four times. I'd say let Lake give us his information first."

"Doesn't bother me having to tell the men. It's telling Nadine that's bothering me."

It had stopped snowing altogether when Sheriff Lake Johnson arrived at his office, though the afternoon sky remained heavy with clouds. The wind had diminished to a brisk breeze.

When Johnson entered his office, every spare chair was taken, and most of the men stood. Jackson DeLong sat in the sheriff's chair behind the desk. Pastor Walker stood near the door with Monte Dixon, and Ivan Charles was half-sitting on the front edge of the desk. Tension was thick in the room as every eye fastened on the sheriff.

Lake ran his gaze over familiar faces to see who might be missing. Almost everyone on the list was there. He swung his gaze to his deputy. "Clay's not back yet?"

"Not yet."

"Who was he supposed to go after?"

"Tom McVicker, Les Osborne, and Darrell Amick."

Lake looked at Tom. "Clay got to you, but not to Les?"

"He didn't find me, Sheriff. I came into town to see you, and Eugene told me you were at the telegraph office. He went ahead and told me about Dan, and that you had called this meeting."

Lake nodded. "Whatever it was you wanted to see me about will have to wait. What about the judge, Monte? You were to contact him."

"I went to his chambers at the courthouse, but he wasn't there. So I went to his house. Mrs. Reed told me he's over at Crackerville and won't be back till about five o'clock."

There was a muffled sound of voices and the thump of heavy boots on the boardwalk. Clay Madison and Darrell Amick entered and closed the door.

"Did you find Les, Clay?" Lake asked.

"I went to all three mines, and nobody knew where either Les or Tom were, Sheriff. All the men at the silver mine could tell me was that Tom had headed for the gold mine. I didn't find them at home either."

Lake looked at McVicker. "We need Les here, Tom. Any idea where he might be?"

McVicker wiped an unsteady hand over his mouth. His throat was dry and his chest ached with fear. "Yes, I have an idea, Sheriff, but I don't think you should wait for him. You'd better go on with the meeting. I'll explain after you've told us what this meeting is all about."

"I'd really like him here," Lake said.

"Believe me. It's best that you go on."

Lake sighed. "Okay, we'll begin."

"Without the judge, Sheriff?" Monte asked.

"Have to. Five o'clock is two hours away. I want these men to hear it all right now. I'll have to tell Judge Reed about it later."

The sheriff had every man's rapt attention as he started with Clay Madison's discovery of Dan Cogan's body that morning. He showed them the note Clay had found on the dresser, and read it to them.

Lake went on to tell them Doc Bristow had examined Cogan's body and said he'd died of heart failure. He told them of the work orders Ivan had shown him. Without question, the note and the work orders were written by the same hand.

George Walz looked at Johnson with a face devoid of color. "Sheriff, are you telling us that you believe Payton has risen from the dead and come back to kill us?"

"I didn't say that, George. But it's my duty to give you the facts. What I've told you about Dan's death and the handwriting are facts. But I do not believe we're dealing with a ghost."

"Well, how do you explain—"

"Let me give you all the facts before you start asking questions. Okay, George?"

"Yeah. Okay."

Lake proceeded to tell them about the fifteen grave markers at the cemetery, each one bearing the name of a man who sat on the jury at Payton Sturgis's trial, plus Judge Reed, John Stranger, and himself. "We left the crosses exactly as we found them, gentlemen," Lake said, "in case any of you want to see them for yourselves."

Everyone agreed they wanted to see the grave markers.

"All right," Lake said, "let's go out there and take a look."

"Before we go, Sheriff," Tom McVicker said, "I should tell you about Les." He stepped forward and stood beside the sheriff before saying, "The reason Les isn't here is because Payton got him about an hour ago." The mine owner told his story, closing off with his fast ride into town.

The men stared at him in silence, unable to believe what they'd just heard.

The next man to speak was Pastor Walker. "Gentlemen, let me say something. I know that by everything you've heard here, it appears we're dealing with something supernatural— a ghost, if you please. I assure you, according to the Word of God, this is not so. I know what the Bible says may not impress all of you, but it *is* true; every word of it. And it's clear on this subject. Dead men don't come back. What we're dealing with is a flesh-and-blood human being. Crafty and cunning, yes. But a mortal being."

"That's right," Lake said. "When this gets out to the town, there's going to be enough fear and panic, even if we can convince them we're dealing with a mortal man. But if they get it in their minds that we're at the mercy of a supernatural being, they'll go berserk.' "

George Walz, obviously afraid, said, "Lake, if this is a flesh-and-blood human being we're facing, tell us how he managed to frighten Dan Cogan to death. And tell us how he duplicated Payton's handwriting. And tell us how Tom McVicker, an intelligent, responsible businessman, could be so grossly mistaken as to who he saw on the bridge with Les Osborne."

Lake pulled at his mustache. "George, neither the pastor nor I can explain all of this. But it will all come to light when we catch this guy. We know, at least, that he resembles Payton, and—"

"He doesn't *resemble* Payton, Sheriff," Tom said. "The man I saw *is* Payton! I've got excellent eyesight, and I'm telling you it was Payton Sturgis I saw on the bridge! And there's something else I forgot to tell you. Payton's neck was bent to the side, as if his neck had been broken, you know."

Lake sighed and looked down, then ran his gaze over each man's face before saying, "I want you men to sit tight right here while Monte and I take a quick ride out to the bridge. I want to check it out. We'll be back in a few minutes, then we'll all go over to the cemetery to take a look at the grave markers."

While Johnson and Dixon were out of the office, Pastor Walker did everything he could to calm the men and encourage them. He read Scripture that stated God's Son was the only one who ever had the power to raise himself from the grave. He then read from Mark 6. When King Herod heard of Jesus Christ preaching in the hills of Judea, he was sure the Preacher was John the Baptist risen from the dead.

"The news of this new Preacher on the scene," Walker

said, "caused many people to believe that Elijah had come back. But listen to verse 16: 'But when Herod heard thereof, he said, It is John, whom I beheaded: he is risen from the dead.' "

Walker looked at the men around him. "Now tell me, gentlemen, had John risen from the dead, or was Herod mistaken?"

"Herod was mistaken," Frank Cosgrove said.

"Right. And when this thing is all over, you men will see that even in the face of what seems to be concrete evidence that Payton has risen from the dead, it will prove to be false."

Tom McVicker set his jaw. "Preacher, I really don't mean any disrespect, but you're wrong. I know who I saw on that bridge. It was Payton Sturgis."

Jackson DeLong stood up behind the sheriff's desk and nodded toward the front window. "Lake and Monte are back," he said, "and they've got a body with them."

The men quickly put on their coats and hats and rushed outside. A crowd was already gathering around the lifeless form of Les Osborne draped over Monte's horse.

Tom McVicker stepped to the body and began to whimper. "Oh, Les! I knew it! I knew it! Payton killed you!" He touched the body and quickly jerked his hand away. The corpse was soaking wet, and the water was turning to ice.

Men and women in the crowd stood looking on, wondering what Tom was talking about. Some picked up the name "Payton."

Lake Johnson kept his voice low as he directed his comments to the men who had been in his office. "We found him under the bridge. He was weighted down with rocks at the bottom of the creek."

McVicker turned to the crowd and cried out, "I saw Payton Sturgis! I saw him on the bridge at the creek! Payton is back to kill every one of us who had a hand in hanging him! Dan Cogan's dead, too, and it was Payton who killed him!"

Lake gave Monte a meaningful look and then raised his hands to the crowd. While Monte spoke to Tom in low tones, trying to quiet him, the sheriff lifted his voice, "Folks, listen to me! We've got a serious situation on our hands, and I'm doing my best to handle it."

"We can see that Les is dead, Sheriff," a man in the crowd said. "Is it true about Dan?"

"Yes, but it's a long story, and there are many details I can't give you at the moment. Right now I want all of you to finish your business and go home. It's not the ghost of Payton Sturgis we're dealin' with, here. Dead men don't come back. You—"

Lake's words trailed off when he saw a small band of Crow Indians on the street. Chief Broken Bow was coming toward him, threading his way through the press. Broken Bow wore a full headdress and was wrapped in a blanket of wolf hides, as were the six braves with him. They wore fur-lined leggings and furry boots.

The chief moved close to Lake and halted. The icy breeze plucked at his headdress. As Johnson looked into the Indian's jet-black eyes, the chief let a smile tug at his stoic features, and he spoke in a heavy, deep tone.

"Sheriff Lake Johnson, Broken Bow asks your pardon for intruding. Broken Bow has seen and heard what has taken place here. He has heard Tom McVicker say he saw Payton Sturgis at bridge. Tom McVicker says Payton Sturgis kill Dan Cogan . . . kill Les Osborne. Sheriff Lake Johnson says dead men do not come back. Though Tom McVicker see ghost of Payton Sturgis, Sheriff Lake Johnson says no."

Turning to McVicker, the chief asked, "When Dan Cogan die, was it snowing?"

"I don't know," McVicker said, "but it sure was snowing when I saw Payton on the bridge with Les."

Clay Madison spoke. "Yes, Chief, it was snowing when Dan died."

"Please. Broken Bow mean not offend Sheriff Lake Johnson, but Tom McVicker and Clay Madison are right. Just as Crow enemies come back from the dead as snow ghosts for revenge, so Payton Sturgis has come from the dead as snow ghost for revenge on men who hang him."

The people watched with keen interest as Lake said, "I don't mean any offense to you either, Broken Bow, but the fact is, dead men don't come back."

"He's right, Chief," Pastor Walker said. "We consider you and your people our friends, and we always want to be your friends. But our God gave us a Book, and His Book teaches that dead men do not come back. We must hold to this. Besides, if a man was going to come back from the dead to bring vengeance on a town for hanging him, it would be Turk Kostin!"

Memories stirred at the mention of Turk Kostin. The hanging of this innocent man was a black mark on Butte City that everyone wanted to forget. The reminder brought special pain to the heart of Jackson DeLong.

Kostin had come to Butte City and opened a wagon repair shop, which he had operated for about a year before he was arrested for murder.

Turk and Banker Brad DeLong (Jackson DeLong's oldest son) had argued publicly in the bank over an alleged error the bank had made on Turk's account. While customers and bank personnel looked on, Turk closed his account, took his money, and stomped out of the place in anger.

That night, Brad DeLong stayed at the bank after hours to catch up on some work. As he walked home after dark, he was attacked from the shadows and bludgeoned into unconsciousness. Steve Nadler and Ernie Davis had just left the Saddlehorn Saloon when they stumbled onto Brad, lying on the boardwalk.

Davis stayed with the unconscious banker while Nadler summoned Sheriff Johnson and Dr. Bristow. They rushed Brad to Bristow's office, where Johnson found that Brad's wallet was missing.

Bristow worked hard to bring Brad around, but he stayed unconscious until two o'clock in the morning. When he came to briefly before dying on the examining table, Turk Kostin's name was on his lips.

Sheriff Johnson awakened Turk at three o'clock in the morning and jailed him, charging him with the murder of Brad DeLong.

Judge Virgil Reed was on a trip back east, and they had to wait almost five weeks to hold Turk Kostin's trial. Turk hired Attorney Donald Fryman of Butte City to defend him. During the trial, Fryman argued that since Brad DeLong was hit from behind, and on a dimly lit street, it was hardly possible that he could have seen his assailant. In his semi-conscious state, he had assumed it was Turk because of their heated argument earlier in the day.

Kostin pleaded his innocence, admitting he was angry at Brad, but stating emphatically that he never would have killed him. When questioned about where he was at 9:30 the previous night, Turk told Johnson he was at the Fred Sanders ranch four miles outside of town, repairing one of Sanders's wagons. He had started at 7:00 and worked on the wagon until about 11:30.

Sanders and his family were in Billings at the time, and couldn't back Turk's statement. Sheriff Johnson found that the wagon had been repaired, but there was no proof as to when Turk repaired it.

In spite of Turk's plea of innocence, the jury accepted Brad DeLong's dying testimony and returned a guilty verdict.

Three days after Turk Kostin was hanged, two local ranchers, William Stone and Clyde Moore, returned from a long business trip to St. Louis, Missouri. When they heard about the murder, the time period in which it happened, and of Turk's execution, they went to Sheriff Johnson.

They had ridden from town together on the night of the murder. They had purchased stagecoach tickets at the Wells Fargo office late that day and were scheduled to leave Butte City at six o'clock the next morning.

As they rode toward their neighboring ranches, they passed the Sanders place and saw Turk working on the wagon at the side of the house by lantern light. He was easily identifiable at that short distance, but he had not looked in their direction. He had not known they were there.

The testimonies of Moore and Stone cleared Kostin and convicted the judge and jury of hanging an innocent man. Sheriff Johnson was sick at heart, as were the rest of the townspeople.

The sheriff remembered that a drifter named Woodrow Pike was in town at the time of the murder and had been seen in town up until the day of the trial. Johnson formed a posse and found Pike in Crackerville with Brad's wallet in his possession. He was brought back to Butte City, tried, and hanged.

Now, Turk Kostin's name on the lips of Pastor Bob Walker cast a pall over the crowd.

CHAPTER

SIX

Pastor Walker looked around the crowd, and said, "If a man *could* come back from the dead to get even with people who took his life, wouldn't Turk come back? Why hasn't he? For the same reason Payton hasn't. Nobody comes back from the grave."

People exchanged glances, checking out each other's reactions. Some were nodding; others just looked frightened.

Chief Broken Bow moved his head back and forth slowly. "You will soon see that Broken Bow is right, Pastor Bob Walker. The snow ghost who caused Dan Cogan to die, and who drowned Les Osborne, is Payton Sturgis. He has come back to have his revenge on those men who brought about his death, even as he vowed to do before he was hanged."

Walker was about to reply, but Lake Johnson cut in. "We can stand here and argue till dark, but it won't change anything. If you men who were on the jury want to go to the cemetery, let's do it now."

Lake picked a couple of men out of the crowd and asked them if they would take Les Osborne's body to the undertaker. The men were also to inform Ivan Charles of the meeting called for that night at the town hall.

The crowd huddled together and watched Johnson, his deputy, and the marked men head north up Main Street on foot. Bob Walker went along, with Chief Broken Bow and his braves following.

It was 4:15 when they topped the hill at the cemetery. The dismal sky was spitting snow again. Johnson, Dixon, and Madison led the way, halting when they arrived at Payton Sturgis's grave. The wooden crosses that bore the names of the killer's intended victims still stood in a straight line.

Each of the men found his marker, the symbol of his own death. Suddenly Jackson DeLong let out a growl, yanked his marker out of the ground, and threw it in a ditch some thirty feet away. The others looked at each other, then almost in unison they did the same.

When all of the markers were in the ditch, and the men were gathered beside Payton's grave again, Bob Walker said, "Men, believe me, you have nothing supernatural to fear. There's a killer, yes. But he's no ghost. Keep this in mind when you go home and talk to your families. The man Tom saw with Les at the bridge was mortal. Our sheriff and his deputy are going to track him down. It may take some time, but they'll catch him, and he'll hang."

"Monte and I are going to have some help," Lake said. "You all know I was at the Western Union office earlier. I sent a wire to Chief U.S. Marshal Solomon Duvall in Denver, asking the whereabouts of John Stranger."

The mention of Stranger's name brightened the men's faces.

"Duvall wired me back and said Stranger is pursuing a killer outlaw in the mountains of Colorado at the moment, so there's no way to contact him. However, Duvall will have Stranger wire me as soon as he returns to Denver. He didn't think it would be too much longer. Of course, in the meantime, Monte and I will do everything we can to catch the so-called snow ghost ourselves. I want you to bring your families to the town hall tonight. I want to meet with them and do what I can to encourage them. Be there at seven-thirty."

The Crow chief left his braves and approached Johnson. "Sheriff Lake Johnson, Broken Bow does not understand."

"What's that, Chief?"

"How does this man make himself look like Payton Sturgis?"

"I can't answer that. I don't know."

The chief paused for a moment, then: "Broken Bow has suggestion."

"Yes?"

Pointing to Payton Sturgis's grave marker, the Crow leader said, "Sheriff Lake Johnson should open the grave. See if Payton Sturgis still in there."

The sheriff's face stiffened. "I will do no such thing. Payton is dead, and his body is still down there, Chief, under six feet of cold ground."

Broken Bow smiled tightly. "Tom McVicker know he saw Payton Sturgis. Sheriff Lake Johnson can soon learn that it is snow ghost of Payton Sturgis Tom McVicker saw."

Tom worked hard at keeping his voice steady. "He's right, Lake. You'll see."

Blacksmith Lawton Haymes spoke up. "Let's get home to our families, men. They've no doubt heard this horror story by now. They'll need us."

Fresh snow fell, stirred by the rising wind, and the frightened men talked in low tones among themselves as they walked back to town.

Judge Virgil Reed drove his one-horse buggy along the road from Crackerville toward Butte City. It was close to five o'clock, and he had promised Edna he would be home by five.

The wind was picking up. Periodically the judge wiped the snow from his face, wishing for the heat of summer. When he passed a massive boulder with jagged outcroppings of rock on one side, he knew he was five miles from home.

He had gone about half a mile when off to the left of the road, just outside the edge of the trees, he saw a pack of wolves. Their heads turned toward him in the fading light of day. They remained motionless, studying horse and driver.

The leader of the pack threw one last flick of his amber eyes at Reed, then loped along the edge of the trees and darted into the shadows of the timber. The others, gray splotches in the falling snow, ran effortlessly after him.

The buggy dipped into a low spot, then climbed to the crest and leveled off after about sixty yards. Movement caught the judge's eye up ahead. He squinted. Sure enough, it was a man on foot, standing along the side of the road. He was waving his arm.

The man's heavy coat and a wide-brimmed hat were heavily flecked with snow. The hat was tilted low in the front, and partially obscured the man's face.

The judge reined to a stop and peered at the man. "Howdy, there, fella. You want a ride into town?"

"Sure could use one," came a half-whispered reply, as the tall man climbed in and sat beside Reed's portly frame. He kept his face partially averted.

Judge Reed snapped the reins and put his horse into motion. The man sat in silence. Reed looked at him and said, "You look vaguely familiar. Do I know you?"

"I've been around."

"Well, tell me, what are you doing out here on the road this far from town in this snowstorm?"

The voice came again. Silken. "I'm out here to kill *you,* Virgil!"

The man's mouth twisted in a wicked sneer, and the judge could see the man's angular features as he lifted his face into full view and pushed back his hat.

"*Payton!*"

The blond man seized Reed's wrist with a grip like a steel vise, and hissed, "Time to face up to what you did, Virgil! Time to pay!"

"No! Please, Payton! I . . . I was only doing my duty after the jury found you guilty! I'm sorry! Please don't hurt me! I'm sorry!"

"Not as sorry as you're going to be!"

It was closing time at the Silver Bow County Sheriff's Office. Lake Johnson shuffled through some papers at his desk while Monte Dixon swept the floor.

Monte leaned over and swept the small pile of dirt into a dustpan. "Sheriff," he said, "I need to ask you something."

Johnson looked up. "Yes?"

Monte carried the dustpan to a waste can and dumped its contents, then turned toward his boss. "I'm confused."

"How's that?"

"Neither you nor Pastor Walker can explain how this impostor could look exactly like Payton Sturgis. You can't explain how he could possibly match Payton's handwriting. Yet you insist he's not a supernatural being—that he's not Payton's ghost because of what the Bible says. Why? What makes the Bible so special? It was written by mortal men."

Johnson dropped the papers and said, "Yes, God used mortal men to pen the Bible, but He breathed every word they penned." He picked up the Bible on top of his desk. "Monte, this is God's written Word. This is His way of making Himself known to man, and it must be accepted above all of man's ideas and philosophies about life, death, and eternity."

Monte leaned the broom against the wall by the rear door,

then came back to sit in front of Johnson's desk. "Sheriff, I've heard about the Bible all my life, but I really don't know much about it. If it's the Word of God, then it would have to be correct, no matter what subject it discusses."

"Well, son, it *is* God's Word, and it *is* correct, whatever subject it deals with."

"But how do you know it's the Word of God? I've heard learned men say it's not, and that it has errors."

"Nobody's ever proven one error, Monte, though multitudes of skeptics have tried."

"Okay, but can you prove it *is* God's Word?"

"No, and neither can any other man. But God can. He uses the Word itself to prove to any person who honestly wants to know. In the final analysis, we must accept by faith that this Book is the Word of God. It says in Hebrews 11:6 that 'without faith it is impossible to please him: for he that cometh to God must believe that he is, and that he is a rewarder of them that diligently seek him.' You believe that God exists, don't you, Monte?"

"Of course. I know that every effect has a cause. My intelligence tells me that this universe and this earth are not accidents. The cause has to be Someone much greater in power and intelligence than His creatures here on earth."

"Good! You're closer to the whole truth than you might think, Monte. Bible faith is not a blind leap in the dark, as many would have you believe. It is confidence in a believable record that God has given. Romans 10:17 says, 'faith cometh by hearing, and hearing by the word of God.' "

The young deputy nodded, listening with interest.

"Monte, you never saw a skeptic any more hardheaded than Lake Johnson. Two years ago, when John Stranger was here, we spent a lot of time together. He presented the gospel to me, explaining that Jesus had gone to the cross of Calvary for the purpose of paying the sin debt for sinners, so that they might be saved from hell and the wrath of God.

"Well, I gave John fits for a while, but he just kept quoting Scripture to me, and reading to me from the Bible. Pretty soon I began to see how blind I had been. The Spirit of God was driving the Word to my heart, and finally I saw it all, believed what it said, repented of my sin, and opened my heart to Jesus. He saved this old wretched sinner, and now I'm a child of God on my way to heaven."

Monte looked a bit skeptical. "It's that simple, eh?"

"Yes. It's the devil who tries to make it look difficult. In 2 Corinthians 11:3, Paul warned that Satan would try to corrupt people's minds from the simplicity of the gospel. He uses religion and the philosophy of men to corrupt people's minds and make salvation seem difficult. Jesus did the hard part on the cross. It's up to us simply to believe that, repent of our sins, and open our hearts to Him."

Eager to reach his new deputy for Christ, Lake Johnson showed him Scripture passages regarding the cross, the blood, the resurrection, heaven, and hell.

When Johnson finished, he was still holding the closed Bible in his hand. "Well, Monte, what do you say?"

Monte rubbed his jaw. "I'll have to think on it, Sheriff. You've given one horse a whole load of hay to digest. But if what you've read about hell and the wrath of God is so . . . I need to know about it."

"I understand," Lake said. "Once I was where you are. Tell you what. How about coming to church with me Sunday? Faith comes by hearing the Word of God. Pastor Walker is an excellent preacher. He doesn't use big words that only a university professor could understand. His preaching is simple and to the point, and his sermons are jam-packed with Scripture. How about it?"

Monte grinned. "I'll do it."

"Good!"

"I'll do it for *two* reasons, boss."

"Two?"

"Uh-huh. I've noticed a young lady around town, and I finally asked somebody about her. I was told her name is Jessie Westbrook, and that she goes to church."

"That's right. Her parents are faithful members of the church, and fine Christian people."

"So would it be wrong for me to go to church to hear the Bible preached *and* to see if I can meet Jessie?"

"I guess not. As long as it's in that order!"

The door opened, and Edna Reed entered with worry deepening the lines of her face. "Oh, Sheriff, I'm so glad you're still here! I was afraid you might have left the office already."

"What is it, Mrs. Reed?"

"It's Virgil. He was due home from Crackerville at five. I'm worried sick, what with this snow ghost story going around town. Virgil's name is on that list!"

"Now, Mrs. Reed," Lake said, "we don't want to panic every time somebody's a little late getting home. The judge has been late returning from Crackerville before, hasn't he?"

"Well . . . yes."

The sheriff put a comforting hand on Edna's shoulder and said, "The judge will no doubt be home any minute. He may even be there now."

Edna nodded. "You're right, Sheriff. I panicked."

"I can understand why. This Payton Sturgis thing is going to have the whole town on edge. Especially the families of the men on the list. You go on home now."

She turned toward the door and then stopped. "Sheriff, you want us at the town hall at 7:30, right?"

"Oh! Yes. How did you find out about the meeting?"

"It's all over town. You're going to have a big crowd. Everybody wants to hear what you have to say. I heard that even some of the folks from the ranches are coming in."

"Well, that's fine. It's open to everybody."

"Virgil and I will see you then, gentlemen," Edna said, and was gone.

Monte looked at his boss with concern in his eyes. "I sure hope you're right, Sheriff. I hope the judge is all right."

"Yeah, me, too. All I could do was try to encourage her. And now, Deputy Dixon, since I'm a widower and you're a bachelor, how about we eat supper together?"

"Sounds good to me, boss," Monte said with a grin. "Long as you're buying."

When the lawmen entered the Meadowlark Café, someone called out, "There's the sheriff! Let's ask him!"

Men and women left their tables to converge on Lake, all talking at once.

"Wait a minute! Wait a minute!" Lake said, throwing up his hands. "Monte and I came in here to eat. You folks know about the meeting at the town hall in about an hour, don't you?"

All acknowledged that they did.

"Then you come to the meeting and I'll do my best to answer everybody's questions."

Lake noticed that Merlin and Hilda Loberg, the café's owners, and their new cook, Herb Guthridge, had come out of the kitchen.

"Evenin', folks," he said.

"Howdy, Lake," Merlin replied. "We've been listening to our customers since we started serving supper. We've only picked up bits and pieces of what's happened. Could you just tell us one thing right now?"

"What's that?"

"Word is that you've sent for John Stranger. Is he coming?"

"Well, I don't have definite word yet. Chief Duvall's wire said that Stranger's somewhere in the Rockies west of Denver, hunting down a killer. As soon as he returns, Duvall will have him wire me."

Disappointment showed on faces all around the café.

One man ventured a question. "Sheriff, I heard that in spite of all the evidence that Payton Sturgis has come back from the grave to fulfill his threat, you and Pastor Walker don't believe it's him. Is that right?"

"Lennie," Johnson said with a sigh, "Monte and I have got to eat right now, or we'll be late to the meeting. I'll answer you at the meeting, because I'm sure a whole lot of people want to ask the same question. Okay?"

"Sure, Sheriff. Maisie and I will be there."

Lake Johnson and his deputy took a table, and with no further interruptions, ordered and ate their meals.

At 7:25, the town hall was packed with men, women, and children. It appeared to Sheriff Lake Johnson that just about everybody who lived in Butte City and the outlying ranches was there. It was standing room only.

Monte Dixon leaned close and said, "Sheriff, I don't see Judge and Mrs. Reed anywhere."

At that moment Pastor Bob Walker approached them.

"Hello, Pastor," Lake said.

"Reverend," Monte said.

Walker greeted them both and said, "Phyllis and I spent about an hour with Martha Osborne. She's taking Les's death pretty hard. Phyllis and Nadine McVicker are staying with her. Tom and Nadine are going to take her to their home for the night, after the meeting."

"I'm sure that'll be a help to her, Pastor," Lake said.

Walker looked at the clock on the wall. "Well, I'll get out of your way. Time to get started."

"Pastor, have you got your Bible with you?"

"Yes, my small one's right here in my coat pocket."

"How about before I start answering questions, I have you come up and ask the Lord to help us bring this killer to justice?"

"All right."

"Then, would you read some of those Scriptures that show that nobody comes back from the dead, and comment on them?"

"Be glad to."

"Thanks. That may answer a lot of questions the people have. Save them asking. And stay close, please, in case I need help with Bible questions."

"Of course."

" 'Preciate it."

Lake stepped to the podium and raised his hands for silence. All but the crying babies cooperated. "Folks, I know that many of you are frightened by what has happened in our town. I want you to know that Deputy Dixon and I are going to do everything we can to bring this horrible chapter in the life of Butte City to an end. I will do my best to answer all your questions, but before we get to that, I've asked Pastor Walker to come and lead us in prayer and then tell us what the Bible says on the subject of ghosts. What he has to say will be a comfort to all of our hearts if we will listen. Pastor . . ."

The preacher stepped to the podium. When he finished praying, he opened his Bible and read several passages to the crowd so that everyone would understand what God said about death and about the fact that dead men do not come back from the grave.

"In closing," Walker said, after some twenty minutes of speaking, "let me encourage all of you to—"

A high-pitched cry suddenly filled the room. All eyes turned to see Edna Reed rushing up the center aisle, tears streaming down her face. Before Sheriff Johnson could ask her what was wrong, Edna sobbed, "Sheriff! Virgil's horse came into the yard a few minutes ago, pulling the buggy! But my husband wasn't in it! Something's happened to him! Oh-h! Payton's killed him! I just know it! Payton's killed him!"

CHAPTER

SEVEN

The babble following Edna Reed's words crescendoed to an uproar. Women were wailing, children were crying, and men were shouting at the sheriff that he had to do something quick.

The preacher took Edna off to the side of the room and left her with a couple of women from his congregation, who lovingly comforted her as best they could.

At the same time, Lake Johnson returned to the platform and shouted at the crowd until they finally quieted. "Listen to me, everybody!" he said, trying to keep his own emotions under control. "I need a couple of men to ride with my deputy right now and check the road to Crackerville. Since the horse found its way home, Judge Reed must have been reasonably close to town. Maybe he fell out of the buggy and is lying out there on the road. It shouldn't take long to find him."

There were several volunteers, including those whose names were on the killer's list.

Johnson shook his head, saying, "I appreciate you men who were on Payton's jury volunteering, but I'd rather you stayed here. I'll pick some other men to go."

Ranchers Clyde Moore and Fred Sanders offered to go. As Dixon and the ranchers were leaving, Sanders said he had a lantern in his wagon they could take.

When the trio had left, the sheriff quieted the people

again. "Folks," he said, "I want you to know that I'm trying to make contact with our friend John Stranger. As you know, he's the one who figured out who was killing our citizens two years ago. And it was Stranger who brought Payton Sturgis to justice. Until he comes, Deputy Dixon and I will be on this situation night and day. If we haven't stopped this maniac by the time Stranger gets here, I know he will.

"I realize this whole thing is terribly frightening to all of you, and especially to the men who've been marked, *and* to their families. Please, folks, try not to panic."

An elderly man named Jed Wagner spoke up. "Sheriff, what can these men do to defend themselves against this menace? Or the rest of us, for that matter. He may decide to just start killing at random, like Payton did."

Before Johnson could reply, Tom McVicker stood up and said loudly, "There's no way to defend ourselves against a ghost! I'm sorry to stand in opposition against Preacher Walker and Sheriff Johnson, but I saw Payton Sturgis at the bridge, as you all have heard by now! He had my foreman in his clutches, and there was nothing I could do about it. Payton is back, I tell you, and we all might as well face it!"

Mark Westbrook stood up. "Tom, I know you *think* you saw Payton, but Pastor is right. Dead men don't come back!"

"Right!" Jed Wagner agreed, rising to his feet. "I'm thinkin' that maybe Payton wasn't really dead. Somehow, he faked it and took off. He's been waitin' for these two years to come back and kill the men who put him on the gallows!"

There was a stirring among the people. Dr. Bristow, who was sitting with his wife, Sadie, rose to his feet and said, "Payton was dead! I know my friend Jed, like all of us, is trying to solve the mystery, but I'm here to tell all of you, I examined the body. Payton died of a broken neck. I know a dead man when I see one."

"Broken neck is right, Doc!" Tom McVicker said. "When I saw him on the bridge today, his head was bent to one side."

"Tom, the way that rope cracked his neck, there was no way Payton could have lived. Let's be realistic. He died, and he hasn't come back from the dead."

Ivan Charles was seated near the back of the room. Now he stood and called out, "I know a dead man when I see one too, folks! Doc is right. Payton was cold and dead when I laid his body in the coffin and nailed the lid down. I didn't bother to embalm him, but I'll tell you this, even if he had been alive when I nailed the coffin lid down, he sure wouldn't have lasted long in that pine box when it was six feet down under a ton of dirt!"

Tom McVicker spoke again. "Sheriff, we should have taken Chief Broken Bow's advice and opened Payton's grave to make sure the body is still in the coffin."

"Yeah, Sheriff!" a voice called. "That coffin ought to be opened, so we'll know!"

Dozens of voices—male and female—spoke their agreement.

Lake Johnson sighed and rubbed his forehead. He caught the eye of the town council chairman, who sat on the first row, and said, "Jackson, could the town afford to pay for having the coffin dug up?"

Jackson DeLong nodded yes.

Then the sheriff looked at Charles. "Ivan, would you be willing to open the grave at the town's expense?"

"I'd be glad to, Sheriff," the undertaker said. "And there won't be any charge. I want to see the inside of that coffin myself!"

"When do you want to do it, Ivan?"

"How about seven o'clock tomorrow morning?"

"Fine with me," Lake said. "I'll be there, and so will

Monte. How about you, Doc? I'd like to have you there if possible."

"I'll be there," Bristow said.

"It's all right if anyone else wants to be there, isn't it, Sheriff?" Tom McVicker asked.

"Sure. Cemetery's a public place. Anybody can come who wants to."

"I could use some help, Sheriff," Ivan said.

Several men volunteered to help open the grave. Ivan told them to bring picks as well as shovels, because the first few inches of earth would be frozen.

With that settled, the sheriff went on with the meeting. Only a few people asked questions, most of which had to do with how the marked men were going to protect themselves. Johnson suggested they never be alone. Both Dan Cogan and Les Osborne had been alone when they were killed. The marked men also should carry a gun at all times.

"What good are bullets or buckshot against a ghost, Sheriff?" Lawton Haymes said.

"None at all, Lawton," Lake replied, "but since the killer is a flesh-and-blood human being, bullets or buckshot will make him bleed and, if put in the right spot, will kill him."

This led back to questions about ghosts. Johnson turned the questions over to Pastor Walker, who gave biblical answers. Some accepted those answers in the face of the mystery that held them in its grip; others did not.

Sheriff Johnson, concerned that the frightened people might start shooting at anything that moved, warned them not to shoot in haste. When there were no more questions, he asked the preacher to close the meeting with prayer.

As Walker was praying at the podium, Deputy Monte Dixon and the two ranchers slipped in quietly. When the

"Amen" was said, the people began talking in low tones and moving about.

Lake spotted Monte and said, "Hold it, everybody! Monte's back!"

Every eye swung to the deputy.

Edna Reed was seated with several women gathered around her. When she heard the sheriff's words, she sprang to her feet, visibly trembling all over.

When Monte reached the podium he told Lake in a whisper, "We couldn't find a trace of the judge, Sheriff. Fresh snow may have covered evidence of foul play, but there's no way to know for sure."

Lake Johnson's face was solemn as he took a deep breath and said to the crowd, "Folks, Monte tells me that he and his two companions could find no trace of Judge Reed. But this doesn't mean—"

"He's dead!" Edna wailed. "Payton killed him!" She covered her face with her hands and sobbed.

Two of the women tried to comfort her as Pastor Walker and the sheriff hurried over to assist them.

While the preacher gripped her hands, Lake said, "Mrs. Reed, there's nothing more we can do tonight. You understand that."

Edna nodded, unable to control her sobs.

"We'll cover the entire road between here and Crackerville tomorrow morning, just as soon as we've opened Payton's grave," Lake continued.

"You'll find my husband's body!" Edna wailed. "He's dead! I know it! Payton Sturgis killed him!"

Lake stepped back and let the preacher talk to her. When Edna grew quiet, Walker spoke with the other women, and one said that she and her husband would take Edna home with them for the night.

Just before Edna was led out the door, Lake cautioned the people once more about giving in to panic. They began filing out into the cold night.

Jessie Westbrook was standing with her parents as they put on their coats. Monte Dixon, feeling a momentary burst of confidence, stepped up to her and said, "You're Jessie Westbrook, aren't you?"

Jessie had long black hair and large brown eyes. "Yes, I am, Deputy Dixon," she replied, smiling. "I haven't had the pleasure of meeting you yet. May I say welcome to our town? I'm sorry for this awful development. You probably wish you'd never come here."

"Not at all. I enjoy working for Sheriff Johnson, and I'm glad I can be here to do my part to help clear up this situation."

"I appreciate your attitude, Deputy," she said. "Really, Butte City is a great place to live. You'll like it once this ghost thing is settled and the culprit is caught."

"So, Jessie, you don't believe it's Payton Sturgis's ghost?"

"Absolutely not. I can't believe that and believe my Bible, too. So I'll just stick with my Bible. How about you, Deputy? Do you think it's Payton's ghost?"

"Oh . . . uh . . . no. No, I don't. Like you say, we can't believe the Bible and believe in ghosts."

"So you're a Bible-believer? That's wonderful!"

"Well, I don't know too much about it, but Sheriff Johnson has been helping me."

"Oh. So you're not a Christian?"

"Uh . . . no. But I'm giving it consideration. Sheriff Johnson has asked me to go to church with him on Sunday. So, I'm coming to hear Pastor Walker preach."

"I'm so glad you are, Deputy. The greatest need you have is to know the Lord Jesus."

"I'm beginning to realize that. I . . . uh . . . I'll look forward to seeing you at church, Jessie."

"And I'll look forward to it, too," she said, smiling at him sweetly.

Dawn's dismal gray sky was no comfort to the citizens of Butte City as they woke to the painful remembrance that there was a killer in their midst. The snow had stopped falling a short time before dawn, but mild wind gusts were picking up the newest flakes and swirling them upward only to fall again.

Windows in houses and business buildings were coated with frost. The towering conifers that lined the streets in the residential areas and surrounded the town seemed to feel the weight of gloom that was in the hearts of its citizens. The massive trees stood with heads bowed, yielding to the heavy snow that clung to their branches.

At 6:15, Sheriff Lake Johnson was in his office, building a fire in the potbellied stove, when Monte Dixon came in followed by Dr. Bristow, his wife Sadie, and Ivan Charles. Lake had asked them to come early so they could be the first ones at the cemetery.

The sheriff greeted them, then smiled at Sadie and said, "So you want to see the skeleton in the box too, m'lady?"

"I'm not eager to, Sheriff," she responded softly. "Just curious."

Lake adjusted the damper, dusted off his hands, and said, "Well, let's go."

Ivan drove the Bristows in his funeral coach while the lawmen rode their horses. As they traveled north out of town, they saw a few brave souls moving about outdoors. Most of the citizens were still inside where it was warm, but Lake knew they were getting ready to go to the cemetery. Even the

Christians in town wanted to be there when the lid was removed from Payton Sturgis's coffin.

As the wagon and saddle horses drew near the snow-covered crest of the hill, Doc Bristow said, "Ivan, you don't really think you'll find it empty, do you?"

"Doc, this whole thing has me strung tight as a telegraph wire. I'm not sure of anything any more. Let's just say that if Payton's bones aren't in that coffin, I'm going to be a whole lot more frightened than I have been up to this point, and I'm not on the list, nor did I find a grave marker with my name on it."

"Speaking of those grave markers," Lake said, "we threw them in the ditch just beyond Payton's grave."

"Good! Only better place would be in the stove in my apartment. They'd make good firew—" The undertaker's eyes bulged. "Sheriff, I thought you said you threw those markers in the ditch."

Lake's mouth fell open at the sight of fifteen crosses stretching out in a row. They were back in their original position.

Lake goaded his horse and trotted him through the snow to the site of Payton Sturgis's grave. Monte Dixon was right with him. Lake raised himself in the saddle as if pulling away from something. Then Dixon heard him gasp. Beneath a thin coating of snow was a dirt mound about three feet wide and nearly six feet long. At the head of the grave, the inscribed wooden marker read:

JUDGE VIRGIL J. REED

The lawmen dismounted, eyes fixed on the fresh grave, as the wagon drew up. "What is it, Sheriff?" Doc Bristow asked, trying to see past the two saddle horses.

Lake turned and said in a tired voice, "Come and see."

While the doctor helped his wife out of the funeral wagon, Ivan Charles hurried to see what had drawn the lawmen's attention. He stopped abruptly when he saw the new grave. Seconds later, the Bristows drew up, and Sadie's breath caught in her throat.

"I'll get my shovel," Ivan said, shaking his head.

People from town were coming up the hill as Ivan quickly dug down about two feet through the comparatively soft dirt and found the portly body of Judge Reed.

The four men freed the body from the hole and lifted it to the snow-laden ground. They brushed away as much dirt as possible from the clothing. Doc knelt in the snow and did a quick examination.

"Single knife puncture in the chest," Doc reported. "Long blade went straight through his heart. He died instantly."

"Let's put the body in my wagon," Ivan said, his voice trembling.

Monte helped Ivan carry the corpse to the wagon and lay it in the back. Ivan quickly covered the body with a tarp.

The earliest people to arrive were close enough to see that the body was that of Judge Reed. They passed the word to those behind them, and fear spread through the group. Sheriff and deputy tried to calm those who were already gathered at the site.

The name of Payton Sturgis was on most lips, and the ghost theory was fast becoming a reality in many minds. Some were saying that old Jed Wagner may be right—the fiend might just start killing at random.

While Lake and Monte worked at trying to calm the growing crowd, they noticed Chief Broken Bow and six braves at the rear edge of the crowd. More townspeople were coming up behind them. Edna Reed was riding in a buggy with two other women.

Suddenly a voice cried out, "Sheriff, you've got to do something! You're being paid to protect this county, and especially this town! The killing must be stopped!"

Loud voices rose in agreement.

Lake, whose own nerves were frayed, said loudly, "I'm doing everything I can, but I can't be in more than one place at a time. How am I supposed to know where the killer is going to strike next? Be reasonable!"

A piercing shriek cut the cold morning air, and every eye went to Edna Reed. She had made her way to the side of Ivan Charles's wagon. Now she held up the tarp and screamed her husband's name hysterically at the top of her voice. Bob and Phyllis Walker rushed to her side. Doc and Sadie joined them and said they'd take her to the office and give her a sedative.

The men who had volunteered to help Ivan open Payton Sturgis's grave moved in eagerly with their picks and shovels, the crowd at their heels.

Lake raised his hands to quiet the crowd and said, "Now, folks, I hope you will give us a little space to do our work. When I was elected to this job, I took an oath to uphold the law in this county to the best of my ability. I hate what's going on here as much as you do. And I might remind you that I'm on the killer's list, too. Monte and I will do everything possible to stop this killer, and if possible, we'll have John Stranger here soon. Please bear with me. I need your help, not your criticism!"

"That's right, Sheriff!" called out Milo Wilson. "Listen to him, you people! We need to back this man, not buck him!"

"Well spoken, Milo!" Pastor Walker said.

Other voices joined in, shouting their agreement.

Encouraged, Lake Johnson said, "You people came here to watch Payton's coffin opened. You still want that?"

The crowd affirmed that they did.

The sheriff gave the signal and Ivan Charles and his helpers swung their picks to break up the frozen ground.

The people huddled in a tight circle, their eyes fixed on the spot. Soon the men were past the frozen ground, and digging with their shovels. When the shovels scraped wood, tension mounted.

They cleared the dirt and lowered ropes into the rectangular hole to attach to the coffin handles. Ivan and his helpers, including sheriff and deputy, got a good grip on the rope.

"All right, now," Ivan said, "we have to lift it evenly. On the count of three, we all lift at the same time to keep the coffin level. Is everybody ready?"

The men nodded.

"All right," Ivan said. "One . . . two . . . *three!*"

The ropes went taut, and the coffin began to rise from the hole.

Monte Dixon blinked and said, "Doesn't feel heavy enough to have a body in it, Ivan."

Charles gave him a tight grin. "Skeletons don't weigh very much, Deputy."

The coffin swayed slightly against the ropes as it reached the earth's surface.

"All right, men," the undertaker said, "let's set it down." The coffin settled into the snow with a crunching sound.

Ivan hurried to his funeral wagon and returned with a hammer and chisel. The crowd stood breathless while he tapped his way around the thick wooden lid, loosening the nails. The nails squeaked with each lift of the chisel. Finally the lid was loose enough for Ivan to finish removing it with his hands.

Ivan gave the lid a yank, and it came free. As soon as the lid was off there were gasps of horror at the sight of an empty coffin.

Susan Cosgrove, the hotel owner's wife, cried, "See? I knew it! Tom McVicker told us he saw Payton! He's escaped the grave and come to kill my husband!"

Frank took her in his arms and turned her toward their wagon, saying, "Let's go home, honey."

Most of the crowd stood speechless.

Pastor Walker stepped up to Ivan and said, "What do you make of it?"

Charles shook his head, his face showing the shock he felt. "Preacher, I don't know. I buried Payton's lifeless body in this coffin two years ago. George Walz and Ernie Davis helped me nail down the lid, lower the coffin into the ground, and cover it up."

"That's right," George said. "We buried that cold-blooded beast, just like Ivan says."

"But he's escaped the grave and come back!" Roberta Amick wailed. "He's come to kill Darrell and make me a widow, just like he did Edna and Martha and Elaine!"

Pandemonium broke out. Lake Johnson tried to settle the crowd, but to no avail. Women were screaming and some passed out, and the men were trying to care for them and comfort them. Lake turned to see Broken Bow looking at him with stoic eyes. "It is as I told you, Sheriff Lake Johnson," came the chief's deep voice. "Payton Sturgis has come back as snow ghost."

Jed Wagner, who was standing close by, cried, "Best thing for you marked men to do is make a run for it. Get outta town!"

The Crow chief spoke loudly. "No! It would be foolish for anyone to try to run from snow ghost! He would only follow them! Take comfort in one thing. Snow ghosts only come for their victims when snow falls from sky.'"

Althea Kevane cried out, "There'll be enough snowstorms before winter is over for Payton to kill every marked man!"

Sheriff Johnson waved for the crowd to quiet down and said, "People, listen to me! This is a mystery neither I nor my pastor can fathom, but I'm telling you the killer is not Payton Sturgis! Dead men don't come back!"

"Then where's his body, Sheriff?" Eva Walz demanded.

"I don't have an answer right now, Eva, but this killer is not a ghost. I'll do everything in my power to catch him. And as soon as possible, I'll have John Stranger here to help!"

CHAPTER

EIGHT

The small log cabin nestled in the shelter of the snow-crusted evergreens, high in Colorado's Rocky Mountains. Snow had fallen the day before, and the cabin was surrounded by a world of white that brilliantly reflected the sun's morning light.

A stream of smoke rose from the chimney, carried south by the slight breeze out of the north. Deer and elk foraged for food in the surrounding timber.

Jake Bowman stood on the back porch, hands thrust deep in the pockets of his sheepskin coat. Shaggy hair sticking out from under his hat matched the silver of his full beard and mustache. The cold air made his breath plume out like steam from a boiling kettle.

Jake watched the barn door until it opened and the tall man emerged, leading his huge black gelding. Jake squinted against the light of the rising sun and smiled toothlessly, admiring the horse, its beautiful black saddle and matching bridle, and its owner.

The tall man dressed in black from his boots to the low-crowned hat on his head had twin jagged scars on his right cheek. His eyes were gunmetal gray, and his well-trimmed mustache matched his black hair. On his hip, under the long greatcoat, he wore a bone-handled Colt .45 Peacemaker in a low-slung black gunbelt. A leather thong secured the holster to his leg.

The tall man led the gelding to the edge of the porch and extended his hand. "Thanks a heap, Jake. I really appreciate your hospitality. Sleeping in your cabin beside a warm stove sure beats burrowing into a snowbank. And thanks for breakfast."

As Jake clasped the man's hand, he said, "It's me who needs to be thanking *you*, John Stranger. Thank you for carin' 'bout an old lost sinner like me, and takin' the time to show me from my own dusty Bible 'bout Jesus dyin' for me, personally, on that cross. I'd have left this world lost when my time came if you hadn't led me to the Lord."

Ebony nickered as his master swung into the saddle. Stranger smiled and said, "Jake, if we don't meet again on earth, we'll have us a reunion at the pearly gates."

The old man's wrinkles deepened as he showed his gums in a grin. "We sure will, my friend. We sure will. I hope you catch that killer purty soon. What'd you say his name is?"

"Leo Tupa."

"An' how many folks did you say he murdered?"

"We've got proof of eleven. Eight men and three women."

"Well, even one conviction will get him a noose when you catch him, that's for sure. So you think you're close on his heels, huh?"

"Yes. He's headed for Leadville. He has no idea I'm on his trail, so I've got a little surprise for him."

"Well, God bless you, John. Go get him."

Stranger wheeled Ebony about and waved. "God bless you too, Jake."

Stranger guided Ebony down the slope through the deep snow. Before entering the dense timber, he drew rein and looked up toward the cabin and saw the old man still standing there. He lifted his hand again, then turned west toward Leadville and its elevation of over ten thousand feet.

Horse and rider were soon climbing through a three-foot depth of snow. The majestic mountains glistened like polished silver, sparkling with the sun's brilliance reflected from countless frozen crystals.

It was just after noon when John Stranger emerged from the heavy forest east of Leadville and guided Ebony past long rows of cabins that made up the section of town where the miners lived.

The wooded slopes surrounding the town were marked by the spiderweb tracery of spindly limbed aspen trees and dark-shadowed fir, their needles dark green beneath clumps of snow.

When Stranger reached the wagon-rutted street that was the center of Leadville and its business district, he turned right and let his gaze sweep both sides of the street. Traffic was heavy, and the boardwalks were crowded with shoppers.

The business district was only two blocks long, yet in that length Stranger counted five saloons. He stopped in front of the Bulldog Saloon and left Ebony tied to the hitch rail, then crossed the boardwalk into the saloon's dark interior.

Stranger always felt ill at ease in saloons and only entered them when duty called. A man who carried the Holy Spirit of God in his bosom was like a fish out of water in such places.

The Bulldog was relatively quiet for a drinking and gambling place in a town like Leadville, even at midday. Since there was no tinkling piano playing, the low rumble of voices sounded louder than usual. Five men stood at the bar, drinks in hand. Behind the bar stood a short, plump, red-nosed man who looked like he might be drinking up all the profits. Stranger headed his way.

The chubby barkeep looked Stranger up and down, smiled, and said, "Yes, sir. What'll it be?"

"Just some information."

The smile drained away.

"I'm looking for a fella named Leo Tupa. T-U-P-A. Not hard to spot. He's short, stocky, and wears a close-cropped beard. His upper lip is missing. Knife fight. Gums show all the time where the lip used to be. Late thirties. He been in here?"

The bartender frowned. "You the law?"

"What difference does it make? I asked a simple question. Has the man been in here?"

"Not that I recall. I don't look at every man's upper lip when he comes in."

"Okay, thanks," Stranger said, and turned to leave. He could feel the bartender's eyes on him all the way to the door. Outside at the hitch rail, as he was untying Ebony's reins, he heard the saloon door open.

"Hey, mister!" a voice called.

John paused and looked back. "Yes, sir?"

The man came close and said, "I was at the bar and couldn't help overhearing your conversation with Eddie. The guy you described was in the Lucky Horseshoe Saloon up the street yesterday. I got a feelin' he's been in the Bulldog, too. Anyway, I heard this guy with no upper lip tell somebody in the Horseshoe that he's stayin' at the hotel. He's kind of a mean-lookin' dude."

Stranger grinned. "You get his name?"

"No, sir."

"Well, thank you for the information. I appreciate it."

"Glad to help," the man said, turning back toward the saloon door. Stranger was already in the saddle when the man stopped and called out, "Hey, mister!"

Stranger eyed him in a friendly manner. "Yes?"

"*Are* you a lawman?"

Stranger grinned, touched the brim of his hat, and rode on. He weaved the big black through street traffic and soon arrived at the Rocky Mountain Hotel.

Desk clerk Wiley Manners was a small, bald-headed man in his mid-sixties. The tall man in the long black coat caught his attention as soon as he came through the door.

"Need a room, sir?" Manners asked, looking at Stranger over his half-moon spectacles.

"Might. Right now, I just need some information."

"If I can supply it, I'll be happy to, sir."

John reached inside his coat and withdrew a folded, official-looking paper. He held it so the clerk could read it and said, "This paper is from the Chief United States Marshal's Office in Denver. It shows that I have been authorized by Chief Duvall to track down and capture an outlaw killer by the name of Leo Tupa."

Manners quickly scanned the writing and said, "I see that, Mr.—Mr. Stranger. This Leo Tupa's a bad one, eh?"

"Cold-blooded, heartless killer. Wanted in two states and three territories."

"He must be a bad one, all right. What can I do for you?"

"I was told a few minutes ago that he's staying here in the hotel."

"We don't have anyone here by the name of Leo Tupa, sir."

"The man I'm looking for is in his late thirties, short and stocky, and wears a close-cropped beard. He has no upper lip. Lost it in a knife fight years ago. Mean look in his narrow-set eyes."

"Well, Mr. Stranger, you're describing Robert Nelson. He's . . . ah . . . registered here by that name."

"What room is he in?"

"Room twelve, upstairs. About halfway down the hall on the right side. He came in and registered midafternoon yesterday. Said he's waiting for a man named Duane Mead to arrive in town today or tomorrow."

"Is this Nelson in his room?" Stranger asked.

"Yes, sir. He was out all morning, but he came in about fifteen minutes ago."

Stranger looked over his shoulder at the staircase to the second floor.

"This Duane Mead. He's a bad one too, huh?" Manners asked.

"Yes."

"You know him?"

"Never met him. But I know about him. He's a gunslinger. But worse, just like Tupa, he's a cold-blooded murderer. I'm not surprised to learn they run together."

Manners grinned. "Birds of a feather, right?"

"Right. Tell me, are there any guests upstairs in their rooms at the moment?"

"Yes, sir."

Stranger scrubbed a hand over his mouth. "Mmm. Then I've got to take him without gunplay if possible."

"Now?"

"Now. Tell you what. If you'll help me, I think I can take him without a shot being fired."

"All right."

"Good. Here's what we'll do . . ."

Leo Tupa lay on the bed in his hotel room with a whiskey bottle in his hand. Periodically, he removed the cork and took a pull. After a while, he reached over and set the bottle on the bed stand.

"Better not put down too much of this stuff," he told himself. "Need a clear head when Duane gets here."

Tupa let his mind settle on Duane Mead. The infamous gunfighter had told Leo last week in Denver that he had a foolproof plan to swindle a miner here in Leadville. Could he really bilk a man out of his claim?

Duane had told him it would take two men to pull off the scheme, but when it was done, both of them would be so rich they'd never have to scrape for a dollar again. It was hard for Tupa to understand why a man who was so eager to work his way up the roster of top gunfighters in the West would take the time to swindle himself a gold mine.

Oh, well, Tupa thought, I won't mind bein' rich as long as it doesn't make me turn to mush so I don't enjoy killin' somebody now and then.

Tupa heard the sound of footsteps in the hall. "Duane?" he half-whispered, turning his face toward the door.

The footsteps stopped at his door. And then he heard a knock.

"Who is it?"

Wiley Manners's muffled voice came through the door. "Mr. Nelson, you're expecting Mr. Mead . . ."

"Coming!" Tupa smiled to himself and rose from the bed.

Tupa turned the skeleton key in the lock and twisted the knob, pulling the door open. "Well, it's about time, Duane! I've b—"

Leo was surprised to see a man who was a good seven or eight inches taller than he, square-jawed, broad-shouldered, with a pair of jagged twin scars on his right cheek.

"Who are you?" the outlaw demanded.

"I'm your worst nightmare," Stranger said.

Before Tupa could move a muscle, a fist lashed out and caught him solidly on the jaw and sent him reeling backwards. When he hit the floor, a black cloud began to descend over him. For a brief moment he struggled against its weight, then everything went black.

Leo Tupa heard male voices from somewhere in the black fog that had swallowed him. His head throbbed, and his jaw felt like someone had pounded it with a sledgehammer. Where was he? Who was talking? Why did he feel like he was spinning in circles?

He could hear someone moaning. He wished whoever it was would be quiet. It was irritating. When he ran his tongue over the dry roof of his mouth and the moaning stopped, he realized it was coming from him.

"Looks like he's almost back with us," a voice said.

"Another minute or so," another voice said.

Leo opened his eyes, blinked, and closed them again. The pain inside his head and in the hollow of his jaw was fierce.

"C'mon, Tupa," the first voice said. "Wake up."

His eyes opened again, and he could see a ceiling above him, and a face. A fuzzy face. He was in a room, and the room was spinning in circles. He closed his eyes, willing the dizziness away.

"I'm Lance Adkins, Leadville's town marshal," the same voice said. "You're under arrest."

Leadville! That rang a bell. Sure. Leadville. Duane Mead. The knock on the door. Duane. No, not Duane! Some tall guy . . .

And now, as the fog was clearing and his senses were coming back, Leo realized he was lying on his back against a hard wooden floor, and his arms were pinned beneath him. He tried to move them, but they wouldn't cooperate. Something—*handcuffs!* His wrists were cuffed behind his back.

"You hear me, Tupa? You're under arrest."

A second face appeared. The owner of that face said, "For

murder, Tupa. You're going back to Denver to stand trial for at least eleven counts of murder."

"Who're you?" Tupa said.

"Ever hear of the man they call the Stranger, Leo?" Marshal Adkins asked.

Tupa's head throbbed, but his brain came clear. "Yeah."

"Well, meet the Stranger."

The outlaw squinted, studying John's angular features. "Y-you're the one who—"

"Punched you?"

"Yeah."

"Correct. And I'm the one who's taking you back to Denver."

"You . . . you been trackin' me?"

"Mm-hmm." Stranger took him by the arm. "Come on. Let's get you on your feet."

People on the street gawked as Marshal Adkins and John Stranger ushered a handcuffed Leo Tupa along the boardwalk toward the marshal's office and jail.

The outlaw's voice quivered. "How long you been trackin' me, Stranger?"

"Since a day and a half after you left Denver. You know, when you knifed that man in the back who beat you in the poker game at the Colfax Saloon."

"I didn't knife nobody! What're you talkin' about?"

"That's funny. We have two men waiting in Denver to testify that they saw you do it right under the street lamp at Colfax and Broadway. They were across the street in the shadows, and you didn't see them. You *did* kill Harley Kramer at Colfax and Broadway, didn't you?"

Tupa didn't reply.

"You'll spend the night in Marshal Adkins's nice jail, Leo," Stranger said, as the marshal opened the office door.

"You and I will head out for Denver early in the morning. And for your information—just in case you're thinking you might escape—you will make the entire trip with your hands cuffed behind you and wearing leg irons."

Tupa gave Stranger a hateful look as they moved inside.

"And if you so much as *attempt* an escape, Leo, you'll make the rest of the trip on your belly behind your horse. Fella could get his face scratched up right bad, traveling like that."

Directly across the street from the marshal's office, Duane Mead sat his horse and watched John Stranger and the marshal usher Leo Tupa through the door with his hands shackled behind his back.

Mead had arrived in town just in time to see his friend marched to the jail. Warring emotions stirred within him. He felt anger because Leo was in the hands of the law, but he also felt elation because the man who was with the marshal was John Stranger.

Mead had a narrow hatchet face with a cruel, downturned mouth. His close-set shifty eyes were such a pale blue that they seemed to have no bottom. He was tall and slender, and his body moved with the natural rhythm of a gunfighter.

For the past three years Mead had been inching his way up the "gunfighter's ladder" after outdrawing and killing one of the top names on the roster. He was hungry to become the fastest gun in the West, and now only a few men stood in his way. One of those men was John Stranger.

Mead smiled to himself as he dismounted. Today he would challenge Stranger and leave him lying dead in the snow-crusted street. He had seen Stranger challenged by a gunslick named Benny Wick down in Santa Fe a couple of years ago. Wick was a clumsy fool. He deserved to die at Stranger's hand.

Duane Mead was no fool. That day in Santa Fe he had watched Stranger carefully and memorized the way he drew and fired. Ever since then he had imitated the man's style and found it rewarding. He had taken out every man he faced.

Now it was time to use the unwitting teacher's own style against him. Mead practiced his draw every day to hone it to perfection. This was John Stranger's day to meet his match and die.

When the barred steel door clanked shut on Leo Tupa, he turned to glare wickedly at Stranger and Adkins.

"Better sit down on the bunk and rest your bones, Leo," Stranger said. "You've got a hard ride coming up." Then turning to the marshal he said, "I'll go on over to the hotel and get a room."

"What time you plan to leave in the morning?" Adkins said.

"Let's say six o'clock."

"Okay. I'll feed whatshisname at five-thirty."

"How about supper this evening? Can I buy you a steak?"

"Woe be unto me if I ever turn down free food," the marshal said with a laugh.

Stranger grinned. "What time?"

"I close up at six."

"Then I'll be here at six."

Stranger stepped outside and headed down the boardwalk toward the hotel.

"Hey, John Stranger!" came a booming voice to his right.

John turned to see who was calling his name. The man was standing in the middle of the street, holding a palm up to stop traffic. Wagons and buggies halted on both sides of him, as did men on horseback. It took them only seconds to realize what was happening. People on foot began to gather. Few ever avoided watching a gunfight.

John had never seen Duane Mead, but he'd heard his description. And he knew Tupa had been expecting Mead. Stranger's long black coat was buttoned, and he would leave it that way if possible. But by the look in the man's eyes, he doubted it was going to be possible.

Stranger stepped into the street. "You wanted to see me, mister?" He stopped with some thirty feet between them.

"Yeah," Mead said, his breath making tiny clouds on the cold air. "You know who I am?"

"Should I?"

"Ever hear the name Duane Mead?"

"Guess I have."

"Well, you're lookin' at him."

Stranger moved his head back and forth slowly and said, "You don't want to do this, Duane."

Mead's face contorted with anger. His coat was already unbuttoned. He pushed it behind his holster and took his gunfighter's stance. "It's time somebody took you down, Stranger!"

"Well, it won't be you."

Mead laughed hollowly as the crowd increased in number. "What kind of man is a gunhawk and a preacher all rolled into one? No wonder they call you *strange*."

Stranger's hands were at his sides. The coat was still buttoned.

"I don't consider myself a gunhawk, Duane. A preacher, yes. But not a gunfighter. I'm not like you. I don't go around challenging men so I can have a big name as a gunslick. Now, just let it go. I don't want to kill you, but I will if you force me."

Mead threw back his head and guffawed. "Every man meets his match sooner or later, Stranger, and you're about to meet yours. I'm challengin' you here and now, in front of all these nice people!"

"Don't force me, Duane. You're alive and breathing. Let it stay that way."

"I've been wantin' you for a long time! Now either you draw against me or I'll shoot you down like a dirty, mangy coward!"

Mead's lips curved in an evil grin as the steady-eyed Stranger unbuttoned his coat and tucked it back so he could draw. The two men slowly positioned themselves in the street about forty feet apart and in such a way as to keep the people on the boardwalks out of the line of fire.

"Duane," Stranger said, "one last time. Give it up. I don't want to kill you."

"You won't!" Mead shouted, and his gun hand flashed down.

John Stranger's move was smooth and snakelike. The Peacemaker was out and spitting fire just as Mead cleared leather. Surprise filled Mead's eyes as the .45 slug struck his right shoulder and knocked him flat on his back. The gun was still in his hand.

The crowd looked on in amazement.

Stranger walked toward Mead, thin tendrils of smoke rising from the Peacemaker's muzzle. Suddenly, Mead raised his gun to shoot again and left Stranger no choice. The Peacemaker roared once more.

It was a cold, brisk day, but the sun was shining as Denver County Sheriff Curt Langan and his deputy, Steve Ridgway, sat in the office having coffee.

Steve glanced out the window at the same time John

Stranger drew up to the hitch rail outside. He was leading a second horse with a man in the saddle shackled in handcuffs and leg irons.

"Hey, John's back! And he's got Tupa!"

The lawmen charged out the door to welcome John, who handed Langan the reins of Tupa's horse and said, "I told Leo you'd have a nice uncomfortable cell for him."

"Of course," Curt said with a chuckle. "Steve and I will make it as uncomfortable as possible!"

Tupa set sullen eyes on Langan but remained silent.

"I'll see you gents later," Stranger said. "I've got to report in to the chief."

John halted Ebony and slid from the saddle in front of the federal building on Tremont Street. When he stepped into the U.S. Marshal's Office, Chief Solomon Duvall was leaning over the desk of his male secretary, explaining something on a slip of paper.

The tall, silver-haired Duvall looked up at the sound of the door opening and broke into a broad smile. "Well, howdy, John! Dead or alive?"

"Alive and unharmed. He's checking in at the Langan Hotel right now."

"Good. It'll be the hangman's pleasure to put a noose on his neck. Come on back to my office. I want to hear all about it. And I've got an urgent message for you."

John took a few minutes to tell how he caught Leo Tupa, and how he had to take out Duane Mead. Duvall commended him for a job well done.

Stranger eased back on the wooden chair in front of Duvall's desk and said, "Now, what's this urgent message?"

Duvall leaned forward and said, "I received a wire a few

days ago from Sheriff Lake Johnson in Butte City."

"Oh? What's up?"

"All he said was that when you returned to Denver I was to tell you he needs you desperately, and to mention one name . . . *Payton Sturgis.*"

CHAPTER

NINE

It was mid-morning when a buggy driven by a man in a well-pressed business suit under his overcoat pulled into the parking area of Denver's Mile High Hospital. Peggy Walters looked up from her receptionist desk when the man entered the front door.

"Good morning, sir," Peggy said with a broad smile. "May I help you?"

"Yes, ma'am. My name is Bertram Chadwick. I'm with the Wallace A. Morton Company of Kansas City. We manufacture canes, crutches, wheelchairs, and all kinds of hospital equipment. I'm between trains on my way back home, and I thought while I was in Denver, I would come by and see if I could talk to your chief administrator. I believe his name is Dr. Matthew Carroll."

"Yes, it is, Mr. Chadwick. How long will you be in town?"

"Only until one o'clock, ma'am."

Peggy glanced at the clock on the wall. "The reason I ask, sir, is that at present, Dr. Carroll is in surgery. There's no way to estimate how long the operation will take, but it's quite serious, and he could be there for some time."

Chadwick's eyebrows arched. "Surgery? He's chief administrator of the hospital, and he's performing surgery?"

"Yes, sir. You'd have to know Dr. Carroll to understand, but he still practices medicine, even with the load of running the hospital. He has his private practice in the building just east of the hospital, and he performs surgery on a regular basis. He's the most prominent surgeon in the entire Rocky Mountain region."

"I see. Will it be all right if I wait around for a while? I'd sure like to see him if possible."

"You can be seated over here in the waiting area. If Dr. Carroll comes out of surgery before you have to leave, I'll tell him you're here."

Chadwick fished a business card out of his coat pocket. "Let me give you this. You can show it to him when you tell him I'm here."

"Thank you, sir. I'll be glad to do that."

Chadwick removed his overcoat and derby and took a seat.

A nurse emerged from the hallway behind the reception desk and laid some papers before Peggy. "There you are, sweetie. This will keep you busy for a while."

"Glad to help, Stefanie," Peggy said.

"Pretty nurse," Chadwick said after Stefanie disappeared down the hall.

"That she is. Her husband is Denver County's sheriff, Curt Langan."

"Oh. I see."

The next two hours saw numerous people pass in and out of the hospital, visiting patients. It was almost noon when Peggy Walters's attention was drawn to the front door when it came open and John Stranger stepped inside.

"Hello, Mr. Stranger," Peggy said, smiling warmly.

"How's Miss Peggy today?" he smiled in return.

"Doing fine. I hate to disappoint you, but the lady you're here to see is in surgery with Dr. Carroll. Could be quite some time yet."

"M-m-m," Stranger hummed, rubbing his mustache.

"Well, okay. I'll come back later. If she comes out before I get back, please let her know I was here."

"Will do."

When the tall man-in-black was gone, Bertram Chadwick approached the desk. "Pardon me, Miss, but did I hear correctly? You called that man Mr. Stranger?"

"Yes."

"He's John Stranger?"

"That's right."

He looked toward the door where he had last seen Stranger. "I've heard a lot about him. Some people say they think he's an angel from heaven disguised as a man. They say that sometimes he hands people a silver medallion that says something about him being from some far country . . . like maybe that far country isn't of this world."

Peggy smiled. "I've never seen any of the medallions, Mr. Chadwick, though I've heard about them, too. I have no idea where he's from, but I can tell you for sure . . . he's human."

Chadwick studied her steady eyes for a moment. "Well, you seem to be well acquainted with him. I guess you ought to know."

For the second time Breanna Baylor administered ether to the elderly man on the surgery table, then returned to her position beside the doctor as he began cutting away tissue from a tumor in the patient's midsection. The operation was touch-and-go.

Although the operating room was cool, Dr. Carroll's brow was beaded with perspiration. For probably the dozenth time, Breanna picked up a cloth from the table next to her and dabbed at the doctor's forehead.

After several minutes of watching him skillfully work

with the scalpel, Breanna asked if he thought the tumor was malignant.

"I'm almost positive it's hyperplasia," he replied.

"Good."

After a few more minutes, Breanna once again administered a small amount of ether and then stood ready to assist if necessary.

Breanna looked at Matt Carroll with admiration. He had turned out to be such a marvelous husband to her sister, Dottie. He was a dedicated Christian and a wonderful adoptive father to Dottie's children, James and Molly Kate.

After the mental illness and tragic death of Dottie's first husband, Jerrod Harper, and all the anguish Dottie and the children had suffered, Breanna was thrilled to see them so happy and enjoying life again. Silently she thanked the Lord for His wondrous working in their lives.

After more than five hours at the operating table, Dr. Carroll pronounced the surgery a success. A male attendant wheeled the patient into the recovery room where another nurse would watch over him until he regained consciousness and could be taken to his room.

While they scrubbed their hands at the wash basin, Matt said, "Breanna, have you heard anything from John?"

"No, but I'm hopeful he'll return soon with that Leo Tupa in tow."

"Mm-hmm. From what I've read in the paper, Tupa's a bad one."

"That's the kind Chief Duvall sends John after."

"I can understand why. The man's good at what he does."

"Too good," Breanna said, drying her hands on a fresh towel. "That's why he's gone so much."

A moment later, Breanna and her brother-in-law emerged

from the surgical room into the hall. Near the door, leaning against the wall, was the very man they had been discussing.

"Oh, John!" Breanna gasped, and rushed into his arms. "I'm so glad you're back! Did you get him?"

"Yep."

"Why even ask, Breanna?" Dr. Carroll said, reaching out to shake John's hand. "John always gets his man . . . or men. Is Tupa breathing, or will they bury him today?"

"He's breathing. But not for long. He'll hang in a day or two."

"Are you going to be home for a while?" Matt asked.

John looked into Breanna's sky-blue eyes as he answered, "Until six-thirty tomorrow morning."

Breanna's bright expression dimmed. "So soon, John? What is it this time?"

"I'll explain over dinner tonight. And I've got something very important to discuss with you while we eat."

Breanna looked at Matt and said, "Will you tell Dottie that John is home? I'll have to pass on the invitation to supper this evening."

"Of course. But if you like, you could eat supper at the Carroll house, then have the rest of the evening to yourselves."

John chuckled. "I sure could use some of Molly Kate's hugs. So if it's all right with Breanna, we'll eat at your place."

The meal was over and the adults were sipping a final cup of coffee at the kitchen table. Molly Kate sat on "Uncle" John's lap.

James, her brother, looked across the table, eyes flashing, and said, "Okay, Uncle John, I wanna know all about how you captured that Leo Tupa!"

Dottie, who strongly resembled her older sister, said,

"James, you heard Uncle John and Aunt Breanna say they had things to talk about tonight. Uncle John can tell you about it another time."

"I think we've got time to tell the Tupa story, Dottie," John said.

Molly Kate stayed in his lap while he told about his pursuit and capture of the outlaw and then the shootout with Duane Mead. When he finished, James said, "I can't wait till I grow up, Uncle John! I'm gonna be fast with a gun just like you, and chase bad guys! Only I'm gonna wear a badge."

Molly Kate looked up into John's cool gray eyes. "How come you don't wear a badge, Uncle John? You always chase bad guys."

"I'll have to explain that later, honey," John said, kissing the top of her head. "Right now, your Aunt Breanna and I have to go."

"Not till I help with the dishes," Breanna said.

The two sisters argued about it good-naturedly, with Dottie insisting that she and the children would do the dishes. As usual, Breanna won. Matt and John stayed at the table while the others worked around them.

"So where are you going tomorrow, John?" Matt asked.

Though Breanna was busy at the cupboard, her ears pricked up to hear his answer.

"Montana. I'll take the six-thirty train for Cheyenne City in the morning, then catch the afternoon train to Billings. Union Pacific finished laying track between Cheyenne City and Billings just about a month ago."

"I did read something in the paper about that," Matt said.

"I'll take a stagecoach from Billings to Butte City."

"Butte City . . . isn't that where you were last summer when you almost got caught in that forest fire?"

"I was in Billings. The fire was in the forest country north-west of there."

"Oh. But you *have* been to Butte City. Seems like you once mentioned chasing down an outlaw up there."

"Might have. It was a couple of years ago that I went there to help Sheriff Lake Johnson trap a killer."

"You did trap him, and he hanged," Breanna said, moving toward the table. "You told me all about it. What was the killer's name? Ah . . . something Sturgman, was it?"

"Sturgis. Payton Sturgis."

"Yes, that's it."

"So what's the problem in Butte City now?" Dottie asked, as she wiped off the table with a damp cloth.

"Wel-l-l, they, ah . . . have another killer on the loose in the area. Sheriff Johnson seems to think that since I helped stop Sturgis, I might be able to help with this new guy."

Dottie chuckled. "Come on, now, John. I know why you're *really* going back to that part of Montana. You want to see if you can get a glimpse of that big black horse that saved your life last summer in the fire. What did you call him?"

"He called him Chance, Mom," James said. "Didn't you, Uncle John? 'Cause he was your last chance to make it out of that fire!"

John looked at the small boy and smiled. "That's right, James."

Breanna saw the longing in John's eyes at the mention of the black stallion. She touched his shoulder lovingly and said, "You still think about Chance, don't you?"

"Well . . . yes. You know I love Ebony. There'll never be another horse like him. But I'll admit that a special relation-ship developed between that wild beast and me when he let me on his back and carried me to safety." He paused a moment, then looked at Dottie with a mischievous grin.

"However, sweet sister-in-law, when I go to Butte City, I won't have time to beat the forests looking for Chance, much as I'd like to."

It was nearly 8:30 when John guided the rented buggy around the big house belonging to Dr. and Mrs. Lyle Goodwin and halted. He hopped out, helped Breanna from the buggy, and they entered the cottage behind the Goodwin's house that was her home.

John built a fire in the potbellied stove, while Breanna started one in the kitchen stove and put on the coffeepot.

They sat down in the parlor as the room began to grow warm, and by the soft light that flowed from the lanterns on the end tables by the couch, Breanna looked into John's eyes and said, "All right, Mr. Stranger, out with it."

John blinked, letting an innocent look capture his face. "Out with what?"

"Butte City. Sheriff Lake Johnson. Some killer on the loose. What else is it?"

"Well, Miss Baylor, just how do you know there is something else?"

Breanna leaned close, touched her lips to his lightly, and said, "I just know you, darling. You were holding back something when you answered Dottie's question about the problem in Butte City."

A slow grin worked its way across his handsome face. "You're acting like a wife."

"Well, dear man, I have news for you. I'll *really* learn to read you when I am your wife!"

John's features changed, taking on a serious cast. "Sweetheart," he said softly, "I told you there was something very important I wanted to talk to you about. Let me do that first, then I'll explain about Butte City."

Breanna was surprised to see him rise from the couch and drop to one knee in front of her.

She blinked in puzzlement. "John, what is this?"

He took her hands in his own. "We've been asking the Lord to guide us as to when we should marry. You said you believed the Lord would show me, and that you were ready whenever I got the go-ahead from Him. Well, Miss Breanna Baylor, I have absolute peace in my heart about a date." John swallowed hard. "Miss Breanna Baylor, will you marry me on the first Sunday of next June, at our church, in an afternoon ceremony?"

Tears welled in Breanna's eyes, then spilled down her cheeks. She threw her arms around his neck and said, "Yes! Oh, yes!"

They embraced for a long moment, then John kissed her tenderly, sealing their agreement.

Once again beside her on the couch, he held her hand and said, "The date, darling, is June fourth."

"It'll be the third most marvelous day of my life," she said, sniffling. "The number one most marvelous day of my life was when I met my precious Jesus, and He saved my soul."

"Yes," John said, feeling certain he knew what number two was.

"The second most marvelous day of my life was when I met a tall, dark, handsome man on the Kansas plains in a thunderstorm, and he saved me from being trampled to death by a herd of stampeding cattle."

John smiled.

"And on the third most marvelous day, you will save me from being an old maid!"

They laughed heartily and kissed again.

Breanna squeezed John's hand as she said, "When we talked in the past about getting married, you said we would both have to cut our travels quite a bit in order to have a married life. I can always work at the hospital, or at Dr. Goodwin's office, but what will you do? I realize money is no object, but knowing my John, I know you'll have to be busy."

"The Lord hasn't revealed that to me yet," he said. "All I know is I have perfect peace about us getting married in June. I have no doubt He'll show me His will concerning my occupation sometime between now and when we get married."

"Of course He will," Breanna said.

John smiled at her again. "So when I get back from Montana, we'll talk to Pastor Bayless and set up that Sunday afternoon for the wedding."

Breanna flung her arms around his neck. "Oh, darling, I'm so happy!"

As he held her close, John half-whispered in her ear, "You couldn't be as happy as I am. The Lord has given me the most beautiful and wonderful woman in the world to be my wife!"

After several moments, Breanna settled back contentedly against the couch and looked at John expectantly. "Now, what about the Butte City situation?"

He took a deep breath and said, "You recall the story of when I was up there two years ago . . . some maniac was murdering people at random in the town. Turned out that maniac was Payton Sturgis."

"Yes, I remember."

"Well, it's starting all over again . . . except the killings are not random this time. The killer has named his intended victims, and they're being killed one at a time."

"Is there some pattern to it? I mean, some reason he's picked out his victims?"

John scrubbed a hand over his mouth. "Yeah, and this is the bizarre thing about it. Apparently he left a written list with the first body. The fifteen men on the list are the same men who had a hand in putting his neck in the noose. You know . . . the judge, the jury, and the like."

" 'And the like.' You mean like John Stranger, who tracked him and caught him. And probably like Sheriff Lake Johnson. If it was a twelve-man jury, then the judge, the sheriff, and you would make fifteen."

"Yes, Breanna. That's about the way it stacks up."

"I don't want you to go."

"I have to. I've got to help Sheriff Johnson stop him before he kills every man he's marked. He's killed three already."

Breanna sat silently, studying his eyes for a moment. "John, I love you. I just don't want anything to happen to you. But I also know you, and I understand why you have to go. And that's one of the reasons why I love you so much."

John grinned.

"But there's more, isn't there? What is it you're not telling me?"

He grinned again. "I wonder if all women are as perceptive as you."

"Out with it!"

John let out a sigh and said, "I never told you about what happened at the gallows the day they hanged Sturgis. Never thought it necessary."

The aroma of hot coffee wafted into the room. "Just a minute," Breanna said, springing to her feet. "I'll be right back with the coffee."

Almost immediately she returned with two steaming cups on a tray and offered one to John. She sat down beside him again, with her own cup in hand, and said, "Now, what happened at the gallows?"

"Well, after Johnson put the noose around Sturgis's neck, he descended the gallows steps to the lever. Sturgis refused a hood, so we all saw his face. His eyes bulged and got this insane look as he screamed that he would come back from the grave and kill every man involved in his arrest, conviction, and hanging."

"But we both know that can't happen."

"Right. But most of the townspeople are scared out of their wits. They believe the killer is the ghost of Payton Sturgis. One of the men marked for death is a wealthy mine owner who sat on Sturgis's jury. His name is Tom McVicker. Johnson's wire said McVicker got a look at this killer—a clear view. He swears the killer is Payton Sturgis."

"John, it can't be! You and I know what God's Word says about such things. Jesus is the only one who ever raised Himself from the dead."

"Yes, and He's the only one who ever will. What they've got in Butte City is some smart guy impersonating Sturgis. He's crafty enough to do that, and to find a way to kill his intended victims. He's working so hard at impersonating Sturgis that he only kills during snowstorms."

Breanna frowned. "I won't try to stand in your way, darling, because I know that in your mind you owe those people to come back up there and stop this killer. But I *will* be praying for God's hand on you."

"I appreciate that. And don't worry. The Lord will bring me back to you, alive and kicking. After all, He made us for each other, and we've got a wedding coming up."

They finished their coffee, and John stood to go. He shouldered into his coat and then took Breanna into his arms, holding her tight. "Sweetheart, you've made me the happiest man on earth. Just knowing that you love me, and that in a few short months you will be my wife, will bring me back as soon as possible." He kissed her soundly. "I'll be back from Montana before you know it."

Breanna wrapped her arms around his neck and squeezed

hard. "I won't say good-bye tonight, darling. I'll be at the station in the morning to see you off."

"I'd love that, but I can tell you're tired. You really need to get some rest."

"But I *must* see you off, John. You know, like you *must* go to Butte City."

He kissed her again, looked into her eyes, and said, "How can I argue with such a woman?"

"You might as well learn before we marry, darling, you can't win an argument with me."

John laughed and kissed her one more time, then left.

Breanna stood on the porch, ignoring the cold night air, until the buggy disappeared from sight.

CHAPTER

TEN

John Stranger lay in his hotel room bed, staring at the ceiling. *Breanna.* His heart warmed at the thought of their wedding day and the happiness they would know as husband and wife. Then his thoughts shifted to the task before him.

He rolled over, fluffed up the pillow, and closed his eyes. But sleep wouldn't come. He thought of Dottie's words earlier that evening, "Come on, now, John. I know why you're *really* going back to that part of Montana. You want to see if you can get a glimpse of that big black horse that saved your life."

Chance. If it hadn't been for Chance, John would have died. His mind trailed back to last summer, when he was tracking a gang of killers led by Wilson Kyger. He was riding a borrowed horse in the vast forest country northwest of Billings, when the horse bolted, frightened by an angry mother bear. The horse stumbled and fell, breaking its leg. The only humane thing to do was shoot it. He lay there, remembering . . .

After he put down the horse, John started walking, rifle in hand, saddlebags draped over his shoulder, and a canteen around his neck. He had been in this area before but couldn't remember where the nearest ranch was. He figured to run into one as he continued north toward Red Mountain.

The afternoon passed, and the sun went down. No sign of a ranch so far. It was almost dark when he came upon a small creek that had been reduced to little more than a trickle for lack of rain. He filled his canteen and drank from it as he ate hardtack and beef jerky.

Soon a full moon came over the peaks to the east, spraying its silver hue everywhere. A soft breeze stirred, rustling the limbs of the giant pines. For a while he stood on the bank of the creek, smelling the night smells and listening to the night sounds.

He used his saddlebags as a pillow and stretched out his weary body and closed his eyes. He was about to fall asleep when he heard the shrill whinny of a horse. He sat up and looked around. He heard the whinny again, then he saw him—a magnificent black stallion, wild and beautiful.

The horse stood skylined on top of a craggy bluff with the full moon behind him. He looked at Stranger, his regal head held high and ears forward. The breeze fluffed his mane and tail. Then he bobbed his head and snorted, pawing at the earth.

John rose to his feet. The stallion snorted again, then reared up, pawing the air with his forelegs. He whinnied again and darted off the bluff, vanishing from sight.

"Marvelous, Lord!" John said to his God. "What an animal!"

The next morning, as John proceeded north, the great stallion appeared to him again, this time with a dozen-and-a-half horses following him. At a distance of some thirty yards, the big black looked straight at John, laid back his ears, and reared up, whinnying and pawing the air.

"I sure would like to borrow your back for a while, big boy; I need a ride out of here."

The beautiful beast shook his head, flopping his mane

from side to side before he wheeled and galloped toward the forest with his herd behind him. Within seconds they were swallowed up by the tall timber.

Later in the afternoon, as John walked north under the blazing sun, he caught sight of the stallion again, moving in timber on higher ground. The horse paused for a moment, looked down at the lone traveler, then snorted and tossed his head before disappearing.

Late in the afternoon the timber gave way to a slender meadow with a brook running through it. To the north he could see a narrow gap between trees that led to more open country. He estimated the gap to be some six or seven miles away.

He decided to stay in the meadow for the night, and as he laid his saddlebags and canteen beside the brook, the black stallion broke out of the woods and came prancing toward him with marvelous ease and swiftness, head and tail erect. He came within twenty yards then swerved and climbed to a rock ledge above.

This time the stallion was close enough for John to get a good look, and he marveled at what he saw. The horse was all muscle, grace, and power. Everything about him spoke of unbroken spirit—from the keen intelligence of his expressive eyes and the flare of his nostrils, to the way he held his head and swished his tail. He stood like a monarch as he looked down.

John wondered where the rest of the herd was when, without warning, a male cougar he had seen earlier sprang over the rocks above the stallion and landed on his back. The horse screamed and reared, then bucked, but the cougar's claws were buried deep. The stallion came down to level ground with the cat on his back. John shouldered his rifle, took careful aim, and fired. The cougar fell to the ground and rolled over, still dangerous. As it started to get up, a second gunshot ended its life.

John wanted to check the claw marks on the stallion's back, but when he drew near, the horse galloped away, then came back and stopped just ten feet from this man who had saved his life. He allowed John to pour cool water on the scratches, but when he tried to mount the horse, he shied and bolted.

That night John was awakened by a vicious crack of lightning. For the next hour he watched a fiery display in the sky, some of the bolts coming dangerously close to the ground. Finally it stopped, and he went back to sleep.

Just before dawn he was awakened by the smell of smoke on the wind. The forest was aflame on three sides! The only place the fire wasn't burning was in the gap between the timber to the north. But the wind was forcing the flames further in that direction, narrowing the gap and creating a circle of fire that was fast closing in.

He dropped his gear and ran as fast as he could toward the gap. In his heart he knew that if the wind continued at the present rate, he would never make it.

As he ran with the oppressive heat closing in on him, he saw the big black stallion come charging down an area of solid rock. The herd of wild horses ran behind him, neighing in terror.

The stallion saw John running toward him and skidded to a halt. The herd galloped past their leader, heading for the gap at the end of the meadow. The stallion watched John for a moment, then reared, pawed the air, and galloped after his frightened herd.

"No! Come back!" John shouted. "Come back! You're my only chance!"

The smoke swirled in the wind like a fog, stealing the stallion and his galloping herd from sight. John knew he wouldn't make it now. But he would die trying.

Suddenly, through the roar of wind and fire, he heard a thrilling sound—the rapid, rhythmic beat of hooves. Through the thick smoke ahead of him, he saw a phantomlike form. The black stallion came thundering through the smoke, eyes bulging. He stopped in front of John, whinnying shrilly.

Without hesitation, John grabbed a fistful of mane, and swung aboard. "Okay, big boy, let's ride!"

The heat was unbearable as horse and rider flew across the meadow. The flames were reaching across the small opening just as the mighty stallion thundered through into the open area beyond the burning forest.

John looked back. Behind him the fire flared and the smoke rolled ever upward. It was an unearthly spectacle, but he was alive! He was alive because the great wild stallion, who had never had a man on his back, allowed John that privilege and carried him to safety.

All the other horses bunched up and came to a stop a few feet away. The stallion greeted them with a shrill whinny.

Stranger slid off the horse's back, patted him, and said, "Thank you, big fella. I saved your hide, now you've saved mine. I'll never forget you. And I've thought of a good name to remember you by—Chance. Seems fitting, since you were my last-chance escape from death."

Chance nickered and bobbed his head as if he understood. He turned his head toward the herd, then looked back. John stroked his neck and patted his shoulder. "I know it's time for you to lead your herd, ol' boy. Go on. I'll be fine now."

The stallion nickered and galloped toward a rocky ridge with his herd trailing behind. Soon Chance and his followers topped the ridge and disappeared.

John Stranger fell asleep in his Denver hotel room to the

reminiscent thunder of fading hoofbeats.

The early morning mile-high air had a sharp bite to it as John and Breanna stood on the platform at Denver's Union Station. The big engine's boiler gave off a soft hiss, and black smoke drifted skyward from the cone-shaped stack.

Passengers were already boarding as John held Breanna's hands, looked deep into her eyes, and said, "I love you, my bride-to-be, with all my heart."

"And I love you with all my heart. I'll be praying for your safety. Hurry back. I'll miss you terribly."

As they held each other close, Breanna said, "Wouldn't it be wonderful if somehow you would see that big black stallion while you're in his territory?"

John thought of his reminiscence before going to sleep last night. "It sure would. But the probability of my seeing Chance is pretty remote."

"I wish I could meet him someday," Breanna breathed into his ear. "I'd like to hug his neck and thank him for saving your life."

Suddenly, the engine's whistle blew, followed by the voice of the conductor. "All aboar-r-rd! All aboar-r-rd!"

"I'll be back before you know it," John said, and kissed her soundly.

He moved inside the coach and chose the first empty seat on the platform side of the train. He quickly placed both pieces of luggage overhead, then dropped onto the seat and slid to the window to look for Breanna.

The wheels of the big engine spun on the track, took hold, and there was a series of loud thumps as the couplings felt the forward pressure. As the train began rolling, Breanna threw John a kiss.

She stayed on the platform until the train disappeared

from sight. As she turned and headed in the direction of the hospital, she whispered, "O Lord, please keep my darling John in the protective hollow of Your almighty hand. I love him so very much."

Soon the coach was rocking smoothly, and the steel wheels beneath John clicked to a steady rhythm. He turned from the window and looked around the coach, noting that it was only half-occupied, then eased back in the seat.

He let his gaze drift to the landscape outside and prayed silently, asking the Lord to take care of Breanna and thanking Him for bringing her into his life, for the love that had blossomed between them, and now for the perfect peace in his heart about their coming marriage.

His mind then went to Sheriff Lake Johnson and the frightened people of Butte City. Who could the killer be? How could he possibly look anything like Payton Sturgis?

One thing was certain: This killer wanted revenge against the men who had a hand in Payton's hanging. But who was he? For now, there were too many unanswered questions, but he would find the answers . . .

John's attention was drawn to a young woman who sat directly across the aisle. She was weeping softly, trying to control her tears. John was about to ask her if she needed some help when the coach door opened and the conductor entered, calling, "Tickets, please! Have your tickets ready, please!"

He watched the young woman as the conductor drew near her, punching tickets. She hurriedly dabbed at her eyes and dried the tears from her cheeks. When the conductor stopped at her seat, he greeted her in a friendly manner. She smiled, but didn't speak. After the conductor moved on, the young woman started to cry again.

John rose from his seat, stepped across the aisle of the

swaying coach, and bent down to say, "Little lady, I couldn't help but notice you've been shedding tears for some time. I don't mean to stick my nose in where it doesn't belong, but is there anything I can do for you?"

His compassion and tender manner touched her, and she said, "Please sit down here, sir. I really could use someone to talk to."

As John sat down beside her, she said, "I'm Gayle Strand. And you are . . ."

"Just call me John."

"All right, John," she said, wiping tears from her cheeks. "You are very kind to care about someone you don't even know."

"I just hate to see anyone hurting. But I know that sometimes pain in the heart can be eased by talking about the problem."

The pain in her heart had stripped away any need to choose her words carefully, and she said simply, "I was just jilted by my fiancé in Denver."

"Oh. I'm so sorry."

"I'm from Cheyenne City. I met Greg Martin while I was in Denver a little over a year ago. We fell in love—well, I thought it was both of us. At least, he said he loved me. He came to Cheyenne City several times over the next couple of months, and one night, he asked me to marry him. Then, two months ago, I traveled to Denver to meet Greg's parents.

"We liked each other, and they invited me to come back anytime. I was able to get a few days off from my job in Cheyenne City, so I traveled to Denver yesterday to surprise Greg."

Gayle choked up for a moment, then continued. "Greg has his own house. I hired a carriage at the depot to take me there before going to his parents' house to stay. I . . . I found him with another woman."

Gayle broke down and sobbed, unmindful of the other passengers' stares. When she had regained control of her emotions, she said bitterly, "No offense to you, but I'll never trust another man."

Stranger waited until Gayle had dried her tears, then said, "Gayle, do you know the one Man who will never hurt you, disappoint you, or forsake you?"

She looked at him blankly. "Pardon me?"

"I speak of God's Son, the Lord Jesus Christ. Do you know Him?"

"Well, I know who He is, but I don't understand what you mean, do I know Him. He's in heaven, and I'm on earth. How could I have met Him?"

"In the Person of His Holy Spirit you can know Him, Gayle. And to die without knowing Him is to face God in your sins."

She opened her purse, stuffed the hanky inside, and closed it again. "John, are you saying that if I don't know Jesus—as you put it—that I'll go to hell when I die?"

"That's exactly what God tells us in His Word. Could I show it to you in the Bible?"

"Yes, I'd like to see it."

Stranger crossed the aisle and came back with his Bible. While flipping pages, he said, "Do you know that Jesus often called Himself the Son of man?"

"Yes, I've heard that."

"Look here in Luke 19:10. Jesus tells us why He left heaven and came to earth. Why did He come, Gayle?"

She read the verse silently, then replied, "To seek and to save that which was lost."

"Who would 'that' be?"

"Lost sinners?"

He nodded and flipped over more pages. "Let's see what God had the Apostle Paul write in Romans 1. Look at these words in verse 16, 'For I am not ashamed of the gospel of Christ: for it is the power of God unto salvation to every one that believeth . . .' What was Paul not ashamed of, Gayle?"

"The gospel of Christ."

"Mm-hmm. And what did he say was the 'power of God unto salvation'?"

"The gospel of Christ."

"So would you agree that whatever the gospel of Christ is, therein lies the power of God to save a sinner?"

"Yes. That seems to be what it says."

"All right. Notice that salvation is given to every person who *believes*. See that?"

"Yes."

"Now, look here," he said, flipping pages again. "Jesus said in Mark 1:15, 'Repent ye, and believe the gospel.' Notice that He tells us to *repent* and *believe* the gospel. Do you know what repentance is?"

"I didn't tell you what my job is in Cheyenne City. I'm a schoolteacher. English is my forte. As I recall, repentance is remorse for sin, which includes turning from it. Right?"

"Exactly. Jesus also said to believe the gospel. This is the same gospel that Jesus said He wanted preached all over the world. You with me so far?"

"Yes."

"We have to believe His gospel to be saved, right?"

"That's what He said."

"The next thing, then, is to find out exactly what the gospel of Jesus Christ is. Could you tell me what it is?"

"I'm sure it has to do with His dying on the cross, but I couldn't give you the definition."

Stranger turned to 1 Corinthians 15. "Now, look at verse 1, Gayle. Paul says he is declaring the gospel to his readers. See that?"

"Mm-hmm."

"In verses 3 and 4, we see God's definition of the gospel. He reminds the people in the Corinthian church that he had preached the gospel to them. Read those two verses to me, Gayle."

Setting her eyes on the page and finding the verses, Gayle read it aloud. " 'For I delivered unto you first of all that which I also received, how that Christ died for our sins according to the scriptures; and that he was buried, and that he rose again the third day according to the scriptures.' "

"There's the gospel, Gayle. Do you believe what it says right there?"

"Certainly."

"Okay. We read from Jesus' own mouth that He said He came to seek and to save that which was lost. And you already understood He was speaking of lost sinners." John paused for effect. "Tell me . . . is Gayle Strand a sinner?"

"Yes. I am a sinner."

"Then you are the kind Jesus came to save." John quickly turned to Romans 10:13 and put his finger on the verse. "Just one more verse for you to read. This one explains what you need to do."

Gayle could hardly read the words for the tears that welled up in her eyes. She wiped them away and read the verse aloud. " 'For whosoever shall call upon the name of the Lord shall be saved.' John . . . I want to do that right now."

With joy in his heart, the tall man led a repentant, believing Gayle Strand to Jesus Christ. When she had called on the Lord, John prayed for her, asking the Lord to guide her, bless her life, and use her for His glory.

"Now, Gayle," John said softly. "Remember that when I started this conversation I asked you if you knew the one Man who would never hurt you, disappoint you, nor forsake you?"

"Yes."

"Let me show you something," he said. He flipped the pages of his Bible to Proverbs 18:24 and pointed. "Read me the second half of this verse."

Gayle's eyes were still moist with tears as she read aloud, " 'There is a friend that sticketh closer than a brother.' "

"Who do you suppose that is?"

"I know who it is. It's Jesus!"

John continued to show the now radiant young woman other Scriptures that assured her the Lord would never leave her nor forsake her. She was thanking him for leading her to Jesus when the train slowed down.

"Oh, my!" she said. "We're in Cheyenne City already!"

John lifted Gayle's one piece of luggage from the rack to carry it off the train for her. She thanked him, saying she could handle it.

"I insist," he said. "Gentleman's privilege."

As they waited for some of the other passengers, hurrying to get off, John told Gayle to get herself a Bible, and recommended two churches in Cheyenne City where he had preached in the past. Gayle assured him she would buy a Bible and get into church.

When they alighted and stood on the platform, with people milling on every side, Gayle said, "You never told me your last name, John, nor where you're from."

John reached into his pocket and produced a silver medallion the size of a silver dollar. He placed it in her hand and smiled, then walked away.

Gayle blinked in puzzlement and watched him disappear

into the crowd, then focused on the medallion. It bore a five-point star in its center, and around the edge were engraved the words: *THE STRANGER THAT SHALL COME FROM A FAR LAND—Deuteronomy 29:22.*

CHAPTER

ELEVEN

The Union Pacific train pulled out of Cheyenne City an hour later. As it rolled north toward Billings, clouds were lowering over the flat land. John read his Bible for about an hour, then laid it on the seat beside him. He raised his arms and stretched before easing back against the seat to watch the prairie roll by.

The train was scheduled to make five stops along the way and would arrive in Billings at 10:30 that night. John would spend the night in the Billings Manor Hotel and take the early morning stage west to arrive in Butte City in early afternoon.

As he watched the snow-coated Wyoming landscape, he could see heavy gray clouds gathering around the ragged mountain peaks to the west. The wind was picking up and buffeting the already swaying coach.

Suddenly John's attention was drawn to a herd of wild horses galloping parallel with the train about a hundred yards out. The leader was a huge chestnut stallion with mane and tail like flame. John thought of Chance and wondered if the great stallion still ran the hills and valleys northwest of Billings.

He scooted lower in the seat, stretched out his legs, and closed his eyes. For what seemed like the hundredth time, he thought about Sheriff Lake Johnson and the killer in Butte City.

Well, it wasn't Payton Sturgis, and it wasn't his ghost.

John had seen the man die at the end of a rope, and dead men *stayed* dead. This killer was acting out a play on the stage set by Payton Sturgis.

John's thoughts went back to that cold, windy day almost two years ago, when he arrived in Butte City after receiving Lake Johnson's desperate wire asking him to come.

Two years earlier

The stagecoach wheeled into Butte City with the icy wind knifing out of the northern hills in hissing gusts. The strong wind picked up and tossed needle-sharp particles of ice from the crust of snow on the ground.

When the coach came to a halt in front of the Wells Fargo office, John knew the husky man standing on the boardwalk had to be Sheriff Lake Johnson, even before he saw the badge.

Two middle-aged women had ridden the stage with John. He stepped out of the coach first and helped them down, then smiled at the lawman as he approached.

The sheriff extended his hand and looked up at the man who towered above him. "Howdy, John Stranger! Lake Johnson. Somebody told me you were a long drink of water. They weren't kiddin'!" Johnson winced slightly at Stranger's powerful grip.

"Glad to meet you, Sheriff," John said, tugging at his hat brim as a gust of wind tried to lift it from his head.

The shotgunner atop the stage handed down luggage to the driver. "Here's your luggage, Mr. Stranger," the driver said, setting the two pieces on the boardwalk.

John thanked him, then glanced down the block and saw a sign that said Silver Bow Hotel. He turned back to the sheriff. "You want to talk before I go to the hotel or after?"

"How about during?" Johnson picked up one of John's bags and headed down the boardwalk toward the hotel.

People on the street noted the tall man in black with their sheriff. Everyone they met on the boardwalk spoke a greeting, and most who rode by on horseback or wagon spoke or waved.

"So tell me about these killings, Sheriff," John said. "Had any more since I left Denver?"

Lake Johnson sighed. "Yeah. One more. A nine-year-old boy yesterday mornin'. And, as usual, it was snowin'. Little fella's name was Billy Fisher."

"Nine years old! How was he killed?"

"Strangled. Family lives on the north edge of town. The boy went out yesterday mornin' to feed the chickens and never came back. The mother found him inside the chicken shed. Doc Bristow said he'd been strangled with some kind of thin rope or cord. Not a clue left behind to identify the maniac who killed him."

John shook his head in disgust. "So this makes six murders, right?"

"That's right."

"Were the other people killed the same way?"

John noticed the undertaking parlor up ahead where a hearse was being backed up to the front door. A sign, centered between two doors, read:

CHARLES FUNERAL HOME
and
CARPENTER SHOP
Ivan Charles, Undertaker
and Proprietor

The man in the driver's seat of the hearse climbed down and moved to the rear. As he opened the door he looked at the two men and said in a friendly manner, "Hello, Sheriff. This the man you been tellin' us about?"

The young man wore no hat, and the wind ruffled his straw-colored hair. He was tall and slender. Stranger noted his pale blue eyes . . . so pale that the irises were almost white.

"Yes," Johnson said. "Payton, I want you to meet John Stranger. This is Payton Sturgis, John. He's assistant to Ivan Charles, who runs both the undertaking parlor and the carpentry shop."

"The viewing was over about an hour ago, Sheriff," Sturgis said. "I'm picking up Billy's body to take it to the church for the funeral service."

"Need some help?"

"Oh, no, sir. Ivan's inside. He'll help me." Payton headed for the door of the funeral parlor, then turned and smiled. "Pleasure meeting you, Mr. Stranger."

"You, too," John said with a nod.

As they continued on down the street, Lake Johnson said, "The other five people were killed during snowstorms, as I told you in my wire. A woman was strangled with the same kind of cord or rope as Billy. Two men and a woman were stabbed to death. The fifth victim was a fifteen-year-old girl. There's a creek runs past the town over yonder, and she was found at the bottom with rocks tied to her body. Doc Bristow said her lungs were full of water."

Stranger's face looked pinched. "Sheriff, I'll give it everything I've got to stop this maniac. He has to have something off balance in his brain to kill like this."

"You think he's crazy?"

"Not in the sense that he doesn't know what he's doing. His thinking was clear enough to weight the girl's body down with rocks. But he's got to be crafty to have left absolutely no clues. And it's odd that he only kills during a snowstorm."

They were coming up on the hotel. "Sheriff," John said,

"after I get my room and unload this luggage, I'd like you to take me to the scene of each murder. I want to study the areas closely. That will probably take what's left of today. Tomorrow I'd like to talk to the victims' families, if possible."

"Whatever you say, John. May I ask what you have in mind about talking to the families?"

"It seems, on the surface anyway, that the killings are random. But there may be an underlying pattern. If so, I want to find it."

It took the rest of the day for the men to visit each crime scene. The next day, John spent time with each victim's family, learning all he could about the family and the dead person's habits.

He spent the entire following day in his hotel room, studying the information.

The next morning, Stranger walked through falling snow to the sheriff's office. Upon entering, he found Lake Johnson talking to two men about the man who had come to town to help him track down the killer.

"Ah, here he is now," Johnson said, grinning at Stranger. "We were just talking about you, John."

The sheriff introduced mine owner Tom McVicker and his foreman, Les Osborne, then said, "Well, what's the verdict, John? Have you found a pattern?"

"Only that our murderer has a fetish for killing strictly during snowstorms. And we already knew that. Otherwise, Sheriff, I can't find any pattern whatsoever. He's killing at random on snowy days."

"But not every snowy day," McVicker said.

"We can be thankful for that," Osborne said. "But since we don't know who he is, everybody's vulnerable at all times."

Stranger rubbed the back of his neck and said, "The man is a psychopathic killer, and evidently has no conscience at all. And since he's so erratic, it's impossible to tell who or where he will strike next." He glanced out the window and added, "With the snowstorm descending on us right now, he could be planning to kill again."

Four inches of snow had fallen on Butte City by the time darkness fell, and the snow was still coming down. Lake Johnson and John Stranger were eating supper at the Meadowlark Café, talking to owner Merlin Loberg. Customers listened as the men discussed the main topic of conversation in the town.

Loberg, who stood by their table, looked down at Stranger, and asked, "What's your next move, Mr. Stranger?"

John gave him a tight grin. "No offense intended, Mr. Loberg, but since every man in and around this town is suspect, I really can't reveal my next move."

Loberg snapped his fingers. "Sorry. I should've thought of that. I—"

Suddenly the front door burst open, and Steve Nadler, owner of Nadler's Furniture Store, charged in. He looked around wildly, then darted toward Lake Johnson. "Sheriff! I was sitting in my kitchen a few minutes ago, and I heard a woman scream! It sounded like it came from my next door neighbor's house, the Stoners!"

"Go on," Johnson said, dreading what he might hear next.

"I picked up my rifle and headed over there. I saw a man leave the Stoners' house and run down the street. Even with the street lamps burning, I couldn't tell much about his size or build because of the falling snow. I shouted at him to stop, but he disappeared. The Stoners' door was open, Sheriff. I went in and I . . . I found them dead!"

Johnson told Steve and everyone else in the restaurant to stay where they were, then said to Stranger, "Come with me."

When the two men arrived at the Stoner house, they saw that the couple had been stabbed in the parlor and had fallen there.

Johnson felt sick as he turned his back on the bodies and said, "I'll get the neighbor on the other side to bring the undertaker."

Two days later, the entire population of Butte City and the surrounding area gathered at the church for the funeral service, but most of the people had to stand outside. When the bodies of Todd and Carol Stoner were carried to the cemetery in the hearse, the crowd followed.

Pastor Bob Walker stood by the coffins and lifted his voice to read a brief passage of Scripture above the sound of people mourning. Then he closed in prayer.

People clung to each other in the bleak sunlight and watched as Ivan Charles and Payton Sturgis lowered the coffins into the cold, unfeeling earth.

When the graves were filled in, several people collected around Lake Johnson and John Stranger.

Rancher Ed Compton spoke up. "Sheriff, we've all been told that this tall fella with you was gonna stop the killin'. He sure didn't help poor Todd and Carol!"

Dan Cogan stood close by with his wife, Elaine, and their neighbor, Clay Madison. The sheriff was about to reply when both Cogan and Madison spoke at the same time. Madison nodded for Cogan to go ahead.

"You're not being fair, Ed," Cogan said. "Mr. Stranger has only had a couple of days to work on this. Give him time."

Compton's face twisted. "Yeah, and while we're givin'

him time, somebody else is gonna get murdered!"

Lake Johnson's features darkened and his voice was almost a growl. "If you can do better, Ed, we'd all like to watch!"

The old man's cheeks flushed and he ducked his head slightly. "I'm sorry, Mr. Stranger. I guess I'm so scared I'm just not thinkin' right. Forgive me."

The tall man smiled. "It's all right, sir. I understand."

"Mr. Stranger," a husky voice said. "I'm Lawton Haymes, sir. The town's blacksmith. Would you mind telling us what you're doing to catch the killer?"

John had a strong feeling the killer was someone in the crowd. He spoke loud enough for everyone to hear him say, "I can't reveal my strategy, Mr. Haymes, in case the killer might be listening." He ran his gaze over the assembly and kept his voice loud. "The killer's days are numbered, believe me! I will catch him, and he will hang!"

There was something in Stranger's voice and manner that instilled hope and confidence in the people. A couple of men applauded and it caught on, spreading through the crowd.

One man shouted, "We're glad you're here, John Stranger! We know you'll bring that dirty killer to justice!"

While the people continued to applaud, John let his eyes drift to Payton Sturgis. Payton applauded with everyone else, but John couldn't shake an uneasy feeling about him. He would find a way to talk to Payton in private. If the feeling persisted, he'd talk to Lake Johnson about it.

The next day, Stranger walked about town alone, simply observing people. "Lord," he said under his breath, "You know who the killer is. Help me nail him soon. Right now I feel I need to talk to Payton Sturgis. Would You make a way that I can get him alone?"

He could see the funeral parlor and carpentry shop just ahead. Suddenly the lanky figure of Ivan Charles emerged from the front door of the shop and moved toward him. As they drew abreast, Charles stopped. "Hello, Mr. Stranger. I haven't yet had the pleasure of meeting you personally. I'm—"

"Mr. Charles," Stranger said with a grin, offering his hand.

"Oh, sure . . . you know who I am because of the funeral. Let me say that I'm glad you're here. I appreciate your willingness to come and help us."

"Glad to do it. It grinds me when some vile man preys on innocent victims. I really want to get my hands on him."

"Well, I hope you catch him soon," Charles said, moving on. "I've got to take care of some business at the bank. Nice meeting you."

"Same here," Stranger said, heading toward the same door from which Charles had emerged.

Inside the carpentry shop, Stranger was met with the sweet smell of freshly cut wood. Payton Sturgis was at the workbench, putting the finishing touches on a rocking chair. At first glance Stranger thought he saw animosity in Payton's eyes, but if so, the man covered it quickly and said, "Howdy, Mr. Stranger. Somethin' I can do for you?"

"Not really. I've just always loved wood smells. I was passing by, so I thought I'd stop in for a minute and take a whiff."

Payton chuckled and turned back to his work. "Well, whiff away. There's plenty for everybody."

John looked around for a few minutes, then said, "You do nice work. Build that chair by yourself?"

"Yep."

"You build furniture before you came to Butte City?"

"Nope. Ivan taught me."

"I see." It seemed to Stranger that the young man was churning with emotion as he gave short, quick answers. There was nothing to give Stranger any reason to suspect him of being the killer, but he would bear watching.

"Well, Payton," Stranger said in an amiable tone, "nice talking to you." With that, he turned and headed toward the door. Just then the door opened, and a short, heavyset, middle-aged man stepped inside.

"Oh, hello, Mr. Stranger," he said with a broad smile. "I'm Alan Dickey. I work at the Culpepper Zinc Mine."

"Glad to meet you," Stranger said, shaking his hand.

"I want to commend you for what you're doing to try to catch the killer, Mr. Stranger. God bless you for it."

"Thank you, sir. I'm honored that your sheriff has enough confidence in me to ask for my help."

"I have no doubt you'll catch him, Mr. Stranger. Many's the story I've heard about your prowess for catching killers."

Payton stayed busy with the rocking chair at the workbench. Stranger said loud enough for him to hear, "I want him *real* bad, Mr. Dickey. It's going to be a pleasure to bring him down."

"And I can't wait till it happens," Dickey said. Then he looked across the shop. "Hey, Payton . . ."

Sturgis glanced at him. "Yeah?"

"Is the hope chest done?"

"No."

Dickey's features reddened. "What do you mean, *no?* You know it's Lynette's birthday present, and I told you when I ordered it when I needed it done. You assured me it would be done today. She'll come home from Bozeman in three days, and Saturday's her birthday. Are you gonna have it done, or do I have to talk to Ivan?"

Payton's pale eyes hardened. "Talk to Ivan all you want. I don't care. There are only twenty-four hours in a day, and both of us have been very busy buildin' coffins, with all of this killin' goin' on. I just haven't had time to build the hope chest."

Alan Dickey stomped toward the workbench and shouted, "Why aren't you working on it now, instead of that rocking chair?"

Stranger stayed by the door, watching.

Payton looked at Dickey with steady eyes and replied, "Because the order for this chair came in before you ordered the hope chest, that's why."

"Well, I want that chest done by four o'clock day after tomorrow, Payton!"

Fire flashed in Payton's eyes as he retorted, "I'll get it done as soon as possible, Alan!"

"Well, it had better be by four o'clock Friday, or there's gonna be trouble like you and your boss have never seen!" Dickey pivoted on his heel and moved past Stranger and on outside. Stranger followed and walked beside him as they headed toward the center of town.

"Your daughter live in Bozeman?"

"No. She's just visiting friends there. Her mother died seven years ago, when Lynette was thirteen. With Helen gone, I've had to be both father and mother. Hasn't been easy."

"I'm sure that's true," Stranger said.

"I've got to stop here at the general store, Mr. Stranger," Dickey said, slowing down. "Sure hope you catch that killer soon."

"I'm giving it my best," John said, as they drew up in front of Smith's General Store. "I hope your daughter has a very happy birthday."

Stranger pondered the heated words between Alan Dickey and Payton Sturgis. The tall man couldn't put his finger on it, but there was something about Payton Sturgis that rubbed him the wrong way. Of course, that didn't make him the killer. But it did make him a prime suspect.

CHAPTER

TWELVE

The afternoon stage from Bozeman reached the outskirts of Butte City four hours after Alan Dickey and Payton Sturgis had exchanged heated words. Lynette Dickey had decided to surprise her father and come home early. She sat next to elderly Mabel Tibbs, who would ride the stage on to Crackerville. Across from them were young newlyweds, Alex and Bernardine Clermont, whose destination was Anaconda, where the stage would turn around and head back to Bozeman. All four were covered with buffalo robes to keep warm.

"So Saturday is your birthday, Lynette," Mabel said. "It's nice that you can be home with your father on your birthday."

"I wouldn't have it any other way," the petite brunette said. "Even after seven years, Daddy's still very lonely without Mother. He sounded so depressed in his last letter. That's why I decided to come home two days early."

"And won't he be surprised!"

Lynette giggled. "Maybe I should have let him know—let him do a little housecleaning."

Mabel laughed heartily. "My husband was the messiest male on earth!" Then her countenance fell as she said sadly, "I wish I still had him to clean up after."

Alex pulled the curtain away from his window and peered out. "We're almost there, Miss Lynette. I sure hope they've caught that killer by now."

"Me, too," Lynette said. "It's been a terrible thing. As of Daddy's last letter, he'd killed four people."

When the stage rolled to a stop in front of Butte City's Wells Fargo office, Alex Clermont stepped out into the falling snow and helped the ladies descend the coach. Mabel and the Clermonts told Lynette good-bye and entered the stage office to warm up and wait till it was time for the stage to move on.

Lynette's luggage was light, and she headed on foot for the residential section on the east side of town. As far as she could tell, no one on Main Street had noticed her, and she was glad. She wanted her father to be surprised at her arrival.

A buggy passed as Lynette turned onto her street, but it came from behind. As she drew near home, she reminded herself that the house would need straightening up. After she built fires in both the kitchen and parlor stoves, she would unpack, then clean up the house. Her father usually arrived home from the mine at about five-thirty. She would still have time, then, to get supper started before he arrived.

The young woman stepped onto the porch, set down her bags, and pulled a key from her coat pocket. Inside the house the temperature was cold enough to see her breath. She carried her luggage down the hall past her mother's sewing room, the kitchen, and the spare bedroom. Where the spare bedroom ended, the hall took a right turn. In the L-shaped length of it were doors to her own bedroom, and to her father's.

Lynette entered her room and placed the suitcase and overnight bag on the bed. She removed her hat but decided to keep her coat on until the house warmed up some.

She lit the lantern on the dresser and crossed the hall to light the lantern on her father's bureau. Her next stop was the kitchen, where she lit the cupboard lantern, then built a fire in the cookstove.

After she built a fire in the parlor, she returned to her bedroom and began unpacking. First she emptied the overnight bag, placing the items in dresser drawers, then took her dresses from the suitcase and hung them up in the closet.

She was just closing her suitcase when she heard what sounded like the front door opening. She knew that sometimes her father got home a little early. She quickly put the two bags where they belonged at the back of her closet and stepped into the hall, intending to rush to the door and embrace her father.

Suddenly she heard her father's voice thunder through the house. It sounded like he said, "What are *you* doing here? Get off my porch!"

She couldn't hear a reply. She moved forward cautiously, listening for what might come next. She was almost to the corner of the L when her father bellowed, "Get out of here! If you don't leave—"

Alan Dickey's words were cut off, and Lynette heard him grunt and gasp. Then she heard repeated sounds like something striking powerful blows on human flesh.

Though terror clutched her heart, Lynette carefully peered around the corner, and saw her father on the floor near the open front door. Outside, the falling snow was barely visible in the dying light of day.

She could see a man in a heavy coat, wearing a stocking cap pulled down over his ears, kneeling over her father. His back was toward her. She had to clamp a hand over her mouth to keep from screaming when she saw a bloody knife in the man's hand.

Lynette began to shake as if she'd been struck with palsy.

She pulled back from the corner and flattened herself against the wall. Since there were lanterns burning in the house and fires in the stoves, she knew the killer would search the house for other occupants. He must have followed her father home from the mine or waited within sight of the house for him to come.

Lynette tiptoed back into her room. She hurried to the back window and flipped the lock and tried to raise it. It wouldn't budge. She pivoted, her heart hammering so hard it took her breath away.

Suddenly she heard the killer grunt as if he was lifting something heavy. There was a slight pause, and then the sound of heavy footsteps.

He was coming down the hall with her father's body!

She started to plunge into the closet, but it was so full of clothing, boxes, and luggage, that she would have a hard time hiding herself.

The footsteps were getting closer.

Lynette dropped to her knees and was about to crawl under the bed when she saw the lantern on the dresser. Quickly she stood up to douse the light, but checked herself as she heard the killer round the corner of the hall. She went flat on her stomach and wriggled her way under the bed, her feet toward the headboard.

Lynette closed her eyes, willing the killer to turn left instead of right. She lay with her head to one side, her right ear pressed to the cold hardwood floor. When he stopped in the middle of the hallway, just outside her door, she opened her eyes and focused on what she could see. The bedspread hung below the bed frame about two inches, giving her maybe nine or ten inches of space for surveying the floor.

She could see tan boots and blue denim Levi's from the knees down. Lots of men in and around Butte City wore the same kind of boots, and probably all of them owned blue denim Levi's.

He was just standing there, apparently trying to decide into which bedroom to carry the body.

The killer entered her room. He came toward the bed, his faltering steps indicating the burden he carried. Alan Dickey's ponderous frame landed on the bed and made the slats under the mattress creak. The killer remained there, bending over the body and adjusting its position.

The boots then turned and clomped toward the closet. Lynette was glad she had put everything away, even the luggage. She had left nothing on the bedstead or dresser to indicate she was in the room.

The killer jerked open the closet door as if he thought he might find someone waiting just inside. Lynette imagined him holding the big knife.

He shoved her dresses back and forth on the rods and kicked the boxes and luggage. He uttered a quiet oath, but she couldn't identify his voice.

He left the closet and walked to the back window and stood there for a long moment. Lynette twisted her head to follow his movements. Next, he went to the side window and paused there. The silence of the house seemed to close in on her. Would he look under the bed next?

Lynette's breath was suspended. It seemed her blood had stilled its tides as if to assist the silence.

Abruptly, the killer left the window and headed for the door. Lynette felt immense relief as he moved out into the hall. But her heart stopped cold when he whirled around, came back through the door, and headed for the bed.

Dr. Paul Bristow looked up from the desk as the long, tall figure of John Stranger entered the office waiting room. The two men had not met formally, and now shook hands.

"Dr. Bristow," Stranger said, "I'm leaving no stone unturned, so I need to ask you some questions."

"All right."

"Do you have time now, or should I come back later?"

"Now is fine. I don't have any appointments at the moment, and my nurse and secretary—who is my wife—is shopping. I was just catching up on some correspondence, but it can wait. Grab that chair over there and sit down."

When Stranger had settled on the straight-backed wooden chair, Bristow said, "Now, what do you need to know?"

"I assume that you looked at the bodies of the killer's victims."

"Yes."

"The ones who were stabbed. Could you tell if it was done when they were standing?"

The doctor rubbed his chin thoughtfully. "Well, Mr. Stranger, I—"

"Just call me John."

"All right. Let me think on that, John. I . . . ah . . . hadn't really given any thought as to what position they were in when they were stabbed."

"Okay. Now, those who were stabbed were all adults?"

Bristow nodded.

"Were they of average height?"

"I'd say so. Yes. The woman was shorter than the men. They were both a little under six feet. She was about five-six."

"And where in their bodies were they stabbed?"

"The chest and abdomen."

"All three of them?"

"Yes."

"The stab wounds . . . were they straight in or angled?"

"I see what you're getting at. Well, let me think." Bristow

closed his eyes, picturing the victims. After a few seconds, he said, "The wounds in the chest would indicate that the knife came at an angle—from above their heads. So no doubt they were standing when he first attacked them."

"That means the killer would most likely have been taller than his victims," John said.

"Yes. The abdominal wounds were, well, as if he had lowered his hand and drove them straight in. Now that I think of it, first he must have hit them in the chest two or three times, very fast, then held them up with his free arm while he drove the knife into the abdomen."

"Mm-hmm. Were the abdomen wounds in the lower or upper part of the abdomen?"

"They were in the upper part. Especially on the woman, who was shorter." The doctor thought for a few seconds and added, "I'd say the killer was taller than average, John. Not as tall as you, but probably an inch or two over six feet."

"What about the depth of the wounds, Doctor?"

"Well, I can tell you that the knife had a fairly long blade. The wounds were all deep."

"Would you say the man was strong?"

"Could be. Or he could be somewhat heavy, which would give him more weight behind the thrust."

"Can you think of anything you might have seen when examining the bodies that would tell you anything about the killer?"

The doctor shook his head. "Not about his physical make-up. But by the way he picks his victims at random and kills them in such brutal ways, I can tell you he's a madman. I wish I could give you more to go on, but I can't think of anything else to tell you."

Stranger rose from the chair. "You've helped me a lot, Doctor. This will narrow my search. Thank you."

Dr. Bristow walked Stranger to the door. "If you think of anything else I can do, John, please let me know. I appreciate what you're doing, and I believe you're going to stop this madman."

"With God's help, I will," John said.

Alan Dickey's body pressed down on the mattress and the wooden slats, weighing on Lynette's back. She barely had space to breathe.

She waited for the killer to drop to his knees and find her. The pounding of her heart against her ribs seemed to fill the whole room, and she was sure he could hear it.

The killer leaned over the bed and pawed through her father's pockets for a long moment, then walked away. This time when he reached the hall, he entered her father's bedroom. She heard him rifling through the closet, then he returned to the hall and headed toward the front of the house.

He stopped in the spare bedroom, checked the closet, then went to the sewing room. Seconds later he looked in the hall closet, slammed the door, and entered the kitchen. The pantry door opened and closed. There was a moment of silence, then Lynette heard the killer leave the house through the front door.

The Alan Dickey family had come to Butte City before the mines were in full operation and had built their house in the main part of town instead of where most of the miners lived. The Kevanes lived five doors down from the Dickeys on the same side of the street. Directly across the street from the Kevanes lived pharmacist Milo Wilson and his wife, Jane.

The Wilsons had invited the Kevanes for supper at 6:00 that evening. At 5:45, the Kevanes left their house and headed across the street. They mounted the Wilsons' porch, and Eugene tapped on the door.

Althea picked up movement from the corner of her eye and casually turned her head to look. She saw a man dashing out of the Dickey house, leaving the front door open. He jumped off the porch and ran down the street in the opposite direction. Just as Milo Wilson opened the door, Althea said, "Eugene, look down there."

"Hmm?" He looked at her quickly and then turned back to his host and said, "Hello, Milo. Here we are, hungry as grizzly bears."

"Eugene," Althea insisted, "some man just ran out of Alan Dickey's house! See him? He's running away!"

Both Eugene and Milo caught a glimpse of the running man an instant before he vanished from view.

"Wasn't Alan, was it?" Milo said.

Althea shook her head. "No. He was taller and slimmer than Alan. And he left the door open."

"I don't like the looks of this," Eugene said, "what with the recent killings."

Jane Wilson walked up behind her husband. "What's going on?"

"I just saw a man run out of the Dickey house," Althea said. "And it wasn't Alan."

"I'll get my coat, Eugene," Milo said. "We'd better take a look. Althea, you go inside with Jane. We'll be back shortly."

Lynette waited in case the killer might return. But the house remained silent. Her relief at being alive brought tears to her eyes, and she silently wept as she wriggled out of her hiding place. Her legs would barely hold her as she stood up and looked at her father. He had been stabbed several times in the chest and abdomen. He lay perfectly still, eyes closed. There was no rise and fall of his chest.

Lynette felt for a pulse in his neck then held a shaky hand to her face. Her father was dead.

Suddenly the full impact of it hit her. She fell to her knees beside the bed and sobbed, "Daddy! Oh, Daddy, I love you!" Her grief became so heavy that it rendered her incapable of speech, and she sobbed incoherently as if her heart would break.

She didn't hear Eugene Kevane and Milo Wilson run down the hall. And she was unaware of their presence as they stepped into the room.

The sight of Alan's bloody form lying on the bed and the girl kneeling over her father struck both men hard. They both moved to Lynette's side and touched her shoulder.

Lynette screamed.

"It's all right, honey!" Eugene said, patting her shoulder. "The man's gone. Milo and I are here. Nobody's going to hurt you."

Together they lifted the terrified girl to her feet. She wrapped her arms around Eugene, and sobbed, "He killed Daddy! He killed Daddy!"

"Let's take her to my house," Milo said. "It'll help her to be with Jane and Althea."

Eugene gently took her arms from around his neck and said, "Come on, honey, we'll take you to Milo's house. Our wives are there. We'll bring Sheriff Johnson and John Stranger to see you."

CHAPTER

THIRTEEN

John Stranger and Sheriff Lake Johnson were eating supper at the Big Sky Café. Lake swallowed a mouthful of mashed potatoes and said, "So Doc agrees that the guy we're lookin' for is tall."

"Yes. I'm quite confident our killer is six feet or better, Sheriff."

"Well, if you're right, it'll narrow the field some. Most men who live around here are like me—'bout five-nine or ten."

John took a sip of coffee. "I'll tell you this much. That maniac is going to make a mistake soon. Killers always do."

"The sooner the better," Lake said. "I just hate to think of anyone else dying before—"

"Sheriff!" Eugene Kevane yelled, bursting through the café door. "It's Alan Dickey! The killer got him in his house! Stabbed him to death!"

A moan swept through the room.

"Let's go," Lake said, grabbing his coat and hat off one of the spare chairs at the table.

While John quickly slipped into his coat, Kevane said, "Lynette was there when it happened. She was hiding under her bed."

John did a double take. "Lynette? I heard Alan say earlier today that she wasn't coming home from Bozeman till Friday."

"Well, she's here. 'Bout half out of her mind."

"You didn't leave her at the Dickey house, did you?" Lake asked.

"Oh, no. I'll explain it all as we go, but she's at Milo Wilson's. The Wilsons and Althea are with her."

The café was buzzing as the three men hurried out into the snowy night.

At the Wilson house, Jane and Althea sat on the bed where Lynette lay, trying to comfort her as she wept. Milo stood helplessly in the bedroom doorway. The grieving, frightened young woman seemed to be gaining control of her emotions, then suddenly convulsed with heavy sobs again and wailed.

Jane stroked Lynette's tear-stained face and said, "We love you, honey. We're here to help you if we can. Don't worry, that killer won't be coming here."

Milo heard a knock at the front door. "That'll be Eugene with Stranger and the sheriff." He hurried to let them in.

Seconds later, Lake Johnson and John Stranger entered the bedroom and saw the girl's hysterical state. John turned to Milo and Eugene and asked them to bring the doctor. Lynette needed a sedative right away.

When Milo returned with the doctor twenty minutes later, Lynette was still sobbing and crying out that her father was dead.

Bristow set his black bag on the bed stand and opened it. "I'll need a cup of water to put these powders in, Jane." Then he sat down beside the grieving girl and took her hands. "Lynette, it's Dr. Bristow. I'm here to help you. I want to give you something to help settle your nerves, okay?"

Lynette stopped sobbing and looked up at him through swollen, tear-filled eyes. "That awful man killed my daddy, Doctor. He killed my daddy!"

"I know, honey. Milo told me all about it. I'm just so thankful he didn't find you, too."

Bristow administered the sedative, and soon Lynette had stopped weeping and wanted to sit up. Bristow and Althea lifted her while Jane put pillows behind her back. The doctor looked into her eyes and said, "Do you think you can talk with the sheriff and John Stranger?"

She nodded, setting her gaze on the tall man in black.

After Sheriff Johnson introduced him to Lynette, John said softly, "Lynette, I'm here in town at Sheriff Johnson's bidding to help catch this man who killed your father. I need to ask you some questions."

Lynette drew a shuddering breath, and let it out slowly. "Yes, sir."

"Did you get a look at the man?"

"Not his face."

"What part of him did you see?"

She struggled to gain control of her trembling voice. "When . . . when I first saw him, it was from the hall that leads to my bedroom. And . . . to Daddy's. I was in my room, about to go to the kitchen to start supper. You see, I wasn't supposed to come home till Friday. Saturday's my birthday. I wanted to surprise Daddy by coming home today instead."

"Go on."

"I . . . I heard the front door open and was about to run and hug Daddy, but I heard him say in an angry voice, 'What are *you* doing here? Get off my porch!' "

Stranger nodded. "So he must have known the man."

"It was like he was already angry at the man before he saw him come up on the porch."

"It's good to know that, Lynette. Then what did you do?"

"I left my room and started down the hall to see what was going on. I was almost to the corner, where I could see the front door. Daddy shouted something at the man, but his words were cut off. It was then that I heard . . . I heard—"

Lynette choked up, and it took her a moment to continue speaking. She told Stranger about hearing the man stabbing her father, though she didn't realize that's what he was doing until she peeked around the corner and saw him kneeling over him.

"But you didn't see his face?"

"No. His back was toward me."

"Could you tell if he was tall or short, heavy or thin?"

"He was tall and slender. I stayed back for a minute, then looked again. He was standing over Daddy. He had on a heavy coat and a stocking cap. The cap was pulled down over his ears. It was then I realized I would have to hide. There was no way out of the house without him seeing me."

"So you went back to your room and hid under the bed?"

"Yes. I heard him coming down the hall, and I could tell he was carrying Daddy."

"How much of the man could you see from under the bed?"

"Only his pants and boots. The pants from the knees down."

"John, let's go over to the house and take a look," Lake Johnson said. "Maybe he left a clue this time."

Stranger nodded. "Let's hope so."

"I'd like to go, too, Sheriff," Lynette said. "Maybe I can help."

"You sure you're up to it?" Lake asked.

"I'll be all right. Eugene and Milo covered Daddy's body before we left. It will help if I don't have to see him like—like that."

It was still snowing steadily as the men walked down the street with Lynette between them. The house was warm now from the two fires Lynette had built, and the lanterns burned brightly.

They stepped around the blood just inside the door and followed the droplets into Lynette's bedroom. Alan Dickey's body lay on the bed under a blanket. Lynette avoided looking directly at it.

"So you were right here, under the bed?" Stranger asked.

"Yes, sir."

Both men studied some coagulated blood drops on the hardwood floor. John looked at the sheriff. "I told you that sooner or later this guy would make a mistake."

"What do you mean?"

John turned to the girl. "Lynette, when you were under the bed, did you notice any of your father's blood on the killer's pants or boots?"

"Yes. I never got to see him above the knees, but both pantlegs and both boots had blood on them."

"What kind of pants?"

"Blue denim."

"What kind of boots?"

"Light buckskin. But so many men around town wear those kind."

"Right. But only one pair will have blood on them. He can wash his pants, but blood will soak into the pores of buckskin. He won't be able to get it out."

Footsteps sounded in the hall. "Just Eugene and me!" Milo Wilson called.

"Find anything?" Milo asked, when the two men appeared in the doorway.

"Enough to incriminate the guy if we can find his boots and pants," Johnson said. "He got Alan's blood on them."

"So what do you do now?" Eugene asked. "Search every house in town and a ten-mile radius?"

"Looks like that's our next move," the sheriff said.

John rubbed his jaw. "Actually, our next move is to have Ivan Charles pick up the body, Sheriff."

"Oh. Of course. That's all right with you, isn't it, Lynette?"

The girl nodded silently.

"Lynette," Stranger said, "is there someone in town you can stay with for a few days?"

"She can stay with Jane and me," Milo said. "We'll keep her till that madman is caught. Okay, Lynette?"

"Yes. Thank you, Milo."

"I'll go over to Ivan's place and ask him to come pick up the body," Lake said.

"I can do that for you, Sheriff," John said. "I actually need to go that direction anyway. I've got a hunch about something. There's no way we can knock on every door in town before the killer washes his pants and at least tries to clean up his boots. He might even burn them. I need to move fast. I'll follow my hunch and let you know how it turns out."

"Tonight?"

"Probably."

"Okay. But you'll tell Ivan to come out here before you do that?"

"Will do."

Ivan Charles left his comfortable overstuffed chair to answer the knock on his door. "Who is it?" he called out before sliding the dead bolt.

"John Stranger!"

Snow was still falling outside as Charles opened the door. "Come in, John. Something I can do for you?"

"Pick up a body."

"Oh, no! Another one?"

"Alan Dickey. Killer got him about suppertime."

Ivan's mouth quivered. "Wh-where?"

"His house."

"How?"

"Knife. His daughter came home from Bozeman two days early to surprise him. She was in the house when the killer did it. She hid from him or she'd be dead, too."

"Oh, how horrible! Poor Lynette!"

"She's at the Wilsons, Ivan, so when you get to the house, just go on in. The door will be unlocked."

"All right."

"Will Payton help you pick up the body?" John asked.

"No, I'll handle it by myself. I don't know where he is. I heard him come home about an hour ago. He was there for a while, then left again."

"Oh. Well, I'll be glad to help you." John hoped Ivan would decline the offer.

"Not necessary. I've carried many a corpse by myself, even ones as big as Alan."

"Okay, Ivan. I've got some investigative work to do anyway. See you later."

Stranger moved into the shadows in the alley, staying out of sight until Ivan harnessed his horse at the small barn and drove away in the funeral wagon. He hurried to the door of Payton's room at the rear of the carpentry shop and found it unlocked.

A street lamp shined enough light through a side window for Stranger to spot the glass chimney of a lantern. He picked up a match, struck it, and lit the wick. It took him only a few minutes to find the bloody boots and pants in the closet.

John stepped to the door and checked the alley. No one in sight.

John set the lantern on top of the one small dresser in the

room and jerked open the top drawer. No knife in there. Second drawer. Socks and long johns. Third and final drawer. No knife, but what's this?

John took out a sheet of paper with names listed on it in clear, legible handwriting. The list began with the names of the first eight people Payton had murdered. Each one had been checked off. To one side of the list was Alan Dickey's name. It looked as though it had been added as an afterthought. Just below the last name checked off—Carol Stoner—was the name Ralph Byers, the town's assayer, followed by several other names.

John Stranger's name was at the bottom.

John went through the list of names again. Ralph Byers. Stranger recalled that someone had mentioned Ralph was a bachelor and lived alone. John folded the paper and put it in his shirt pocket, then grabbed the bloody boots and pants before dashing out the door.

He ran down the alley and drew up behind Mark Westbrook's wagon repair shop. There was a stack of wooden boxes leaning against the back wall. John removed the top box, stuffed the boots and pants in the next one, then put the top box in place.

He dashed out to Main Street and looked both ways. Two men were coming his way in a wagon. He ran toward them and waved for them to stop.

"Howdy, there, Mr. Stranger," the man holding the reins said. "Somethin' we can do for you?"

"Yes. Where does Ralph Byers live?"

"He's over on Elm Street at the Fourth Street intersection. Second house from the corner on the southeast."

"Thank you!"

The wagon moved on as John ran for all he was worth toward Elm Street. He prayed he would get there in time.

Payton Sturgis waited across the street from Ralph Byers's house, wishing the man would come home. The house had been dark ever since Sturgis had arrived about an hour ago.

It was Ralph's time to die, and Payton would stay as long as he had to.

It was snowing earlier when he'd killed that mouthy Alan Dickey. Of course, Alan was an extra one. Payton hadn't planned to kill Alan. But after he shot off his smart mouth today, his destiny took shape in a hurry. Destiny had sent Payton to Butte City to fill a certain number of graves. Even Payton didn't know how many yet. There were more on the list, of course, and there might be new ones added. But Ralph Byers was next.

Payton could hardly wait to work down the list to that cocky John Stranger. "The killer was right there in the crowd, you said. Boy, if you only knew! When it's your turn, big man, I'll—"

He heard the whistling before he saw the man coming down the street with his hands in his coat pockets. Sturgis waited until Ralph mounted the porch steps and went inside.

That's it, Ralphie, boy. Light another lantern and make it cozy. Destiny is coming in!

When Ralph's shadow on the curtained window showed Payton he was taking off his hat and coat, the killer touched the knife handle in its sheath on his belt and crossed the street. He brushed snow from his eyelashes and stepped up on the porch.

John Stranger turned the corner onto Elm Street in time to see Ralph Byers invite Payton Sturgis inside. He slipped and slid on the snow as he ran. When he reached the yard, he could hear Ralph's voice raised in anger and fear. He bounded onto the porch and hit the door with his shoulder, crashing it open.

Payton had backed Ralph up against the wall and stood over him with the knife. Now his head jerked around at Stranger's sudden entrance. Eyes wild, he wheeled and lunged, swinging the deadly blade.

Byers backed away as Stranger dodged the blade and seized Payton's wrist with a steely grip. Payton was like a madman. He howled and screamed, showing teeth like fangs as he grappled with Stranger and stumbled across the parlor floor.

Payton was unusually strong, but Stranger used his formidable strength to slam him against the wall. The impact knocked the wind from the killer's lungs. He sucked for air and tried with all his might to free his knife hand from Stranger's viselike grip.

For a moment they were nose to nose, then Stranger jerked Payton and slammed him against the wall again. The man's breath gushed out.

Stranger used both hands to grip Payton's wrist and gave it a violent twist. Payton screamed in agony, and the knife clattered to the floor.

Payton tried to claw John's eyes, but he moved his head in time and took a step back before hitting Payton with a hammerlike fist. Payton's head snapped back and he staggered, swaying on rubbery legs.

Another right jarred Payton all the way to his ankles. His head banged the wall, and he slid to the floor like a broken doll, out cold.

John turned to Ralph and said, "Sir, it really wasn't the smartest thing to do, being out alone on the street at night with a killer on the loose."

Ralph looked embarrassed. "Well, I had my small revolver

in my coat pocket in case I ran into him. I guess I thought I was safe once I was inside the house." He paused. "Guess I wasn't so safe, though, was I? Thank you, Mr. Stranger, for saving my life."

Sheriff Johnson sat at the kitchen table in his small house near Main Street, cleaning his revolver. Two lanterns burned in the room, giving ample light.

He heard the old grandfather clock strike 8:30 and said in a low tone, "Come on, John. Let's not drag this out. I want to know about that hunch of yours."

When the clock struck 8:45, Lake slid the cartridges into the cylinder, snapped it shut, and shoved it into the holster on his hip. He rose from the table and went to the cookstove. After adding wood to the fire, he took the coffeepot from the cupboard, dumped in a healthy amount of grounds, dipped up some water from the water bucket, and set the pot on the stove.

Was that someone on the porch? He headed toward the front of the house just as he heard a knock rattle the door. He touched the handle of his revolver and called, "Who's there?"

"John."

When Lake opened the door, he was surprised to see the limp form of Payton Sturgis draped over John's shoulder. Payton was hatless, and his blond hair hung down, partially covering his face.

"John, what in the world?"

Stranger moved inside and unceremoniously dumped the unconscious man on the floor. "Here's your killer."

"Wh—? Payton? The killer?"

"In person. I found the bloody boots and pants in his room, and I found this." John produced the folded sheet of paper and placed it in Lake's hand.

He quickly scanned the list of names, noting the check marks beside the names of the dead and looked up, aghast.

John nodded. "You'll notice that Alan Dickey's name was added. I was in the carpentry shop today, just checking on Payton—whom I already suspected—and I saw Alan and Payton get into an argument. I'd say Alan was killed because of the argument."

"You already suspected Payton? This was your hunch?"

"Yes."

"What made you suspect him?"

"Gut feeling. You know."

Lake grinned, shook his head, and looked back at the list. "Looks like Ralph Byers was next."

"That's where I caught up with Payton. He was already inside Ralph's house with Ralph backed up against a wall, and the knife in his hand. I mean, I caught him in the act, Sheriff."

Johnson looked down at Payton to make sure he was breathing. "You carried him all the way over here from Ralph's place unconscious?"

"Well, sort of."

"Pardon me?"

"We were almost here when he started to come around. He was getting mean already, so I had to lay one on him again. He'll probably sleep till we dump him in a nice uncomfortable cell over at your jail."

CHAPTER

FOURTEEN

The courtroom was jam-packed on the day of the trial. The sun shone brightly out of a cold, clear sky, sending its piercing beams through the windows. People crowded around the edges of the room.

Every eye turned to watch Payton Sturgis ushered into the room with his hands cuffed behind his back. John Stranger flanked him on one side, and Sheriff Lake Johnson on the other.

Payton felt the people's hatred and disgust. He set his jaw and glared at them, showing his own hatred in return.

He had refused counsel, which suited Donald Fryman, the town's only attorney, just fine. He had no desire to defend the heartless killer.

Johnson seated Sturgis at a small table directly in front of the judge's bench, and cuffed his right wrist to the leg of the table. Both Stranger and Johnson sat with him.

The jury avoided Payton's malevolent gaze as they filed in from a side room. When the door to the opposite side room opened, Judge Virgil Reed appeared in his long, flowing black robe. The people fortunate enough to have seats rose and stood until Reed was seated behind his desk.

The portly judge looked at Payton Sturgis over his half-moon spectacles and said, "Will the defendant please rise?"

Sturgis looked him straight in the eye and said, "I can't

stand up, Virgil. These two guys have me cuffed to the leg of this here table."

The judge's eyes widened as he said, "You do not address me as Virgil, Mr. Sturgis!"

Sheriff Johnson leaned close to Sturgis and growled in his ear, "You apologize to the judge this instant, Payton!"

"And if I don't?"

"It's gonna go real bad for you, that's what."

Stonefaced, Sturgis said, "You're gonna hang me, ain'tcha, Lake?"

"I'm not the judge or the jury," Johnson said.

"Well, you don't think they'll just slap my hands and let me go, do you? No, they're gonna convict me, and fatso there behind the bench is gonna tell you to hang me. Hangin's bad, ain't it? So what's *real* bad? Huh? What more can you do to me than hang me?"

Everyone in the courtroom could hear the exchange between Johnson and Sturgis.

John Stranger spoke from Payton's other side. "Best thing for you to do, fella, is act civil."

Sturgis glowered at Stranger and hissed, "I wish I'd killed you when I had the chance, scar-face!"

The judge's voice was stern as he said, "Mr. Sturgis, you shut your mouth!" Then to Johnson, "Sheriff, if the defendant speaks out of line again, he will be taken from this courtroom and placed back in his cell. He will remain there until he can keep a civil tongue in his mouth."

Sturgis's mouth curved in an evil grin.

"Pardon me, your honor," Lake Johnson said, "but that's exactly what he wants. He'd like to stall what he knows is comin'. I'd like to see the trial proceed in spite of the way he's actin', and get it over with."

Sturgis took a breath and opened his mouth to speak, but

his words froze in his throat. The strong hand of John Stranger clamped down firmly on his shoulder, and steel-like fingers pinched the nerve in its ridge, sending excruciating pain through Payton's upper body.

"You *will* remain silent unless spoken to, Payton," Stranger said.

Payton ejected a groan and mumbled something indistinguishable.

"What's that, Mr. Sturgis?" Judge Reed asked.

Stranger smiled. "He said there will be no more verbal outbursts during the trial, your honor."

A wave of subdued laughter swept through the courtroom.

Payton clenched his teeth in agony as Stranger said, "That *is* what you said, isn't it, Mr. Sturgis?"

Payton glared at him, but nodded.

"That's what I thought," the tall man said. Then to Reed, "You can proceed, Judge."

"Then let's pick up where I started. From where I sit, it appears to me, Mr. Sturgis, that even though you are handcuffed to the leg of the table, you can stand to your feet. Do it."

Payton shoved back the chair and stood up, leaning slightly because the table leg was tapered and the cuff could not come up all the way.

"Payton Sturgis," the judge said in a solemn tone, "you have been arrested for the murders of nine people whose names Sheriff Johnson has written on the paper that lies before you. Have you read their names?"

"Yeah."

Stranger touched Payton's shoulder. "You don't say 'Yeah' to Judge Reed. You say, 'Yes, your honor.' "

The defendant looked toward the judge without meeting his gaze, and said, "Yes, your honor."

"And how do you plead?" asked the judge.

"I ain't killed nobody. It's all a frame."

"So you plead not guilty?"

"Yeah—uh . . . yes, your honor."

A murmur of protest spread through the courtroom.

"You are also accused, Mr. Sturgis, of attempting to murder Mr. Ralph Byers."

"That's ridiculous," Sturgis said. "I never did no such thing."

Ralph Byers, who was seated two rows from the front, jumped to his feet and spat, "You're a dirty liar, Payton! You came to my house like you were there for a friendly visit. I let you in and you pulled a knife on me! If it hadn't been for John Stranger, you'd have killed me!"

Judge Reed tapped the gavel on the desk. "Mr. Byers, you'll have an opportunity to give testimony in a few moments. In the meantime, I ask you to remain silent."

"Yes, your honor," Byers said, and sat down.

Judge Reed looked toward Jenny Haymes, the court reporter, and said, "Let it stand in the record that the defendant is pleading not guilty."

Lynette Dickey was called as first witness. After taking the oath, the judge asked her to tell what happened at her house when she arrived in town on Wednesday. As she gave her story, Payton Sturgis flushed slightly when he heard that she had been in the house when he had killed her father.

"Miss Dickey," Reed said, "as you lay there under your bed, were you able to see the face of the man who killed your father?"

"No, your honor, I could only see his boots and his pants up to his knees. But I'll tell you this, my father's blood was on those boots and pants."

"Can you describe them for the court, Miss Dickey?"

"The pants were blue denim, your honor. The boots were tan-colored rawhide."

"And was your father's blood on both boots and both pantlegs?"

"Yes, sir."

"Did you see anything else that might help you identify the man who killed your father?"

"No, sir."

"All right. You may step down."

Sturgis eased back in his chair as if he had won a victory. Lynette had contributed nothing that could incriminate him.

The judge then called John Stranger to the witness stand. Stranger laid his hand on a Bible and promised to tell the truth, the whole truth, and nothing but the truth, so help him God.

Reed said, "All right, Mr. Stranger, will you please tell the court what you found in the defendant's room at the carpentry shop?"

"I'll more than tell the court, your honor," John said, "I'll *show* the court what I found."

He left the witness stand and bent over a box he had placed next to the wall earlier. When he brought out the bloody boots and pants, Payton stiffened and his face grew pale.

Stranger held up the boots and pants and explained how he had searched the defendant's room shortly after Alan Dickey had been found stabbed to death. He then presented the sheet of paper he'd found in Payton's room.

Stranger had shown the paper to the judge earlier. Now Reed asked him to read the list to the court and identify the names with the check marks next to them.

Ivan Charles had been subpoenaed to appear at the trial with papers he had in his office bearing Payton Sturgis's handwriting. The judge dismissed Stranger and called for Charles to take the stand. After taking the oath, the undertaker presented the samples of the defendant's handwriting. Those papers, along with the "death list" confiscated from Payton's room, were passed to the men of the jury for their examination.

Reed dismissed Charles and called Ralph Byers to the witness stand. Byers gave a detailed explanation of how he had answered the knock at his door on Wednesday evening and found Payton Sturgis on his porch. Payton had said he was just dropping by to say hello, so Byers invited him in. As soon as Byers had closed the door, Payton grabbed him, pulled a knife, and backed him up against a wall. Byers angrily protested, and Sturgis was about to plunge the knife into him when the door burst open and John Stranger overpowered Sturgis, knocking him out.

When Ralph Byers was dismissed, Reed called for the defendant to rise once more. Payton stiffened as if he was going to refuse, but John Stranger laid a hand on his shoulder. He stood up, sliding the handcuff up the leg of the table as far as it would go. Payton looked at the judge impassively and waited for him to speak.

"Mr. Sturgis," Reed said, "with the evidence that has been presented and the testimonies given under oath by Mr. Byers and Mr. Stranger, do you wish to change your plea?"

"No, I don't," came Sturgis's clipped reply. "This Stranger dude was lyin' when he said he found that piece of paper and them bloody pants and boots in my room. Somebody faked my handwritin' on that paper. Probably Stranger, himself. And him and that Byers dude are both lyin'. I was outside on the street when Stranger crept up behind me. I heard him comin' and turned around to see who it was, and he punched me. I tried to fight back, but he hit me again, and the next thing I knew I was in that stinkin' jail cell."

"All right, Mr. Sturgis," Reed said. "You may be seated." Then to the jury, "Gentlemen of the jury, you have seen evidence presented by Mr. Stranger, along with Mr. Charles's evidence of the defendant's handwriting. You have also heard testimony from Miss Dickey, Mr. Stranger, and Mr. Byers. You will now retire to the jury room to arrive at your verdict."

The courtroom was buzzing in a low tone when the jury returned in just under five minutes. Payton Sturgis had not spoken a word to Johnson or Stranger while the jury was out. He sat staring at the wall behind the judge's bench.

The voices quickly faded as the jurymen took their seats. Judge Reed tapped the gavel on his desk and declared the court once more in session. He turned to the twelve jurors and said, "Gentlemen of the jury, have you reached a verdict?"

Darwin Smith rose to his feet. "We have, your honor."

The judge looked toward Sturgis and said, "The defendant will please rise."

Sturgis flicked a glance at John Stranger and saw the look in his steel-gray eyes. He rose to his feet with Johnson and Stranger beside him.

Reed tilted his head to look at the jury foreman over the top of his half-moon spectacles and said, "Mr. Smith, will you please tell the court your verdict? Do you find the defendant guilty, or not guilty, as charged?"

Smith cleared his throat. "Your honor, we, the jury, find the defendant, Payton Sturgis, guilty as charged."

The judge fixed Payton with a steady look and said, "Mr. Sturgis, you have been duly tried in this court and found guilty of nine counts of murder and one count of attempted murder. It is therefore my duty as judge of Silver Bow County to sentence you for your crimes. I hereby sentence you to hang by the neck until dead. Such execution to transpire tomorrow morning at nine o'clock sharp. Do you have anything else to say?"

Sturgis stared coldly at the judge but remained silent.

After a few seconds, Reed said, "Very well. Sheriff Johnson, you may remove your prisoner from the courtroom. Keep him in your custody at the county jail until the set time of execution tomorrow morning."

Suddenly Payton Sturgis came to life and screamed, "No!" He pointed an accusing finger at the judge, then the jury. "I'll kill every one of you! I will! I will!"

As Payton screamed those words, he jerked the hand cuffed to the table so violently that it snapped the leg off the table. When the table collapsed, a woman screamed, and some of the men rose to their feet.

Just as Sturgis grabbed the broken table leg for a weapon, Stranger chopped him on the jaw with a blow so hard it seemed to send shock waves through the room. Sturgis went down like a rotten tree in a high wind and lay still. Stranger picked him up with ease and draped him over his shoulder.

"All right, Sheriff, let's take your prisoner to his cell."

A few minutes after dawn the next morning, John Stranger entered the sheriff's office and found him at his desk. John carried a Bible in his hand.

"Morning, Sheriff."

"Same to you," Lake said. "I don't know how to thank you, John. What a relief to have this thing over with . . . well, almost over with. You sure did the job every bit as well as I anticipated."

"Glad to have had a small part in it."

"A *small* part? Seems to me you were the *whole* shebang. So what's with the Bible? I've heard tell you're as good a preacher as you are an outlaw trapper. You plannin' on preachin' at the hangin'?"

"No. I'd just like to have a few minutes with Payton. No matter how wicked the man is, the Lord Jesus will save his soul if Payton will let him."

"Are you tellin' me that a lowdown killin' animal like Sturgis could be forgiven by God, and still go to heaven when he dies?"

"The grace of God is for all sinners, Sheriff, and the blood of Jesus Christ was shed at Calvary for all sinners. If they will repent, put their faith in God's Son, and call on Him to save them, He will do it."

"Oh. Well, you'll have to stand in line. Pastor Walker is already back there talkin' to Sturgis right now."

Stranger nodded. "Good enough. Do you mind if I wait and see how it turns out?"

"Of course not." Lake gestured toward a chair in front of his desk. "Sit down."

John eased onto the chair, laid his Bible on the desk, and said, "Sheriff, we really haven't had time to talk about anything but the killings and the killer since I arrived in town, but since we have a few minutes, let me ask you something."

"Sure."

"Let's say it was Lake Johnson who was going to die today, instead of Payton Sturgis. Where would you go?"

Johnson fidgeted on his chair. "You mean would I go to heaven or hell?"

"Mm-hmm."

"Well, let me explain, John. Pastor Walker has talked to me about this on several occasions."

"Good for him. I'm listening."

Lake cleared his throat. "I've always had my own ideas

about God and eternity, and heaven and hell."

"I see. Your own ideas based on what?"

Lake shrugged. "Just . . . ah . . . what I think."

John smiled and said, "A hundred men may think a hundred different things, Sheriff. Which one of them is right?"

"Well, I guess each one is right in his own way."

John shook his head. "You know why this world is in such horrible shape, Sheriff? Because of that very kind of thinking. You know I'm your friend, don't you? And that I mean no disrespect."

"Of course," Lake said. "I'm listening."

John smiled at him. "Our Creator has given us a Guidebook for life's journey into eternity." Picking up the Bible, he said, "This is the Guidebook, and it was our Creator who gave it to us. It has absolutes in it. God's absolutes. The law you serve in this county has absolutes, doesn't it? I mean, Payton Sturgis considered what he did to be right for him. This may sound harsh, but if we went by your philosophy, Payton shouldn't be punished by the law for doing what was right for *him*. Get my point?"

"I . . . ah . . . yes. I get your point."

"Make sense?"

The sheriff fidgeted again. "Yes."

"May I read some of God's absolutes to you from His Book?"

"Pastor Walker's done that before, John. I just hadn't quite seen it the way you're puttin' it. Sure. Go ahead."

Stranger read Scripture after Scripture on the subject of salvation. He was reading the story of the cross in Matthew 27 when the cellblock door opened. John stopped reading as Pastor Walker entered the office, shaking his head.

"Didn't go so good, Pastor?" John asked.

Still shaking his head, Walker replied, "The man laughed

in my face. Mocked me when I gave him the gospel and told him that without Jesus he would go to hell at nine o'clock this morning. Said he isn't going to hell, he's going to come back from the dead and get even with every man who had anything to do with sending him to the gallows."

It was John Stranger's turn to shake his head. "If he only knew."

Walker's eyes fell on the open Bible.

John noticed, and said, "The sheriff and I have been talking about salvation, Pastor."

"Wonderful. Has he been a help to you, Sheriff?"

"Yes. Yes, he has," Lake said. "He's shed some new light on my views about life and death. I'm going to give what both of you men have taught me some serious thought."

"Good," Walker said. "You need to give it serious thought. No man knows when he rises in the morning but that he's looking at his last sunrise. If you die without opening your heart to Jesus, you'll go to the same place where Payton Sturgis will be in less than three hours."

Lake blinked in astonishment.

"Well, I must be going," Walker said. "I'll see you two men at the hanging."

When the preacher was gone, Lake screwed up his face and said, "John, why would I go to the same place where Payton's going? I'm not a murderer."

John flipped the pages of his Bible and said, "Let me show you about that."

In tenderness and love, the tall man read Scripture to Lake, pointing out that all human beings are sinners, and that no one goes to heaven for being good. And no one goes to hell for being bad. He opened the Bible to John 3:18 and showed the sheriff that even good people are condemned already because they have not repented of their sin of unbelief and trusted Jesus Christ to save them.

John saw a light come on in Lake's eyes. "John, I've never clearly understood it till now. Will you help me? I want to call on the Lord and be saved."

After Lake Johnson had become a child of God by receiving Jesus into his heart, Stranger rejoiced with him, then said, "Sheriff, I'm going back and talk to Payton. Maybe he's had time to let what the preacher told him sink in."

"More power to you, my friend."

John headed down the short corridor and entered the cellblock. Payton Sturgis was the only prisoner in the jail. When he saw John with the Bible in his hand, he jumped off his bunk, eyes wild, and screamed, "Get outta here, Stranger! I don't want to talk to you, especially with that Bible in your hand! You think you can accomplish somethin' that stinkin' preacher couldn't do?"

John stepped close to the bars, and spoke softly. "It's not that I think I can accomplish what the preacher couldn't, but I just thought maybe you'd think over what he told you and decide to let Jesus Christ save your soul before you die."

Sturgis screamed at John and cursed him violently, telling him to get out. Without another word, John turned and walked away.

The bleak winter sun shone down on Butte City as the whole town gathered on Main Street to watch the hanging. Also attending the execution were Crow Chief Broken Bow and a dozen of his braves. The Indians had great interest in the white man's laws.

The gallows was a well-constructed affair built on skids so that it could be dragged by a team of horses from its normal resting place behind the jail. Steps led up to the eight-foot-high platform. Atop the platform was a trapdoor. Above the platform, a solid wooden beam stretched overhead between two posts. The hangman's noose hung from the beam.

A cold, stiff breeze was blowing as the crowd watched John Stranger and Sheriff Lake Johnson emerge from the lawman's office with Payton Sturgis between them. Sturgis was hatless, and the breeze toyed with his straw-colored hair. He kept his face expressionless, his eyes straight ahead.

The ominous noose danced in the wind as it dangled from the crossbeam of the gallows.

All twelve jurors and their families stood nearby, as well as Judge Virgil Reed and his wife. With them were the families and close friends of Payton Sturgis's victims.

Sturgis's hands were cuffed behind his back, and by his own choice, he wore no coat. The icy breeze drew rose-colored spots to his cheeks.

Sheriff Johnson guided Sturgis to the center of the trapdoor while Stranger stood close by. As Johnson took hold of the swaying noose and dropped it over Sturgis's head, the man's features contorted as if a demonic being had possession of him.

Johnson cinched the rope tight around Sturgis's neck and pulled a black hood from his pocket.

"No! Don't cover my head! I want all those people out there to see my face just before you pull the lever!"

"As you wish," Johnson said, and moved toward the steps.

John Stranger glanced at the wild-eyed man and followed Johnson down the steps. The crowd looked on—some with apprehension, some with guarded anticipation. Others with complete satisfaction.

Dr. Bristow had moved to the foot of the gallows steps. Johnson met Bristow's stolid gaze when he reached the bottom of the steps and moved toward the lever. Stranger, who followed, nodded solemnly at the doctor, then turned and stood beside him.

Suddenly Payton Sturgis let out a loud, shrill cry. "Go ahead, Lake! Go ahead! Pull the lever! But it won't do you any good! Sure, I'll die when I hit bottom, and Ivan will bury me! But I won't stay in the grave! I'll be back! And I'll get you, Lake! And I'll get you, too, Johnny boy! Yeah, and you, too, Virgil!"

The people stood in dread at the words coming out of Payton's mouth. The look in his eyes and the wolfish curve of his lips were frightening to behold.

Payton's voice became a snakelike hiss as he ran his eyes over the faces of the jurymen and said, "You twelve will die, too! I'll come back and get every one of you! I'll—"

Sturgis's words were cut off by the trapdoor opening beneath him. He plummeted downward, his neck snapping with a loud crack when he came to the end of the rope.

CHAPTER

FIFTEEN

Now it was two years later, and John Stranger still felt an icy shiver when he recalled the demonic look in Payton Sturgis's eyes just before he dropped through the trapdoor.

He shook his head as if to throw off the memory, then sat up straight and looked out the train window. The sun was already touching the tips of the mountains to the west, turning the sky a flaming orange.

Passengers getting off at Buffalo began to gather their bags and put on coats and hats. The train chugged into the Buffalo station a few moments later and ground to a halt. The engine stood hissing steam from its sides while a few passengers alighted from each of the three coaches. John was in coach three, just in front of the caboose. He had about an hour before the train departed again. Better stretch my legs, he thought.

While he strolled about the depot platform, his thoughts returned to Payton Sturgis. John was eager to find the man who now impersonated Sturgis and prove to the citizens of Butte City, once and for all, that only one Man in all of history had ever come back from the dead.

The train had been in Buffalo for nearly an hour when the whistle blew and the engine bell started to clang. The conductor called for everyone to board the train. The next stop would be Sheridan, Wyoming, just south of the Montana border.

By the time Stranger entered his car, several new passengers had boarded it, and someone was in the seat he had occupied. He reached overhead, took down his overnight bag, and moved to the rear of the coach. He chose the last seat on the left side of the train. The next four seats ahead of him on both sides of the aisle were unoccupied, as well as the seat directly across the aisle.

John noted that the six lanterns inside the coach had been lit. He glanced out the window and saw that a few stars were beginning to twinkle in the sky.

He eased back in the seat, closed his eyes, and thought about Breanna. His heart grew warm as he pictured her bright blue eyes, flashing smile, and captivating features. He told himself she would be the most beautiful bride ever. He could just see her walking down the aisle on the arm of Dr. Lyle Goodwin—

"Everybody get your hands in the air!"

Stranger blinked, startled from his daydream, and focused on the two men at the front of the coach with guns drawn and bandannas tied across their faces. They wore wide-brimmed hats pulled low over their foreheads.

Stranger eased his hands up with the rest of the people but kept them just above shoulder level.

One of the train robbers was tall and slender. The other one short and stocky. The tall one had a mean look in his eyes as he spoke harshly through his bandanna, "Keep your hands up till we get to you. We'll tell you when to move 'em so you can give us your wallets and purses . . . and take off those rings, necklaces, and watches."

The short one added, "Anybody gets cute and tries to keep somethin' from us, or goes for a gun, we'll shoot you on the spot!"

The terrified passengers did exactly as they were told as

the robbers moved down the aisle, relieving people of their valuables and placing them in a canvas bag.

John watched the two robbers move from seat to seat. The short one was on John's side of the aisle. Stranger slowly inched his way to the edge of his seat while keeping his hands in the air.

The robbers worked hastily, and soon had collected valuables and money from every passenger in the car except for Stranger. "You get his stuff," the tall one said to his cohort.

The short robber fixed his eyes on John and grunted, "Okay, buddy, gimme your wallet."

John moved with the swiftness of a cougar and kicked the robber's gun hand. The gun fired harmlessly, sending a bullet through the coach roof, as it sailed from the robber's grasp and clattered to the floor. At the same time, he slammed the short robber against his partner. Both robbers went down in a heap.

Before the tall robber could react, Stranger had his gun. The robber cursed and lunged. John struck him on the head with the gun barrel and the man went down hard. John smashed him with a rock-hard fist, knocking him out cold.

Stranger looked toward the passengers, who had begun applauding, and said, "Some of you men take these fellas' belts and tie them up." As he spoke, he moved forward in the coach toward the door, figuring the gunshot would bring other gang members to see what had happened. He handed the robber's revolver to a husky young man, and said, "Hold onto this."

Just as Stranger stepped out onto the platform he met another masked man. John surprised him by kicking the gun out of his hand. The weapon sailed out into the night. The outlaw swung a fist, but John seized his arm. With one powerful thrust, he threw the man off the side of the platform. The outlaw hit the ground, cartwheeled, and disappeared.

A second robber exited the back door of coach number two. His eyes widened when he saw the tall man in black, and he lifted his revolver. But he was too slow. Stranger's fist met the man's jaw with the force of a mule's kick, and the outlaw peeled over the side of the platform.

Stranger cautiously opened the rear door of car number two, saw the frightened people looking in his direction, and plunged inside. "Don't worry, folks," he said, hurrying toward the front door, "everything behind me is under control."

"God bless you, mister!" a female voice said, as Stranger hurried through the car.

He had barely stepped onto the platform when the rear door of car number one opened. John caught a glimpse of a masked face, and jumped sideways into the shadows. Suddenly the robber saw Stranger from the corner of his eye and whirled toward him, pointing his gun. John threw a punch and sent the man sailing off the platform into the darkness.

Almost immediately another robber came out the door and saw his friend fall. He sprang forward, swinging his gun barrel at John's head. Stranger sidestepped, and the robber's momentum made him stumble. He fell between the two platforms and was crushed beneath the wheels.

To Stranger's surprise, a third robber emerged from car number one with a gun barrel trained on him. Stranger ducked, and the bullet struck the rear of coach two. Before the outlaw could cock the hammer for another shot, Stranger kicked him in the groin. The man doubled over, and Stranger cracked him with a solid punch that dropped him unconscious to the platform floor. Stranger kicked the man's gun off the platform and dragged his limp form inside car number one.

The people's apprehension turned to relief when they saw

Stranger dragging the unconscious robber.

"Couple of you men come and tie this guy up, will you?" Stranger said. "I'm going up to the engine and see if we've got any more robbers on the train."

While two men headed for the unconscious outlaw, the conductor hastened toward Stranger, holding a bloody bandanna to his temple. "They cold-cocked me, mister," he said. "I just came to a minute ago. What about the rest of them?"

"Two are tied up in car number three, and four . . . ah . . . decided to get off the train. You know of any more on the train?"

"No, sir. But there might be some more with the engineer and fireman."

"I'll go find out," Stranger said, heading for the front door. He passed through the baggage coach and inched along the narrow ledge on the coal car. The train was on a curve, and Stranger could see a row of cottonwoods in the beam of the headlight.

When he reached the rear of the engine, he looked into the cab and saw the engineer on the right side and the fireman just closing the iron door of the firebox, with a scoop shovel in one hand.

Stranger sighed with relief and mumbled, "Looks like we got them all," then began moving again toward the engine.

As the fireman turned to put the scoop shovel away, he spotted the dark figure coming toward him on the ledge and jerked in surprise.

Stranger hung on to the thin metal rail along the side of the car and threw up his other hand in a gesture of peace. "It's all right!" he shouted. "I'm one of your passengers!"

"One of the passengers, Mack," the fireman told the engineer, as Stranger stepped into the rear of the engine cab.

"What can we do for you, sir?" Mack Gibson asked.

"Nothing," Stranger said. "We just had an attempted robbery. Seven of them boarded the train in Buffalo. We've got it under control. The canvas bags they put their loot in are on the train. Nobody will lose a thing."

"Wow!" the fireman said. "I'm sure glad you folks were able to overpower the robbers!"

"Took a little doing," Stranger said with a grin. "Main reason I came out here was to see if they had somebody holding you two at gunpoint."

"We didn't see hide nor hair of them," the engineer said, turning back to his window. "And I'm plenty glad we—"

"What's the matter, Mack?" the fireman asked.

"We got us a fire on the track ahead."

"They've resorted to a flaming barricade so they can get their pals off with the loot." Stranger said.

"I'll have to stop," Mack said, laying his hand on the throttle.

Stranger shook his head. "Best thing to do is ram it. They might have decided to go the barricade route for another reason. Could be a whole passel of them."

"*Ram* it?"

"Ram it!" Stranger said.

"But it'll derail us! If they've got heavy timbers in that fire, it'll throw the engine right off the track, and the rest of the train with it!"

Stranger shook his head. "I'll wager what's burning is only a pile of small tree limbs. Those no-goods are too lazy to cut down or even carry enough heavy stuff to derail the train. It's a bluff, just to make you stop."

Mack thought quickly, then said, "Okay, Mr.—I don't even know who you are. What's your name, stranger?"

"That's good enough."

"Pardon me?"

"Just call me Stranger. John Stranger."

The engineer turned back to his window. "Okay, Mr. John Stranger, we're gonna take your advice and ram it." With that, he shoved the throttle wide open.

"Better brace yourself," the fireman said.

Mack Gibson peered ahead as the thundering train raced toward the flaming barricade. "Hey, John Stranger! Looks like they had another reason for putting up the barricades. I can make out at least five horses!"

They were now less than seventy yards from the barricade, and charging toward it at about fifty miles per hour.

Stranger moved up beside the engineer while the fireman went to the other window. They could see five figures moving hurriedly toward their horses. Mack Gibson reached up and pulled the small rope above his head. The shrill sound of the whistle and the roar of the oncoming train had frightened the horses, and the outlaws were having a time getting into their saddles. Four of them finally mounted the animals and spurred them out of the circle of firelight. The fifth man was still trying to get into the saddle when the engine slammed through the barricade.

Blazing limbs scattered in all directions, and sparks flew toward the starlit sky, fluttering like fireflies.

"Whew!" the engineer said. "You were right! But I don't mind telling you, I was more than a little scared!"

"I guess you know a lot about outlaws, sir," the fireman said.

"I've had enough experience with the criminal mind to do me a lifetime," John said with a chuckle.

"So what are we going to do with the ones you've got tied up in the passenger cars?" the engineer asked, as he slowed the train to its normal cruising speed.

"When we stop in Sheridan, we'll turn them over to the

county sheriff—let him take it from there. If they're wanted by federal authorities, he can call in a U.S. marshal."

"I'll just be glad to get those no-goods off my train," Gibson said.

"Too bad we can't put 'em off like Mr. Stranger did the other ones," the fireman said. "Some hard bumps would do 'em good."

Stranger and Gibson laughed, dispelling the tension of the last half hour.

At the same time John Stranger was delivering the surviving train robbers to the sheriff in Sheridan, a snowstorm hit Butte City after three days of sunshine. Dan Cogan had been buried, and his widow, Elaine, was in deep mourning at home. Several family members had traveled to attend the funeral and were staying with her.

Deputy Sheriff Monte Dixon walked down Main Street amid the falling snow and entered the general store. Darwin Smith, the proprietor, was stocking a shelf and turned to see who had entered. He managed a slight smile and a greeting.

Dixon looked around at the empty store. "Morning, Darwin. Business a little slow?"

"Yeah . . . it's the snowfall. People in this town are scared to be out. Afraid they might run into that snow ghost. Can't say that I blame them."

"Me neither. I'll sure be glad when this horror is over."

"Not as glad as I will. At least you're not on the death list."

"The way I see it, Darwin, nobody's really safe in this town. Who knows but what that madman might just decide to kill anybody he sees."

"That's what most people are sayin'. That's why the whole town is scared stiff." Smith paused, then asked, "What can I do for you?"

"Just wanted to pick up some lye soap and a new razor."

"All right. I'll get them for you."

Smith was behind the counter taking Dixon's money when the door opened and Frances Westbrook and her daughter, Jessie, entered, brushing snow from their coats.

The sight of Jessie made Dixon's heart flutter.

"Good mornin', ladies," both men said in unison.

Frances nodded her understanding, but said, "We must keep things as normal as possible, even with this snow ghost lurking about. There are quite a few people on the street right now."

"Oh. Well, good. I'm glad to hear it."

Smith and Frances struck up a conversation, and Jessie told her mother she would pick up the things they needed.

Monte moved along with Jessie as she picked up items and carried them for her. As they moved slowly along the shelves, Jessie said, "I was glad to see you at church last Sunday, Monte. Did you enjoy the service?"

"Yes. I really like the way the people sing the hymns with so much enthusiasm."

"That's because we've got something to sing *about*. Did you like the pastor's preaching?"

"He speaks plain and clear, that's for sure."

"Are you going to come back and hear him again?"

"Oh, sure." Monte hesitated, then said, "Jessie, could . . . could I take you out for dinner some time?"

Jessie was quiet for a moment. She pulled an item off a shelf, handed it to him, and said, "Monte, let me ask you a question."

"Sure."

"Are you a Christian?"

"Well, ah . . . Sheriff Johnson has been talking to me a lot about it. And what I heard on Sunday helped me understand better, Jessie. But . . . no. I'm not a Christian."

Jessie looked into his eyes in a tender manner, and said, "Monte, you are a nice person. I like you very much. What I'm about to say is not meant to offend you, so please don't take it that way."

"All right . . ."

"When a person becomes a Christian, there's a tremendous change in his life. He looks at life totally different than he did before he asked Jesus to save him. It's not that Christians think they're better than anyone else, but because of the change Jesus makes in us, we find when it comes to dating, we're only comfortable with another Christian. I . . . I hope I'm making sense."

Monte blinked. "Go on."

"Well, Monte, a person is going to marry someone they date. I mean, nobody marries someone they haven't gotten to know. And the best way to get to know someone is to spend time with them."

"Of course, Jessie."

"Well, according to the Bible, it's wrong for a Christian to marry someone who's not a Christian. This would only be asking for trouble in the marriage. A marriage that isn't compatible is no marriage at all. It wouldn't last. Again, it isn't that I think I'm better than some young man who isn't saved. I'm only a sinner saved by the grace of God. But an unequal yoke just doesn't work. So, to guard against making a big mistake in my life, I only date young men who know the Lord. Am I making sense?"

"Well . . . I guess this is all so new to me that it's kind of foggy. I will say that I really like you, and I would really like to get to know you better. And for sure I'd like to take you on a date. But I respect you, and I respect your way of thinking.

Guess there's a lot more for me to learn about being a Christian and all."

"Monte, the main thing about becoming a Christian is that you need to be saved. Just like the rest of the human race, you need your sins forgiven and cleansed so you don't go to hell when you die. Jesus went to the cross and shed His precious blood for our sins. He paid the penalty God demands must be paid for sin. When we understand that, and believe it, He will save us if we ask Him."

Disappointment showed in Monte's eyes, but he said, "Jessie, I've got questions about all this that I need answered. It's all so new to me. I mean I've heard *about* being saved and knowing Jesus Christ, but there's a lot I still don't understand."

"The best person to talk to is Pastor Walker, Monte. You need to go to him right away and get your questions answered."

"All right. I'll ask him for an appointment next time I see him."

"Better yet, why don't you just go to his office right now and talk to him? Salvation is not something to put off. When God talks about a time for salvation in His Bible, it's always *now*. He warns us not to boast about tomorrow, because we don't know what a day may bring."

"Okay, Jessie. I've got some errands to run for the sheriff, but I'll go see Pastor Walker as soon as I can."

CHAPTER

SIXTEEN

Monte Dixon left the general store and ran the errands for Sheriff Johnson before heading back to the office. He was amazed to see so many people on Main Street in spite of the snowstorm, although they hastily moved in and out of the stores and shops.

Dixon could see fear on their faces as he overheard snatches of conversations about the snow ghost.

Darrell Amick, owner of the leather and saddle shop, suddenly darted out of his shop and ran toward him, waving his arms. He slid to a stop in front of the deputy and said breathlessly, "Monte, I just saw the snow ghost! I saw him, I tell you! He was in the alley behind my shop, just standing there glaring at me!"

Passersby on the boardwalk stopped to listen.

"Did you get a good look at him?"

"Yes! It was Payton Sturgis!"

"Did he make a move toward you?"

"No. It was like he wasn't expecting me to open the back door of the shop. Like I'd surprised him. It was only a few seconds till I slammed the door and ran. But he just stood there glaring at me. I'm one of the jurors, you know! My name's on that death list!"

"Let's go tell the sheriff, Darrell," Monte said.

"You sure it was Payton?" asked a man in the group gathered around them.

"It was Payton, all right."

"But you only saw him for a few seconds," an elderly woman said. "And you were looking through this snowstorm, too. How can you be so sure it was Payton?"

"I know Payton when I see him, Mrs. Humphries. It was him!"

"Excuse us, folks," Monte Dixon said, ushering Amick away, "but we've got to get to the sheriff's office."

Lake Johnson was at his desk when the door opened and his deputy entered with Darrell Amick on his heels.

Johnson took one look at Amick's face and said, "What happened, boys?"

"It's Payton, Sheriff!" Amick blurted. "I saw him! I opened the back door of my shop a few minutes ago and he was standing not more than twenty feet from me!"

Johnson rose from the chair. "You mean it was this so-called snow ghost who *looks* like Payton, Darrell."

"No, sir! I'm telling you, it was him!"

Johnson reached for his coat and hat. "Darrell, you stay here. Monte and I will go take a look."

They entered the alley with guns drawn. The back side of the stores and their slanted porch roofs held many shadowy hiding places with boxes stacked high. Nothing moved as the lawmen slowly made their way to the rear of the leather and saddle shop. They scanned the ground for footprints but could see none.

"You suppose he hallucinated, Sheriff?" Dixon asked.

Johnson brushed snowflakes from his eyelashes. "I wouldn't say that. It's snowin' hard enough to cover tracks made even a few minutes ago. I've no doubt he saw the killer. But it wasn't Payton Sturgis. C'mon. Let's get back to the office."

The two lawmen had barely reached the street when banker Jackson DeLong came toward them. "Sheriff, I heard from some of the people on the street what's going on. Did you find anything in the alley?"

"Nothin'," Johnson said.

"Just as I thought. We're going to have a lot more of this. People's imaginations are running away with them."

"Darrell swears it was Payton Sturgis," Monte said.

"Bah! We've got a killer around here, but it's not Payton!"

"I agree," Johnson said.

"Well, so do I," Dixon added, "but this guy has got to look exactly like Payton. Darrell's not the first one to say so."

A loud gunshot reverberated in the air.

"Came from the residential section east of Main," Johnson said. "Let's go, Monte!"

The two men broke into a run. When they reached the first block beyond Main, they saw people heading east across their yards through the falling snow. In the next block they heard a voice wailing and crying. Soon they saw a gathering at the small house of retired miner David Ellsworth, and more people filing through a gate into the back yard.

Johnson took the lead with Dixon on his heels. They pushed past the people and found Ellsworth on his knees, bending over the body of a man on the ground. Johnson recognized Mike Yarbrough, the eighteen-year-old son of Ellsworth's next-door neighbors. They could see a bullet hole at the right shoulder of the boy's mackinaw, and blood seeping through the cloth.

Johnson could see that the boy was still breathing, and he turned to the crowd. "Couple of you men help us get Mike to Doc Bristow's office." Then to the elderly ex-miner, "Dave, what happened?"

Ellsworth's gnarled hands were trembling. His lips quivered as he said, "I . . . I thought he was that . . . that snow ghost, Sheriff! Mike was comin' down the alley, here. I've been carryin' my Colt .44 with me since this snow ghost thing started. I stepped out on my back porch to fetch the galvanized tub by the door, and all of a sudden I see this tall, slender figure comin' at me. I wasn't wearin' my spectacles, so I couldn't make out his features, but I figured it was Payton comin' to kill me! So I shot him. When he fell, he called out that he was Mike Yarbrough so I wouldn't fire again. Oh-h! If I'd only known it was Mike!"

The old man broke down and sobbed.

Four men picked up the wounded man just as Dale and Marlene Yarbrough drove into their yard. When someone yelled that their son had been shot, they jumped from the wagon and fell to their knees beside him.

Moments later, the Yarbroughs sped in their wagon toward Doc Bristow's with Marlene bending over her son.

The sheriff turned to Jackson DeLong and said, "You need to call for a meeting at the town hall tonight. We've got to warn people to keep their heads. If we don't get a handle on this, somebody else is gonna get shot, and maybe not be as fortunate as Mike."

"You're right," DeLong said. "I'll set it for seven o'clock and get the message out right away."

The storm had blown out, leaving stars twinkling in the cold night sky, as the uneasy citizens of Butte City filed into the town hall. The place was packed.

At precisely seven o'clock, council chairman Jackson DeLong called the meeting to order with Sheriff Johnson standing beside him. First DeLong asked Dr. Bristow to give a report on Mike Yarbrough's condition. Bristow told them he had removed the bullet from Mike's shoulder. No bone was broken, and Mike would be fine in a few weeks.

DeLong then turned the meeting over to Lake Johnson, who did his best to convince the people they must keep cool heads or someone else was going to get shot.

When the sheriff was finished, DeLong ran his gaze over the frightened faces and said, "Folks, we are *not* dealing with a ghost. We're dealing with a flesh-and-blood human being who's somehow making himself resemble Payton Sturgis. It's a whole lot easier to handle the fact that the killer is a man rather than some spook who's come back from the grave."

Merlin Loberg stood up and said, "You're asking these people to believe that he's an earthly being, but neither you nor Sheriff Johnson have any evidence to back up your statements."

A man near the back called out, "Yeah, Sheriff. Give us some answers!"

Johnson and DeLong exchanged pained glances, then Johnson said, "Frank, we don't have any answers."

Loberg was still on his feet. "*I* have an answer, Frank. It's simple. Payton Sturgis has come back like he said he would, and he's here to get revenge!"

Many voices murmured agreement.

"Listen to me!" Johnson called above the rumble of voices. "You people have got to keep calm! If you don't, some other innocent person is going to get shot!"

Lawton Haymes jumped to his feet. "I'll tell you this much, Sheriff, I take my shotgun with me while I'm walking to my shop, and it stays only inches from my hands while I'm working! If that Payton skunk comes near me—ghost or no ghost—I'll blow a hole in him big enough to drive a wagon through!"

People leaped to their feet and cheered.

When the noise subsided, Darrell Amick said, "Sheriff!

Jackson! You can deny that Payton has come back from the dead all you want, but *I saw him!* He was standing no more than twenty feet from me in the alley behind my shop! Sure it was snowing, but I got a clear look at him! His eyes were full of hatred! I'm telling you, it's not some earthly maniac plaguing us, it's Payton Sturgis! Chief Broken Bow is right! Payton has come back as a snow ghost!"

Tom McVicker stood up. "I saw Payton, too, Sheriff! It was snowing, but not so heavily that I couldn't make out his features! Everybody here knows that he killed Les Osborne while I hurried to you for help."

"Face it, Sheriff!" came a voice from the back. "Payton is back!"

Pastor Walker moved up beside the sheriff and whispered in his ear. Johnson nodded and said to DeLong, "Pastor Walker would like to speak to the people."

DeLong gestured for Walker to move to the center of the platform. The pastor once again tried to convince the people that no matter how much it seemed that Payton was back from the dead, according to the Bible, it simply wasn't so.

When Walker finished speaking, Cliff Morgan, owner of the *Butte City Sentinel*, rose to his feet. "May I say something, Jackson?" He turned so that all could hear him. "I've kept this snow ghost thing very low-key in my newspaper. I've just reported the facts about the killings. Pastor Walker, you know that even though I don't come to the church, I have deep respect for you."

Walker nodded.

"But even an actor from the Broadway stage in New York City couldn't make himself look exactly like Payton. Yet these men who have seen the killer are credible witnesses. If they say it's Payton, how can we dispute them? Especially when you can't tell us how a man could look exactly like

Payton and perfectly duplicate his handwriting."

"Cliff," Walker said, "I take my stand on the Word of God. The Bible makes it clear that no man can come back from the dead. You'll see that, once this killer is caught."

A man shouted, "If the dead don't come back, why was Payton's coffin empty?"

"All these questions will be cleared up when the killer is caught, believe me," Walker said.

"Sheriff," another man called, "speaking of catching the killer, when is John Stranger supposed to arrive?"

"He'll be on the stage from Billings tomorrow."

Suddenly Eva Walz entered the hall, crying out, "Dr. Bristow! It's George! He's in the buggy, and he's hurt bad! The snow ghost stabbed him!"

Both Doc and Sadie Bristow jumped from their chairs and hurried outside. Sheriff Johnson ran up the aisle and touched Eva's arm to detain her. He led her to a seat and urged her to sit down.

"Tell me what happened, Eva," he said.

She took a deep shuddering breath and let it out. It seemed to settle her down somewhat, and she began to tell the sheriff, and anyone close enough to hear, what had happened. "George saddled up this morning and rode to Cardwell on business. He was supposed to be home by about three o'clock. I got worried when he wasn't home by four.

"When George wasn't home by suppertime, I hitched the horse to the buggy and started east. It had stopped snowing by then, but it was getting dark. I looked up the road and saw George's horse. When I got to it, I found him lying in the snow with blood everywhere. He was conscious but couldn't get up. He said Payton Sturgis had come out of the woods from behind him and jerked him out of the saddle, stabbing him repeatedly with a big knife. Payton apparently thought

George was dead, because he left him lying there and ran back into the woods."

Sadie Bristow had returned and made her way to Eva's side. "Doc thinks George will make it, Eva," she said. "He needs a couple of men to help him get George to the office."

The people in the town hall were showing signs of panic when Sheriff Johnson turned to the council chairman and said, "Jackson, you and Pastor Walker do what you can to calm these folks. I've got to go see about George."

It was almost noon the next day when Lake Johnson and his deputy entered the Wells Fargo office. Agent Tim Wiley looked up and said, "Howdy, Sheriff . . . Monte. Wire came from Billings early this mornin'. The stage left there on time. They always put on a fresh team of horses at Bozeman. I expect 'em in here just any minute."

"Glad to hear it," Lake said.

"I'm really looking forward to meeting John Stranger," Monte said.

"I guarantee you'll like him," Wiley said. "Only ones that don't are killers, robbers, and other types of no-goods. Ivan and Bill stopped by a couple hours ago. Said Doc got George stabilized. You heard anything more?"

"Yes," Lake said. "We just left Doc's office, and George is doin' fine for a man who was stabbed five times."

The familiar sound of tinkling harness and horses blowing met their ears. The brilliant sunlight reflecting off newly fallen snow made the men squint as they watched the coach's arrival.

Wiley and Dixon greeted the stagecoach driver and shotgunner as they climbed down from the box. The first person out of the coach was a short, stout middle-aged man. Another man alighted behind him. They told the driver they would be right back, and not to leave without them.

The final passenger was a tall, broad-shouldered man in black. When he stepped out, he smiled at Lake Johnson and said, "Hello, Sheriff."

"John!" Lake extended his hand. "Am I ever glad you're here!"

Monte stood close by and cleared his throat loudly.

Johnson turned and said, "John, I want you to meet my new deputy, Monte Dixon."

"Oh, so you finally got yourself a deputy, eh?"

Dixon felt as if an electric current went through him when he grasped John Stranger's hand.

"Glad to meet you, Monte," John said, and grinned. "My heart goes out to you, though, having to work for this scalawag."

Dixon laughed. "Oh, he's not so bad."

"Well, I'm glad you think so. Just wait'll you really get to know him."

"Okay, okay, John," Lake said, cuffing him on the shoulder. "Don't give away my secrets."

The shotgunner set down two bags beside Stranger. "There you go, sir."

John thanked him, then said, "Well, Sheriff, I guess the first thing is to get my hotel room. While we're walking, bring me up to date."

"All right. But before I forget, Ernie Davis will let you have a horse free of charge while you're here."

"Mighty nice of him," John said.

As the three men made their way toward the Silver Bow Hotel, Lake described everything that had transpired since the snow ghost business had begun.

A block away from the hotel, they met up with Jessie Westbrook and Lynette Dickey. Lynette hurried to Stranger and surprised him with a light embrace.

"Oh, Mr. Stranger," she said, "it's so good to see you again! We've all been looking forward to your return. Especially Sheriff Johnson."

"Amen to that," Lake said.

"We're praying hard that the Lord will help you catch the killer, Mr. Stranger," Jessie said.

"Thank you, ladies. You just keep praying."

"We will," Jessie said, then turned to the deputy. "Monte, did you have your meeting with Pastor Walker?"

"Not yet. I've been too busy. But I'll see him just as soon as I can."

"Don't wait too long, please," she said, touching his arm.

"I won't. I promise."

The two young ladies moved on, and when they were out of earshot, Lake said, "Monte, what were you gonna see the preacher about?"

Dixon blushed. "Jessie . . . ah . . . wants me to talk to him about salvation."

"So that's what she meant about not waitin' too long."

"Yeah."

"And you shouldn't wait too long, Monte," John said. "If you want, I can talk to you about it right away in my hotel room."

"Oh. Well, ah . . . thank you, Mr. Stranger. I really don't have time right now. I've got some important things to do. Sheriff, I'll see you at the office later."

Lake watched Monte hurry away, then said to John, "He's runnin' from the Lord, just like I did."

"Yes, Lake, I remember."

Moments later, the sheriff and Stranger entered the hotel and greeted Frank and Susan Cosgrove, who were behind the front desk. John pulled out his wallet to pay a few days in advance, but the Cosgroves told him there would be no charge, no matter how long he was in town. Stranger thanked them and headed up the stairs with Johnson at his heels.

"Let me tell you about the eyewitnesses who have seen the killer, John. Each one says that it was Payton."

When the sheriff had told each eyewitnesses' story, John said, "I want to talk to each one myself, but before I do, I want to visit Ivan Charles. He knew Payton better than anyone else in town. I'll drop by your office after I've talked to him."

Ivan Charles and his assistant, Bill Pollard, were constructing a coffin when Stranger entered. Charles smiled and moved toward him, extending his hand.

"John! Welcome! I'm sure glad you're here!"

"Thank you, Ivan," John said, then set his gray gaze on the assistant. "New man since I was here, eh, Ivan?"

"Sure enough. This is Bill Pollard. Shake hands with John Stranger, Bill."

After shaking hands with Pollard, Stranger said, "Ivan, I need to talk to you. Could we go to your office?"

"Sure. Come this way."

They crossed into the funeral parlor and went to the back where Charles kept his office. Ivan invited Stranger to sit down.

"Now, John, what can I do for you?"

"As you know, I'm here to help Sheriff Johnson track down the killer. I need you to tell me what you know about Payton's family."

"There is no family, John."

"No family at all?"

"No. Payton told me his parents were dead and he had no living grandparents, uncles, aunts, or cousins. He said virtually nothing about his childhood, and never told me when his parents died. Why do you ask?"

"All the eyewitnesses who say this snow ghost is Payton . . . are they credible, sensible men?"

"Every one of them."

"Then it seems to me Payton had a brother who looks very much like him, or even maybe an identical twin."

"John, Payton and I were close. He told me there were no siblings in his family. He was an only child. In fact he often used to say how much he wished he had a brother or a sister. No, John. It can't be a brother, much less an identical twin."

Stranger shook his head slightly, pondering what Ivan had just told him.

Ivan continued, "Let's say he did have an identical twin brother. How would the twin know all the men on the death list by sight? And how would the twin duplicate Payton's handwriting and signature?"

"I'm just exploring every possibility. So what do you make of it, Ivan? You don't believe this killer is Payton come back, do you?"

"Well, I can't explain how the killer is making himself look like Payton, and I can't explain how he duplicates Payton's handwriting. Did the sheriff tell you about Payton's coffin being empty?"

"Yes."

"Well, add that to these other things, John. I just have to say that I'm beginning to think maybe it really *is* Payton come back."

Stranger was silent for a few moments and then said, "I'm going to get to the bottom of this, and when I do, you'll see that this killer is not the ghost of Payton Sturgis."

"I hope you're right, John. But right now, I'm leaning the other way."

Stranger thanked the undertaker and headed up the street toward the sheriff's office. As he walked, he prayed, "Lord, You already know who this killer is and how he's disguising himself as a dead man. Help me to catch him and end the bloodshed and the terror in this town."

Several times people on the street stopped him to talk about the murders and to thank him for coming to help them.

When Stranger entered the sheriff's office, Lake Johnson was at his desk, sorting through the mail. "Learn anything from Ivan, John?"

Stranger pushed back his black, flat-crowned hat and sat down in a chair facing the desk. "My reason for questioning Ivan was to see what I could find out about Payton's family. I wanted to know if there were any brothers—especially an identical twin brother. I just can't come up with any other explanation for this killer looking like Payton."

"And?"

"Ivan said Payton told him he had no brothers or sisters. He was an only child, and there were no living relatives."

"John, you and I both know the dead don't come back. But what do you think we're dealing with here?"

"We'll know when we catch him," John said. "Remember when we were trying to catch the killer before, and I told you they always make a mistake?"

"Yeah."

"Well, I'm going to pressure this dude till he makes a big one."

CHAPTER

SEVENTEEN

John Stranger left the sheriff's office and walked to Ernie Davis's stable to pick up a good saddle horse. When he'd saddled up, he trotted the horse out of town to the McVicker silver mine and found Tom McVicker in his office.

After they had greeted one another, Stranger said, "Tom, I want to hear it straight from you. Tell me exactly what happened the day you saw the man you identified as Payton Sturgis on the bridge."

When McVicker had told every detail, he said, "I mean no disrespect to you, John, or to anyone else who refuses to believe that Payton has come back from the dead, but I saw him. It *was* Payton."

"I intend to prove that it wasn't, Tom," John said.

Tom frowned. "I assume the sheriff has shown you the work orders written by Payton when he was alive, and the death list in the same handwriting."

"Yes."

"Well how do you explain that?"

"I can't right now. But I will. There's a rational explanation for all this, Tom, and it will come to light when we catch the killer."

"I sure hope I'm wrong and you're right. A mortal man will be a lot easier to stop than a man who's returned from the dead. But I know what I saw, and I saw Payton Sturgis."

Stranger's next stop was the Bristow Clinic. Sadie Bristow was sitting at the desk in the waiting room. "Good morning, Mr. Stranger. What can I do for you?"

"Would it be possible for me to talk to George Walz?"

"I think so. My husband is with a patient in the examining room right now. George is in the clinic patients' room next to it. But let me ask the doctor first."

Sadie returned and said, "You may go in, Mr. Stranger. Doctor says George is a little groggy from the laudanum, but he should be able to talk to you."

In just a few minutes Stranger returned to the waiting room.

Sadie looked at him inquiringly. "Was George clear-minded enough?" she asked.

"Just barely. I wanted to hear straight from him about his experience on the road with the so-called snow ghost."

"Does he still believe it was Payton Sturgis who stabbed him?"

"Yes, ma'am. Well, I've got a few more interviews, so I'll be going now. Thank you, ma'am."

Stranger's next stop was at Darrell Amick's leather and saddle shop. There were two customers at the counter. Stranger waited until both men had left the shop before he asked Darrell about the man in the alley.

Amick showed Stranger where the man had stood, and told him of the hatred burning in the man's eyes. A fearful expression came over Darrell's face as he recounted the incident. "I'm telling you, John, it was Payton. I'm sure of it." Then he snapped his fingers. "Something else just came to me . . ."

"What's that?"

"His head was cocked to one side. You know, like something was wrong with his neck. Payton died of a broken neck at the end of a rope. I tell you, John, it's Payton! I know it's him!"

Stranger nodded. "I'm going to prove it isn't him, Darrell."

"I hope you're right," Amick said, "but more than anything, I just want to see this horror end."

"So do I, Darrell. Thanks for talking to me."

When John Stranger entered the office of the *Butte City Sentinel*, there was a young man at the front desk, and John could see two men through the open door of a rear room, working at the printing press. A sign above a door just outside the room identified the private office of Cliff Morgan.

The young man stood up and smiled. "You're John Stranger, aren't you?"

"That's me," John said.

"I wasn't here two years ago when you caught Payton Sturgis, sir, but I've sure heard a lot about you. My name's Simon Rivers."

"Glad to meet you, Simon," John said, shaking his hand. "Is Mr. Morgan in?"

"Yes, sir. I'll tell him you're here."

Simon hurried to his boss's office. Within seconds, Cliff Morgan stuck his head out the door and said, "Hello, John! Come on back."

When Stranger was seated, Morgan said, "What can I do for you?"

"I'd like to buy a full page in tomorrow's paper."

Morgan's eyebrows arched. "A *full* page?"

"Yes, sir. The cost doesn't matter, but I need that page."

"I assume this has something to do with your pursuit of the killer."

"Precisely."

"And what do you want to put on the page?"

"A letter to the killer, and I want it in as large and bold a type as possible."

Morgan picked up a pad of paper and handed it to Stranger. He pushed a pencil within reach, and said, "Write it, and I'll print it."

When John had finished writing the letter, he turned the pad of paper around and slid it toward Morgan.

The newspaper owner scanned the message:

TO THE LOWDOWN KILLER IN BUTTE CITY

I know you're masquerading as the late Payton Sturgis, but you're not fooling me. I'm on your trail, and sooner or later, I will catch you. And when I do, you will die at the end of a rope. When they drop your coffin in the ground, you won't come back any more than Payton Sturgis did.

John Stranger

Morgan gave John a steady look and said, "You know this will probably incite the killer to come after you."

John grinned. "That's exactly what I want."

Morgan sighed. "Okay, John. It'll be on page three tomorrow morning."

The next morning, John Stranger, Lake Johnson, and Monte Dixon stood together poring over page three of the *Sentinel* spread out on the sheriff's desk. Johnson shook his head slowly and clicked his tongue. "This oughtta do it, John," he said. "You'd better keep a sharp eye. He'll probably try to sneak up on you like he did George Walz."

Monte looked at the tall man with admiration. "So what's next, Mr. Stranger?"

"I'm going to ride through town, cover the fringes, and see if that snake will show himself."

"You want one of us to follow you?" Lake asked. "You know, stay back a ways?"

"I appreciate the offer, Sheriff," Stranger said, "but if he picked up on it, he wouldn't make his play. No, I've got to do this alone."

"You be careful," Lake said. "He's pretty smart."

"Mm-hmm. But they always make a mistake, Sheriff. This dude will make one, too."

Three days passed without incident. On the morning of the fourth day, a snowstorm blew in. Once more, the people of Butte City—especially those on the death list—began looking over their shoulders. But the next morning dawned clear and cold, with no action from the killer. People wondered if John Stranger's letter had scared him off.

John returned to the newspaper office and paid for another full-page letter:

TO THE COWARDLY KILLER

What is it, Mr. Snow Ghost? Are you afraid to come after me? Maybe the yellow in your belly comes from the wide yellow stripe down your back. Meet me man to man, or I'll stay on your trail till I find you. When I do, I will personally drop the noose over your head.

John Stranger

The morning after the second letter was published, John got out of bed and padded toward the small table where his shaving mug, soap, and razor lay. Something on the floor caught his eye. A folded sheet of paper lay partially under the door. He moved to the doorway and picked up the paper. In bold letters, it read:

Don't threaten me, you high-minded fool! I will kill you, I promise! You just won't know when or how it's coming. Pleasant dreams!

Payton Sturgis, alias Snow Ghost

An hour later, Stranger entered the sheriff's office with a broad smile on his face.

"That's a chessy-cat grin if I ever saw one," Johnson said. "What's that in your hand?"

"Take a look," John said, laying it on the desk.

Lake read it. "Looks like your plan is workin'."

"He's angry now. The madder I can make him, the quicker he'll slip up."

"How'd he get this to you?"

"Slipped it under my hotel room door. I found it when I got up this morning."

"So he was brave enough to enter the hotel. You ask the Cosgroves if they saw anything?"

"They didn't. But the lobby door is never locked, and their night clerk sometimes dozes behind the desk."

Lake pulled a key out of his pocket and unlocked the top drawer of his desk. He took out the work orders Ivan Charles had given him, along with the death list found in Dan Cogan's bedroom. He placed them next to the note John had just handed him. "Same handwritin', John. Matches perfectly."

"I figured it would."

Monte Dixon entered the office from the cellblock and saw the papers on the desk. "What've you got there, Sheriff?"

Lake extended the sheet of paper toward him. "Little love

note the killer left under John's hotel room door."

Dixon read it quickly. "I think you've got him a bit worked up, Mr. Stranger."

"That's the plan. He'll make his play soon, I'm sure."

Lake stood up. "John, I hear Pastor Walker has asked you to preach both Sunday services tomorrow."

John nodded, then to Dixon, "Monte, you'll come hear me preach, won't you?"

"Well, ah . . . sure. Sure, I will."

"Good. I assume you haven't had your talk with Pastor Walker yet."

Dixon blushed. "I just haven't been able to get around to it."

"But you *will* be in the services tomorrow?"

"Yes, sir. I will."

"Good. See you then."

On Sunday John Stranger wove the gospel message into his teaching on what the Bible says about men coming back from the dead. Deputy Monte Dixon, who sat by Jessie West-brook, was obviously under conviction when Stranger gave the invitation. It was the same during the evening service. Again Monte resisted the wooing of the Holy Spirit.

When the service was over and the people were crowded around John, Jessie took Monte by the hand and pulled him aside. She looked up into his eyes and said, "Monte, I've watched the Word of God pierce your heart today. The Holy Spirit has spoken to you, hasn't He?"

Monte cleared his throat nervously. "I don't know exactly what you mean by that, but—"

"I mean, you're miserable inside. I saw you wiping your forehead. That gnawing discomfort down deep inside is the convicting power of the Holy Spirit. He's trying to draw you to Jesus. Why don't you just give in and open your heart to Him?"

Monte looked perplexed. "Well, Jessie . . . I just don't feel I'm ready."

She held his gaze and asked, "Are you ready to die?"

"No," he said softly.

"Monte, death can come to anybody at any time. A man who wears a badge is even more vulnerable than most. Outlaws consider that badge a target."

"Jessie, I can't argue with that. But I want to make sure it's from my heart when I do it. I want to get to know you in the worst way, and I could go through the motions of becoming a Christian just to date you. But I want to be honest with God and with you."

Jessie smiled. "That's admirable, but for the sake of your own eternal destiny, you had best get down to business with the Lord and let Him save you."

"I'll really think about it, Jessie. I promise."

Jessie laid a hand on his arm, concern showing in her eyes. "Don't keep putting Jesus off, Monte. God says in His Word, 'Boast not thyself of tomorrow; for thou knowest not what a day may bring forth.' "

Monte bit down on his lower lip and nodded.

When a snowstorm blew in on Monday afternoon, John Stranger rode through the town and around its outskirts all day long to draw out the killer. Nothing happened.

When night fell, the snow was still coming down. There was barely a breeze to stir the snowflakes as they fell.

Later that evening, Sheriff Johnson was at the Silver Bow Hotel with John. He sat in the room's only overstuffed chair, while John stood at the window overlooking the street. He could see little movement below. Periodically, a wagon or

212

buggy would pass, but no one was out walking.

"Sure is a pity this town has to live in such fear, Sheriff," John said over his shoulder.

"All except our town council chairman," Lake said. "And his wife, too, as far as that goes."

"Oh?"

"Both Jackson and Myra are surprisingly unemotional about it. They both want to see the killer caught, of course, but because they're positive we're not dealing with a ghost, they seem to have no fear that this killer can get to Jackson."

"I hope the killer doesn't realize that. He'd consider such an attitude a challenge."

"Well, both the DeLongs have spoken openly around town about it."

John considered this information, then said, "Who knows whether he picks up on what's going on in town or not? Certainly he can't be moving in our midst. If he looks like Payton, he'd be too easy to spot."

"Yeah, unless it's a disguise he can take off." The sheriff was quiet a moment, then said, "If it's not a disguise, how does he know what's goin' on? He's got to be an outsider. How would he know the faces of the men marked for death?"

Stranger turned from the window. "Only one way."

"And what's that?"

"He would have to have an accomplice who's an insider."

"*What?* No way, John. I know every man, woman, and child in this town. There's nobody in Butte City who would be a part of this horrid nightmare."

Stranger shrugged his wide shoulders. "Just a thought."

Myra DeLong sat across the supper table from her husband. For the entire meal they had discussed the killer and just who he might be.

"I wish everybody in this town would listen to the sheriff and John Stranger," Myra said. "Pastor Walker, too. They wouldn't be half so frightened if they faced the fact that there is no snow ghost walking these streets."

"People are funny, dear," Jackson said, placing his coffee cup in its saucer. "Sometimes they like to believe the worst."

Myra patted her lips with a napkin. A smug look crossed her face as she said, "The very idea of anyone believing that a corpse could somehow slip out of a coffin six feet under the ground and go around killing people is gross superstition, and it's beneath the dignity of any rational, thinking person."

"I couldn't agree more, dear. Well, let's get the dishes washed and dried and spend the rest of the evening together in the library."

"No, my love," she said. "I will do the dishes. You go on. I'll join you in a little while."

Myra was almost finished with the kitchen clean-up when she noticed a smudge on the window where the curtains were parted in the middle. She wadded up a dish towel, drew back the curtain, and wiped at the smudge.

She could see the snow falling outside, and something else close to the window. She dropped the dish towel and froze. Her thundering heart seemed to fill her ears and she felt a scream escape her lips.

Myra was still screaming when her husband ran into the kitchen. He seized her by the shoulders and demanded what was wrong.

"It . . . it was *him!*"

"Who?"

"Payton!"

Jackson guided his terrified wife to the nearest chair at the kitchen table. "Sit here, dear. I'll take a look."

He moved swiftly to the window, pulled back both curtains, and peered out into the snowy night. Lantern light from the kitchen showed him a wide area at the side of the house, but there was nothing out of the ordinary.

Myra wailed in terror. "Oh-h! It was Payton! It was! He *has* come back from the dead!"

"Honey, you've got to get a grip on yourself. It hasn't been more than a half hour since we both agreed the killer is not Payton."

"It *is* Payton! He's come to kill you or maybe both of us!"

"Myra, it wasn't Payton you saw out there. You just imagined the whole thing. I just looked out the window. There's nobody there!"

"He *was* there! I saw him! His head leaned to one side like his neck was broken. Nobody can tell me it wasn't Payton!"

Jackson went to a corner in the kitchen and picked up a Winchester .44 repeater rifle. He worked the lever and jacked a cartridge into the chamber. "I'm gonna find that dirty rat, whoever he is, and kill him!"

"No, Jackson! Don't go out there! He'll kill you! Your name is on that list!"

Jackson DeLong opened the door and stood on the porch, gripping the rifle. He looked back at Myra and said, "Close the door and lock it. Don't open it for anybody but me."

"But—"

"Close the door and lock it! *Now!*"

Jackson stepped to the edge of the porch and looked into the falling snow. He could see only as far as the light from the lanterns would allow. He waved the rifle muzzle and shouted, "C'mon, you! Show your ugly face! I know you're out there! Let's get this over with!"

Silence.

Jackson stepped off the porch. "What is it, pal? You got a

yellow belly just like John Stranger said in the paper? Is that it?"

Myra leaned her back against the door, listening to her husband shout challenges to the killer. His voice began to fade, and she knew he was moving farther from the house.

Tears streamed down her cheeks as she murmured, "Please, Jackson. Please. Come back inside."

Now she could no longer hear his voice. She turned and lay the side of her head against the door, listening intently.

"Jackson," she whimpered. "Let me hear you."

Panic washed over Myra like a cascade of ice water. She fumbled with the lock. An aching tightness seized her throat, and she ejected a wordless cry at the stubborn lock.

Finally the lock slid open and she flung open the door. Fighting her shortness of breath and the hammering in her chest, she wailed, "Jackson! Ja-a-ckson! Where are you? Answer me!"

She heard only the soft whisper of the naked tree limbs bending in the cold wind.

"Jackso-o-n!" she wailed.

Myra's hammering heart seemed to stop when she saw the figure of a man coming toward her through the falling snow.

CHAPTER

EIGHTEEN

Panic nudged the back of Myra's brain. She wanted to turn and dart into the house, but her feet refused to move. She tried to force down the acid rising in her throat.

Suddenly a familiar voice called, "Mrs. DeLong, it's Deputy Monte Dixon!"

Myra's knees almost gave way in relief. She began to crumple just as Monte rushed up and grasped her shoulders. "Mrs. DeLong, it's all right. I'm here. I was just leaving the McVicker house down the street when I heard you screaming. What's wrong?"

Myra worked her mouth for a few seconds, trying to find her voice, and finally gasped, "It's the snow ghost! He was right outside my kitchen window. It was Payton Sturgis!"

"I heard you calling for your husband, ma'am. Where is he?"

She pointed toward the darkness. "He went out there."

Monte turned her toward the open door. "Go inside and bolt your doors, ma'am. Make sure every window is locked, too."

Myra nodded and moved inside, almost as if she were in a trance.

Monte pulled his gun and looked to the right and left of the porch. When he heard Myra slide the bolt, he hurried down the steps and moved to the north side of the house. He saw nothing but deep shadows and falling snow.

He made his way to the south side. Just as he reached the corner of the house, he saw the running figure of a tall, slender man coming toward him. It took the man a couple of seconds to see Monte. When he did, he jerked a knife from its sheath on his waist without breaking stride.

"Stop or I'll shoot!" Monte shouted. He took a step sideways and slipped. As he tried to regain his footing, the man passed by the parlor window, and Monte saw his face. The man's eyes were fierce and demonic, and his teeth were bared like those of a wild beast. He was coming straight at Monte with the knife.

Monte slipped again and fell in a sitting position. He fired his gun but missed his target. Before he could ear back the hammer again, the man leaned over and slashed at him with the knife, going for his throat.

Dixon rolled in the nick of time as the blade slid past his ear. He rolled once more, expecting the killer to lunge again. By the time he had his gun cocked and aimed, the killer was running toward the street.

Monte rose to his knees and fired at the fleeing figure, but he was off balance and missed. He steadied himself as best he could in the slippery snow and fired a second time, and a third. The killer disappeared into the snowy night.

Monte scrambled to his feet, sucking hard for air, and saw Myra's face peering out of the parlor window. At the same time, several dark figures rushed toward him from the street.

Tom McVicker's voice cut through the falling snow, "Monte, is that you?"

"Yes!" he replied, heading toward them.

"You all right?" McVicker asked.

"Yeah. It was the killer. He . . . he almost got me with his knife. He came from the rear of the house. Myra was on the porch, screaming for her husband, when I arrived. She said she saw Payton Sturgis outside the kitchen window, and her husband grabbed a rifle and ran outside, shouting for the killer to show himself. Then he seemed to vanish."

"Steve Nadler went for the sheriff," McVicker said. "He should be here shortly."

Monte nodded, then looked in the direction where he had first seen the killer. "We'd better look in the back yard. Couple of you men might go get your wives. I've got a feeling Mrs. DeLong is going to need some comforting."

Merlin Loberg spoke up. "I'll go in there now. She shouldn't be alone another minute."

They could hear the sound of running feet on crunching snow, and Lake Johnson and John Stranger came running up. The sheriff was breathing hard as he drew near the small group of men. He turned to his deputy. "What happened, Monte?"

Monte told the story quickly and Johnson looked at his deputy anxiously. "You're okay?" he asked.

"Yes, sir. He was trying to slash my throat, but he missed."

A shaky female voice came from the front porch. "Sheriff, did you find my husband?"

"Not yet, Myra. John Stranger and I just got here. You go back inside with Merlin. We'll be with you shortly."

Myra resisted Merlin Loberg's attempts to shepherd her back inside the kitchen, and said, "It was Payton Sturgis, Sheriff! I saw him through my kitchen window! It was him! His head was angled to one side like his neck was broken!"

"You go inside and sit down, Myra," Johnson said. "We'll be back soon."

Merlin guided Myra into the house, and the sheriff led the group of men toward the back yard.

"Monte," Stranger said, "did you get a good look at him?"

"Yes, he was tall and slender. His eyes were like . . . like I'd picture the devil's eyes. That's about all I saw before he swung the knife. Of course, I never saw Payton Sturgis, so I can't tell you whether he looked like him or not."

Sheriff Johnson headed for the corner of the house and then stopped short. The others gathered behind him. Lantern light from two windows showed them Jackson DeLong, lying facedown with his head close to the back door. His right arm was stretched out, and his lifeless hand lay against the bottom of the door.

Johnson and Stranger forged ahead of the others, and Stranger put his fingers against the side of the banker's neck. "He's dead, Sheriff."

Johnson turned to the others and said, "I need a couple of you men to go after Ivan. I don't want Myra to see this." Two men hurried away.

Something on the shadowed door caught John's attention. He squinted and leaned closer. "Sheriff, look at this."

On the lower panel of the door Jackson DeLong had written *Payton* with his finger. He'd used his own blood as ink. The last part of the *n* went all the way to the bottom of the door.

"The skeptic became a believer before he died," Tom McVicker said. "I told you it was Payton, Sheriff. How many more witnesses do you need?"

Sheriff Johnson looked as if the fight had gone out of him.

"Tom," Stranger said, "I understand why you feel as you do, and I'm in sympathy with your heartache over losing Les. I've no doubt that the man you saw, and the man the other eyewitnesses saw, looks exactly like Payton. But I'm going on record, as Pastor Walker and Sheriff Johnson have done. When this horror is over, you'll see that the man you saw was not the ghost of a dead man. He is a vengeful *living* man."

McVicker sighed. "John, you don't know how bad I want you to be right."

"Well," Lake said, sighing, "it's time to tell Myra. I'll take John with me. Monte, if you and these other men will wait with the body until Ivan comes, I'll appreciate it."

"Of course," Monte said.

When the sheriff and Stranger drew near the front of the house, they could see many of the neighbors standing in the yard.

A man called out, "What happened, Sheriff? Some of us heard Myra screaming, and we all heard shots. It took us a while to get up the courage to come over here. Somebody saw you and Mr. Stranger running down the street."

"The killer stabbed Jackson, and Ivan's on his way to pick up the body. We're on our way now to tell Myra."

The stunned people on the street watched their sheriff and John Stranger mount the porch. One of the women with Myra was watching through the parlor window and hurried to open the door. Seconds later, Ivan Charles's wagon appeared.

The DeLongs' neighbors stood frozen in disbelief at what was happening in their town. One woman wept loudly and asked no one in particular, "When is this terrible thing going to end?"

After delivering the news to Myra DeLong, and making sure she would be taken care of by her friends and neighbors, Sheriff Johnson, his deputy, and John Stranger went back to the office to talk. Monte's hands had begun to shake, and his face had lost all color.

"What's wrong, Monte?" Johnson asked. "You don't look so good."

The deputy took off his hat and ran trembling fingers

through his hair. "I . . . I just keep seeing that knife coming toward my throat. He barely missed me. If that blade had laid my throat open . . ."

"You'd have died," Lake finished for him.

"It was the hand of God that spared you," Stranger said.

"Don't I know it!" Monte said. "If I had died, I'd be in hell right now."

"That's right, Monte," John said. "The Lord was giving you a warning not to put off salvation any longer."

Tears welled up in Monte's eyes. "I see that, Mr. Stranger," he said, his voice quavering. "It was just last night after the church service that Jessie talked to me about it. She was concerned that I hadn't responded to your preaching and opened my heart to Jesus. She quoted a Scripture. Something . . . ah . . . about not boasting about tomorrow because we don't know what a day will bring forth."

"Yes. Proverbs 27:1."

Monte drew in a shuddering breath. "She told me that yesterday, and today I almost went to hell. Mr. Stranger, I want to be saved right now."

Lake Johnson wiped away tears and listened as John Stranger led Monte to Jesus Christ. Afterward, Monte wept with relief as the two men shared their joy with him.

Tuesday morning arrived with a cloudless sky. A fresh blanket of snow covered the town, and the air was biting cold.

John Stranger left the hotel and headed for the sheriff's office. He was near his destination when Lynette Dickey and Jessie Westbrook emerged from the pharmacy and saw him.

"Good morning, ladies," he said, touching the brim of his hat.

They returned the greeting. Then Jessie said, "Mr. Stranger, we heard about poor Mr. DeLong, and that Monte had a close call with the killer. Was . . . was it *real* close?"

"The killer took a swipe at his throat with a knife. Barely missed."

"But he's all right?"

Stranger smiled. "Jessie, he's more than all right. The Lord used that close call to get his attention and shake him good. I had the privilege of leading him to Jesus last night."

Tears welled up in Jessie's eyes. "Oh, praise the Lord! Praise the Lord! Isn't that wonderful, Lynette?"

"Sure is, honey," Lynette said, giving her friend a hug.

"Monte's going to make his public profession of faith in church next Sunday morning," Stranger said. "The Lord really did a work in his heart. A great deal of it was because of what you told him, Jessie. You've been a very effective witness."

"I'm glad I could have a small part in his coming to the Lord," she said.

"You had a *big* part, little lady."

She smiled exuberantly. "I want to see him and tell him how happy I am for him! Do you suppose he's at the office, Mr. Stranger?"

"I imagine so. Let's find out."

When Stranger and the two young ladies entered the office, Lake Johnson was pouring himself a cup of coffee at the potbellied stove. "Well, good mornin'," he said.

"Good morning, Sheriff," Jessie said with a bright smile. "Is Monte here?"

"Why, yes. He's in the cellblock."

The door to the cellblock opened, and Monte Dixon entered the office. He smiled at Jessie and started to speak, when she surprised him by dashing up and planting a quick peck on his cheek. "Oh, Monte, Mr. Stranger told us what happened last night! I'm so glad!"

Monte blushed as he touched the place where she had kissed him. "Nobody's as glad about it as I am, Jessie," he said. "You were so right. We don't know what a day can bring forth. God was plenty merciful to me last night."

"I know a little about that kind of thing, Monte," Lynette said. "I didn't open my heart to Jesus until after Payton Sturgis killed my father and came real close to killing me."

"Some of us are a bit stubborn," Lake Johnson piped up.

Stranger grinned. "You especially, Sheriff."

"Don't I know it," Lake said, clearing his throat.

Jessie turned to Lynette. "Well, we'd better be going." Then to Monte, "We just wanted to tell you how happy we are that you're a Christian now."

"Thanks," he said, thinking how absolutely beautiful she was.

Jessie started to turn, then paused, and said, "Monte . . ."

"Yes'm?"

"You can come calling on me now, if you wish."

Light danced in Monte's eyes. "Really?"

"Yes. Really."

"How about tonight?"

Jessie giggled. "Okay. Drop by about eight o'clock."

The killer held the Wednesday edition of the *Sentinel* open to page three, twisting the edges of the paper with fingers clenched tightly. He trembled with fury as he read the bold-lettered message again.

TO THE FAKE PAYTON STURGIS

Your days are numbered, coward. I'm going to get you.

John Stranger

CHAPTER

NINETEEN

Only two of the seven men gathered in Eugene Kevane's barber shop were there for the barber's services. The shop happened to be a good place for socializing, and the topic of discussion today was John Stranger's third message to the snow ghost.

"I appreciate what Stranger is doing to draw the killer out," Darwin Smith said, "but if the killer gets him, we'll be right back where we were."

"There's something about Stranger that tells me he'd be a hard man to kill," Ralph Byers said. "He's not exactly your average man."

Kevane nodded as he clipped attorney Donald Fryman's hair, and said, "I've heard stories about Stranger taking on five and six outlaws at a time. They're buried, he's still breathing."

"Takes a lot of courage to challenge a cold-blooded killer like he's doing," Frank Cosgrove said. "No man has eyes in the back of his head."

"That tall fella is some kind of preacher," rancher Fred Sanders said. "I was glued to the pew both times he preached. I think he might have some kind of special angel watchin' over him. He's plenty sharp right by himself, but from some of the stories I've heard about him, he's come through some real scrapes—the kind, let's say, that the average lawman wouldn't survive."

"He's the man we need, then," Donald replied. "This snow ghost is no ordinary killer."

No one spoke for a moment, then Fred looked at the three men whose names were on the death list and said, "I've heard that some of the men on that list are thinkin' about leavin' town till Stranger nails this dude. You fellas know anythin' about it?"

"George Walz said something to me about it the day before he was attacked," Frank said. "I'm sure he wishes now that he'd left that day."

"I think maybe Darrell Amick has that on his mind," Donald said. "I really couldn't blame any of you marked men if you left town till this thing is over."

Ralph gave a negative shake to his head and said, "From what Broken Bow says, running from the snow ghost won't do any good. He'll just come after you."

Eugene was now running a comb through Donald's hair, giving it the final touch. He paused and looked at Ralph. "Whether you believe it's Payton's ghost or not, you've got to admit one thing. This is the strangest situation you've ever encountered in your life."

Light snow fell in Butte City that evening when John Stranger returned to his hotel room after eating supper with Lake Johnson. Monte Dixon had been invited to the Westbrook home for supper.

John was thinking of Breanna, and missing her, as he placed the key in the lock and opened the door. The room was dark except for faint light coming through the window from a street lantern below. When he stepped inside, he felt something under his boot.

John picked up the folded sheet of paper and closed the door. He crossed the room to the dresser and lit the lantern and unfolded the note.

> Your tough talk doesn't scare me, scar-face. I'm so mad
> at you I might decide to kill you even when it isn't
> snowing. YOUR day is coming. You just don't know
> when. Maybe tomorrow. Maybe the day after tomorrow
> after I kill another man of the jury, or even the sheriff.
> Who knows?
> Nobody but me.
> The snow ghost will win. Pleasant dreams!
>
> Payton Sturgis, alias Snow Ghost

Lawton Haymes was working late in his shop with the
doors and windows locked. Burlap sacks hung over the windows so no one could see inside. He had lit four lanterns to
give him plenty of light. He pumped the bellows at the fire pit,
making the flames roar as they grew hotter.

There was a loud knock at the big double doors, followed
by a loud voice. "Lawton! Lake Johnson here! You in there?"

Haymes left the bellows and picked up his single-barrel
twelve-gauge shotgun. He leaned close to the door and
called, "Sheriff . . ."

"Yeah!"

"I've told you about my family. What's my mother's
maiden name?"

"Scott."

Haymes threw back the latch and opened one side of the
double doors. Johnson nodded his approval and said, "Don't
blame you for bein' cautious. You okay?"

"Yeah."

"Aren't you workin' kinda late?"

"Clyde Moore needs two sets of horseshoes tomorrow. I
have to get them done tonight."

"Well, keep the doors locked and be real careful when you go home."

Lawton raised the shotgun and said, "That blood-hungry killer gets in my sights, he'll get ventilated."

Johnson grinned. "Okay. See you tomorrow."

"Sure enough, Sheriff. Thanks for your concern. And you better be careful, yourself."

"I will. Goodnight."

"Sheriff!" The voice of John Stranger floated down the street.

Both men peered through the falling snow as Stranger hastened toward them. He waved a folded sheet of paper at Johnson. "Got another note from you-know-who. Thought you'd want to see it. He mentions you."

"Come in out of the snow, fellas," Haymes said.

Johnson and Stranger stepped inside the blacksmith shop, and Haymes closed the door after them. Johnson read the note, then handed it to Haymes.

While the muscular blacksmith read it, Johnson said, "You've got him mad for sure, John."

Stranger nodded eagerly. "That's what I wanted. I just hope he's so mad at me he'll come after me next."

Lawton handed the note back to Stranger. "This guy means business."

"He's already proven that," Stranger said.

Johnson turned toward the door. "Bolt this behind us, Lawton."

"You can count on it."

Lawton Haymes watched the two men walk away in the falling snow, then closed the big door and bolted it. He returned to the fire pit and leaned the twelve-gauge against a wooden post. Next to the post was the small water tank where he cooled the horseshoes when forging them. Soon he was pounding a red-hot horseshoe on the anvil next to the fire pit, dipping it periodically into the water tank as he formed it.

About an hour had passed since the sheriff and John Stranger had left. Lawton placed a finished horseshoe on the bench next to the anvil and started another shoe.

Suddenly he heard a woman's high-pitched scream. He turned from the bench and dashed to the door. When he had shot the bolt and jerked the door open, he realized he'd left the shotgun behind. He started to go back for it, but the screams were heart-wrenching. He ran out of the shop and looked up and down the street.

Four doors down he could see Althea Kevane leaning out a second-floor window above the barber shop. When she saw Haymes, she shouted, "Payton was on the street. It was him! It was Payton!"

"Which way did he go, Althea?"

She pointed up the street to her left. "That way! He was right in front of your windows when I happened to look out!"

Even as she spoke, men and women who lived above their businesses left their apartments to come out in the street. Every man among them had a gun.

Lawton looked up at Althea again. "Where's Eugene?" he asked.

"He's at Pederson's gun shop with Milo Wilson and Darwin Smith. T.J.'s outfitting them with more guns."

Now the people were pressing in, asking what the screaming was about.

While attention was focused around Althea, a tall, lean figure slipped around the far corner of the blacksmith shop and moved through the door Lawton had left open. He paused and peeked around the edge of the door to make sure no one had seen him. All eyes were still on the barber's wife.

He pulled the door closed. When he saw the shotgun leaning against the post, he picked it up and bent over the wet earth beside the water tank. He broke open the weapon, removed the live shell from the chamber, and crammed mud into the barrel till it came within three or four inches of the muzzle.

He used his bandanna to ream the mud from the chamber, then replaced the shell and snapped shut the chamber. He wiped away the mud that had spilled on the stock and barrel and leaned it back against the post exactly the way Haymes had left it.

He bent over and smoothed out the spot where he had gathered the mud, then hurried to the door. He opened it a crack and peered out into the snowy night. The crowd had gotten larger. Althea was now on the street in her coat, and her husband was just arriving, along with T. J. Pederson, Darwin Smith, and Milo Wilson.

Sheriff Johnson and John Stranger were also among them.

The tall figure eased outside and kept a watchful eye on the crowd as he placed the door precisely as Lawton had left it, then hastened around the corner of the building.

At sight of her husband, Althea began to weep, and her words tumbled from her lips so rapidly he couldn't understand her.

"Wait a minute, honey," Eugene said, putting an arm around her. "Slow down. You're safe now. Sheriff Johnson and Mr. Stranger are here."

"We've picked up bits and pieces," Johnson said, "but we need to hear from Althea, then Lawton."

The frightened woman nodded and took a few seconds to calm herself. Georgene Pederson, T.J.'s wife, slipped up to Althea and took her hand. "It's all right. Take all the time you need," she said.

Althea began to speak more slowly. "I was sitting in my overstuffed chair, reading today's *Sentinel*, and I stood up to stretch. I stepped to the window to look down in the street. It was deserted at first, then I saw movement in front of Lawton's shop. It was a man. He was standing in front of a window, trying to see in. He happened to turn and look my direction and saw me standing at the window.

"He ran toward me. His head . . . his head was bent unnaturally to one side. He stood right below the window and shook his fist at me. It was Payton! I know it was Payton!"

Eugene squeezed her shoulder. "Stay calm, honey."

Althea licked her lips and continued. "I was terrified. He made as if he was heading for the door of the apartment. I opened the window and started screaming. When he heard me scream, he ran up the street and disappeared."

Georgene Pederson turned to her husband and threw her arms around him, saying, "Oh, T.J., I can't stand this any longer! We've got to get away from here!"

Sheriff Johnson lifted his voice above the babble of frightened voices. "Listen, folks! I want all of you to go home and bolt your doors! Right now!"

Jane Wilson clung to her husband's arm and said, "Sheriff, maybe some of us won't make it home! That horrible snow ghost is prowling the streets at this very moment! Milo's on his list!"

"It's all right, honey," Milo said, patting her hand. "I've got two guns on me. If that dirty devil snow ghost comes at us, I'll blow him to smithereens. Come on. Let's do as the sheriff says. Let's go home and bolt our doors."

The other men flashed their weapons, telling their wives they were going home, too.

As the crowd broke up, Althea pressed close to her husband. "Let's get inside, Eugene."

As they turned to go, Lake Johnson turned to the blacksmith and said, "Lawton, I'm going to accompany the Wilsons home. You lock yourself in your shop. Don't come out till I come back to walk you home."

"I've got my shotgun in the shop, Sheriff. You don't need to bother about me."

"No bother. Althea said that maniac was at one of your windows until she screamed and he ran away. That's too close. I'm walking you home."

"I'll come back too, Sheriff," John Stranger said, as he walked away beside Darrell and Roberta Amick. "Meet you back at the blacksmith shop in a few minutes."

"Okay, John." Sheriff Johnson turned back to Lawton. "Get inside right now. Don't open the door for anybody but John or me."

The blacksmith hurried to the front door of his shop, which stood open as he had left it. His eyes probed the dark shadows. He hurried inside, swung the door shut, and slid the bolt.

At the fire pit, he added coal to the fire, then worked the bellows to get the fire hotter. He had to finish Clyde Moore's order before going home. He hoped word of what had just happened on the street hadn't reached Jenny. She'd be scared out of her wits.

Lawton was still pumping on the bellows when he heard a high-pitched cry at the door.

"Lawton, help me!" came a feminine sounding wail. "It's Althea! Help me!"

The blacksmith dashed to the door and jerked it open. A surge of terror ran through his body with the force of a gale.

"*Payton!*"

The killer used Lawton's sudden fright to shove him backwards, then stepped inside and bolted the door.

It took Lawton only seconds to get control of himself. Just as the killer slid the bolt, he dashed to where his shotgun leaned against the post. He grabbed it, snapped back the hammer, and leveled it at the intruder.

Horror rocked him as he eyed the man before him and stammered, "Don't you m-move, Payton! Or . . . or I'll blow you to shreds! We're gonna wait right here till the sheriff and John Stranger get back. Then you're goin' to jail!"

"I've come for you, Lawton. It's your time to die."

Lawton waved the gun. "Apparently you forget who's got the gun here!"

The killer chuckled. "You can't kill me, Lawton. I'm already dead. It's time for you to join me in the realm of the unliving."

"No! Turn around and unlock that door, or I'll blow you apart!"

The man took a step toward the blacksmith and said, "Put the gun down, Lawton. It'll do you no good."

"Stop!" Lawton shouted, raising the shotgun to his shoulder and sighting along the barrel. "Don't take another step! I'll shoot!"

The killer's eyes were wild, full of evil. "Promise? You'll really shoot if I take another step?"

Lawton's hands trembled, but he kept the weapon aimed at the man's chest. "Yes! Don't you move!"

"I told you, Lawton, you can't kill me. I'm already dead." He reached out a hand and said, "It's time, Lawton. Come." He took another step.

Lawton gritted his teeth. "I told you!" he said, and squeezed the trigger.

The twelve-gauge exploded with a roar.

★ ★ ★ ★ ★

A few minutes earlier, John Stranger and Sheriff Johnson had met on Main Street about two-and-a-half blocks from Lawton Haymes's blacksmith shop.

"Georgene's pretty hysterical," Johnson said. "She wants her and T.J. to leave town right now. He tried to reason with her—said they'd have to close the shop. She said she didn't care. If the snow ghost killed T.J., she'd have to close the shop anyway. Can't blame these women for being so frightened. I'm sure if my wife was still alive, she'd—"

A loud roar split the night air, reverberating along the clapboard buildings.

"Sound like a shotgun to you?" Johnson asked.

"It was loud enough," Stranger replied, "but it didn't have the usual deep-throated sound. Sure could've come from Lawton's shop, though. Let's go!"

As they drew near the blacksmith's shop, people were looking out of their upstairs apartment windows, and some men were already outside.

They could see one of the double doors standing open with lantern light fanning onto the ground. John swung the door wider and allowed the sheriff to move past him.

Both stopped short when they saw Lawton sprawled face up on the floor. The shotgun lay beside him. Stranger knelt down and saw that Lawton's face was covered with blood, and blood was bubbling from his nostrils.

"He's alive, Sheriff," he said, reaching underneath the man to pick him up. "You go get Doc, and I'll head for the clinic."

Johnson picked up the shotgun as Stranger stood up, cradling the unconscious blacksmith in his arms. The gun was split apart where the chamber met the hammer mechanism, and blackened from the explosion.

He examined it more closely and said, "There's mud in the barrel, John. Somehow the killer was able to pack it without Lawton knowin' about it. No doubt showed himself just so Lawton would try to use it on him. The dirty—"

"Let's go," John said. "Lawton needs attention quick."

Thirty minutes later, a large crowd huddled in the cold night air outside Dr. Bristow's office. Clouds of vapor rose from their mouths as they talked in hushed tones. Street lamps flickered, casting dark shadows between buildings on both sides of the street. Death seemed to lurk in every shadow, leaving a quiet fatalism hanging over the people like fog.

Inside the clinic, Dr. Bristow and his wife, Sadie, worked feverishly on Lawton Haymes, while Sheriff Johnson, Deputy Dixon, John Stranger, and Pastor and Phyllis Walker sat in the waiting room with Jenny.

Phyllis sat next to Jenny, holding her hands and speaking in soothing tones. At the same time, Stranger and Johnson spoke quietly to Monte Dixon, filling him in on details of what had happened on Main Street. Dixon had heard the shot from the Westbrook home.

"Oh, Phyllis," Jenny sobbed, "Lawton's going to die!"

Pastor Walker left his seat and knelt in front of Jenny, saying, "Let's pray right now that the Lord will spare Lawton's life."

Phyllis held Jenny in her arms as the pastor prayed. When he finished, John Stranger took up the prayer, asking God to let Lawton live and to allow the sheriff and him to catch the killer soon so the carnage would stop.

CHAPTER

TWENTY

Word had spread through the town, and many more people had come to join the vigil outside Dr. Bristow's office. Other than Lawton Haymes and his critical condition, the conversation centered around the dreaded snow ghost and what he would do next.

Fear slithered through the crowd as they counted off the dead—Dan Cogan, Les Osborne, Jackson DeLong, Judge Virgil Reed. Although George Walz had survived the snow ghost's attack, he was bedridden at home, and he and Eva lived in constant fear that the killer would come to finish him off.

And now Lawton Haymes was fighting for his life.

While the people stamped their feet and worked their arms to keep the blood circulating, several low-voiced conversations were going on at the same time.

"Let's go, T.J.," Georgene Pederson said to her husband.

"All right, I'll take you home," he said.

"I don't mean just take me home. I mean so we can pack and get out of Butte City. I want us to leave tonight. We'll go to Billings and stay till this dreadful ordeal is over."

"Honey, we can't go to Billings. Who'd run the shop and do the gunsmithing? We'd go broke in no time."

"I'd rather have money trouble than to stand over your

grave!" she said, her voice shrill.. "You've got to get out of town! Go! I'll do the best I can with the store. I can't do the gunsmithing, but I can sell hardware."

The Pedersons had other people's attention now.

"I'm not going without you," he said, trying to keep his voice down. "What if that beast took it out on me by killing you?"

"Then let's go together, but let's do it *now!*"

Frank Cosgrove leaned toward them and said, "Don't do it, Pedersons. You can't fool the snow ghost. He can follow you anywhere!"

"Frank, he won't even know we're going," T.J. said.

"Oh, but he will!" came Ivan Charles's voice as he moved closer to them. "T.J., Payton'll catch you out on the Billings road just like he caught Judge Reed on the Crackerville road! Don't go!"

Tom McVicker turned to the frightened couple and said, "Ivan's right. Payton will get you for sure if he finds you two by yourselves on the road."

"He won't find us," T.J. said. "We'll be gone before he knows it. Come on, honey."

Roberta Amick looked up at her husband and said, "We ought to go with them, Darrell."

Darrell shook his head. "No, honey. It was Payton I saw behind the shop. I know it. If he can get out of his grave, he can find us wherever we go. We're staying right here."

After nearly two hours of waiting, the small group inside the clinic jumped to their feet when the surgery room door opened.

Dr. Bristow's face looked strained. As he pulled the door closed behind him, Jenny said in a tremulous voice, "Is Lawton going to live, Doctor?"

Bristow elbowed sweat from his brow. "Yes, Jenny, I believe he'll live, but—"

"But what?"

"Let's sit down."

Jenny's features tightened with apprehension. "But *what,* Doctor?"

"It's his eyes, Jenny. Lawton is blind."

Jenny felt as if her legs were rooted to the floor. "Blind? Permanently blind?"

"I didn't want to say anything until I examined him, Jenny. There was so much blood on his face when these men brought him in . . ."

Jenny's face was a mask of anguish. She opened her mouth to cry, but no sound came out.

"I'm so sorry, Jenny," Dr. Bristow said softly. "I wish I could tell you there was hope that Lawton will see again . . . but the gunpowder burned through the corneas of both eyes. The pupils and irises have been destroyed."

Phyllis tightened her arm around Jenny's shoulders, saying, "Honey, at least Lawton is alive. We must be thankful for that."

Jenny drew a shaky breath and nodded. "Yes. I'm very thankful he's alive. But . . . but how will he make a living? Blacksmithing is the only thing Lawton knows."

"Jenny," John Stranger said tenderly, "you and Lawton are Christians. You are God's born-again children. He says in His Word that he will provide for you. None of us can say why the Lord allowed this to happen to Lawton, but He will not forsake you now. In the Psalms David said, 'I have been young, and now I am old; yet have I not seen the righteous forsaken, nor his seed begging bread.' Your heavenly Father will take care of you and Lawton."

Jenny nodded slowly.

"I like that verse, Mr. Stranger," Monte Dixon said. "I'll have to mark it in my Bible. Where did you say that's found?"

"Psalm 37. It's full of encouraging words for God's people, Monte. You ought to study the whole psalm thoroughly."

"I will, Mr. Stranger."

Pastor Walker took Jenny's hand, and she lifted her eyes to his face. "Jenny," he said, "all of us in the church love you and Lawton. We'll do everything we can to help you."

"Thank you, Pastor."

"The whole town will rally behind you, Jenny," put in the sheriff.

"I want to see my husband," Jenny said hoarsely. "Doctor, can I see him?"

"Not just yet; Sadie's cleaning him up. You go on and sit down. Besides, it'll be a while before Lawton wakes up from the ether. I'll be back shortly." He turned and went back into the surgery room.

Stranger looked at Lake Johnson and said, "I'll go outside and let the people know what's happened."

"Monte and I will go with you, John," Lake said.

While the Walkers remained with Jenny, the two lawmen and John Stranger stepped outside. The low rumble of voices cut off at sight of the three men.

"Folks," Stranger said, "Dr. Bristow just told Jenny and the rest of us that Lawton is going to live."

"Wonderful!" came a man's voice.

"There's something else . . ." Stranger continued. "Lawton is blind."

Someone moaned, and several cried out in protest.

Tom McVicker spoke up. "Is there any hope that someday his sight might return?"

"No. Doc said the blast destroyed his pupils and irises."

Frank Cosgrove turned to Stranger and said, "T.J. and Georgene have gone home to hitch up their buggy and head out of town."

"You mean to get away from the killer?"

"Yes, sir."

"I tried to warn them, John," Tom McVicker said, "but they wouldn't listen."

Without another word, John whirled and ran as hard as he could toward the hardware store and gun shop. He knew the Pedersons lived in an apartment above their place of business and had a small barn in the alley behind it. Sheriff Johnson and his deputy took off after him.

When Stranger reached the corner of the block, he did a quick left turn and darted to the alley of the next block, sprinting toward T.J.'s barn. The double doors stood open, and a shaft of lantern light illuminated the alley. When Stranger was within two hundred feet of the barn, he saw a figure emerge from the shadows beneath the overhang of the building next door.

He ran for all he was worth, shouting, "T.J.! Look out!"

The figure turned and looked at Stranger, then bolted into the shadows on the far side of the barn and vanished.

Stranger ran past the barn door and into the shadows where the killer had disappeared. He could barely make out footprints in the fresh snow, but he could tell that the killer had run through the yard behind Pederson's barn toward the street.

He followed the tracks to the edge of the street and looked both ways, but there was no sign of anyone. He looked down, but there were too many footprints and wheel marks in the street to distinguish them from the killer's.

When Stranger returned to the barn, T.J. was standing at

the door, holding a shotgun, with Georgene behind him.

T.J.'s voice trembled as he said, "I heard you call out the warning, John. Were you chasing the killer?"

"He came out of the shadows on the other side of the alley and headed for the barn door. He was after you, no doubt about it."

"Oh, T.J.!" Georgene gasped.

"When he heard me shout, he turned to look at me, then dashed to that side of the barn. He ran to the street back there but got away from me."

"How did you happen to come here in the first place?" Georgene asked.

"Frank Cosgrove told me you two were getting ready to leave town. Somehow, this guy knows everything that goes on around here. I was afraid he'd come for you."

Pederson's horse neighed, sensing the tension of the moment. Rapid, muffled footsteps sounded in the alley.

"That'll be the sheriff and his deputy," John said.

Johnson and Dixon pounded to a stop, puffing from the hard run. The sheriff was out of breath and let Monte Dixon speak for him.

"John, we heard you holler," Monte said. "What was that about?"

"I was trying to warn T.J. that the killer was just outside the barn door."

"You saw him?"

"Yes. And when he saw me, he took off. I chased him, but he had too much of a head start. He knew T.J. and Georgene were planning to leave town tonight."

"It was my fault, Mr. Stranger," Georgene said. "I pressed T.J. into leaving. I just didn't want to see him killed."

"Nobody can fault you for that, ma'am," Stranger said.

The gunsmith looked perplexed. "If he's a mortal man—

which I believe he is—how can he know so much about what's going on in Butte City?"

"He's got someone working with him," John said.

"Sure would explain a lot of things," Sheriff Johnson said.

"One thing's for sure," John continued, "the mystery will be solved when the man is caught. And I intend to bring that to pass very soon."

Lake Johnson studied Stranger's eyes. "You got somethin' else planned, John?"

"I'm going over to Cliff Morgan's house right now. If he can work it for me, there'll be another little note to the killer in tomorrow's paper. I'm going to work on his ego. He'll make his big mistake soon."

The killer shook with rage when he read the *Sentinel* the next morning. "You die, Stranger!" he hissed aloud. "You die tonight! You hear me? You die tonight!"

His breathing grew ragged as he read the letter again:

You ran away last night when you saw me coming. What is it? The yellow from the stripe on your back and the yellow from your belly seeping into your backbone?

We'll find out at nine o'clock tonight. I'll be in the barn at the Dan Cogan ranch. Since you're up on everything that happens around here, you know that Elaine Cogan left two days ago to live with relatives in Billings. The place is deserted. I give you my word I'll be there alone. No more gutless sliding notes under my hotel room door. Come out from your snow ghost cloak and fight like a man.

Are you man enough to meet me one-on-one, or are you the coward I think you are? We'll find out at nine o'clock tonight. I'll be there all alone. If you don't show up, the front page of this paper will scream your cowardice tomorrow morning.

Yours expectantly,
John Stranger

Lake Johnson and Monte Dixon leaned over the desk, marveling at the letter on the *Sentinel*'s front page.

"John," Lake said, raising his head to look at the tall man, "you've tapped his ego button for sure with this. He'll have to come after you."

"Do you really plan to go alone, Mr. Stranger?" Monte asked.

"Yes, I do."

"But this guy's a psychopath. You don't have to keep your word to him. Let's hide a dozen or so men out there on the Cogan place and take this guy when he shows up."

"Can't do it, Monte," Stranger said. "I told him one-on-one, and I meant it. I'll be out there alone at nine o'clock tonight, just like I said."

Johnson rubbed his jaw. "John, I just wish there was a way we could give you some back-up."

"I appreciate that, Sheriff, but if I'm going to catch him, I've got to meet him man to man, just the two of us."

That same morning, Jenny Haymes was sitting beside her husband's bed in the clinic. Lawton's head was wrapped in a bandage and his face was covered except for openings over his nose and mouth. Dr. Bristow was with them.

Lawton gripped Jenny's hand and rolled his head back and forth on the pillow, saying, "Jenny, you can't spend the rest of your life married to a blind man. That's no life for you."

Jenny squeezed his hand tenderly and said, "Lawton, that's foolish talk. I love you with all my heart. You're alive.

That's what matters most. What kind of wife would I be if I deserted you now?"

"But—"

"No *buts,* Lawton Haymes. We'll get through this together. Lots of people have been blinded and lived happy and fruitful lives."

"She's right, Lawton," Dr. Bristow said. "You mustn't give up. There's too much to live for."

Lawton's lips quivered. "Live? How can I make a living for Jenny and me without my eyes? Blacksmithing is all I know."

"We're God's children, honey," Jenny said. "He will take care of us."

Lawton was silent for a moment, then said, "God could have kept that dirty killer from packing my shotgun with mud, but He didn't. Why, Jenny? Why, Doc?"

"We don't always have an explanation for what God allows," Bristow said.

Jenny spoke with confidence as she said, "That's where faith comes in, darling. The Lord saved us by faith. We walk the Christian life by faith. Now we have to rely on that faith to see us through this hard time."

"But we only have a few dollars in the bank," Lawton said. "You can't run the shop. What are we going to do?"

"We're going to trust the Lord."

Sadie Bristow partially opened the clinic door and looked into the room. "Doctor," she said, "our patient has a couple of visitors. The sheriff and John Stranger."

Dr. Bristow looked at Lawton. "Would you like to see them—I mean, do you want any visitors yet, Lawton?"

"I guess I don't mind if it's just those two."

Sadie turned back toward the waiting room and said, "You can go in, gentlemen."

Johnson and Stranger entered and quietly stepped up beside the bed.

"How's he doing, Doc?" Lake Johnson asked.

"As well as can be expected," Bristow replied. "He's feeling some depression right now."

"I'm sure I would, too," Stranger said. Then to the man in the bed, "Lawton, we're just glad you're alive."

"Thank you, John." Lawton turned his bandaged face in the direction of Stranger's voice. "I want to thank both of you men for getting me to Doc after the shotgun exploded."

"It was the least we could do," Stranger said. "How are *you* doing, Jenny?"

"I'm all right. I'll be better when I convince Lawton that the Lord will take care of us."

"I just don't know how I'm going to make a living," Lawton said.

"The Lord can provide a way," Stranger said. "I realize it must be a horrible thing to be in your place, and since it's never happened to me, I can't say I understand everything you're feeling. But I can say that Jesus loves you and Jenny. He has many ways of providing for His children. You want to tell him, Sheriff?"

"Tell me what?" Lawton asked.

A little frown of puzzlement appeared on Jenny's forehead as she waited to hear what the sheriff would say.

"John and I just came from a meeting at the town hall, Lawton. The city council voted Mark Westbrook new chairman of the council. Since you're a council member, you'll remember that about a year ago we started talking about restructuring our town's governing system. And you recall that last June the townspeople voted unanimously to move ahead with it, expecting that it would all come to pass in about a year and a half."

"Yes, I remember."

"Well, the council has the power to go ahead with it as we see fit."

"Yes . . . ?"

"So, we met this morning and voted to set up the mayor's office within about a month. We want you to be our mayor."

Jenny's eyes welled with tears as she waited for her husband's reaction.

"Me?" Lawton said. "But I'm blind."

"Yes, you are. We figure a blind man could do the job if he had a good secretary. So we're offering the secretary job to Jenny, if she'll take it. The town is growing, and the people have agreed to a tax so we can have a mayor and pay him a good wage. The council agreed that we'll match whatever your net was on the shop this past year. As the town continues to grow, so will the salary. How about it?"

It took Lawton a while to gain his composure. When he finally spoke, his voice trembled as he said Jenny's name.

"I say let's take the jobs, honey!" she said, her smile brilliant through her tears.

Lawton turned toward Johnson, his voice steady now. "All right, Sheriff, you can tell the council they have a new mayor. I'll be on the job when the town's ready, if Doc says I can do it by then."

"I don't see any reason you can't," Bristow said.

Jenny wept for joy and hugged Lawton. "See, honey? I told you the Lord would take care of us!"

As Lawton held his wife, he said, "Lord, forgive me for doubting You. I'm sorry."

John Stranger cleared his throat. "Ah . . . Jenny . . . Lawton."

"Yes, John?" Lawton said.

"Well, the Lord put something on my heart during the night. He has blessed me abundantly in a financial way. And . . . well, I felt led to go by the bank when it opened this morning and make a little deposit in your personal account. I have the receipt right here. I'll give it to Jenny."

Jenny looked at John quizzically, accepted the receipt, then her eyes popped, and she barely choked out the words, "Ten thousand dollars!"

CHAPTER

TWENTY-ONE

Lawton echoed Jenny's words. "Ten thousand dollars? Oh, John. You can't give us that kind of money. You—"

"I already did," John said, laying a hand on the blind man's shoulder. "Take it as from the Lord, Lawton. Everything I have is His anyway. So it was the Lord's gift to you. You're not going to tell Him he can't provide for you in this way, are you?"

"No, I can't do that. But how can Jenny and I ever thank you, John?"

"By accepting it."

Jenny sprang from the chair and embraced Stranger, thanking him over and over.

"The real joy is mine, Jenny," Stranger said quietly. "Remember, the Lord said it is more blessed to give than to receive. So today I am a blessed man."

"Doctor . . ." came Sadie's voice from the office door.

"Yes, dear?"

"Pastor Walker is here to see Lawton. Will one more be too much?"

Lawton answered for the doctor. "No, it won't, Sadie. Send him in."

Pastor Walker entered in time to see Jenny turn from John Stranger and wipe away tears. His apprehensive eyes shifted to Lawton, then to Johnson.

"It's okay, Pastor," the sheriff said. "Jenny's shedding happy tears. The Lord has just blessed Jenny and Lawton in a wonderful way."

Walker's face lit up. "Well, good! I want to hear about it, but first, Sheriff, I need to talk to you in private."

"Sure, let's step outside."

When the two men were gone, Jenny said, "Oh, Mr. Stranger, you've lifted a real load off our shoulders. There's no way we can sufficiently thank you."

"Just thank the Lord," the tall man said, and grinned.

"How's the pain, Lawton?" Dr. Bristow asked. "You can have more laudanum if you need it."

"I was starting to hurt again, Doc, but when I heard Jenny read the amount of that receipt, the pain almost went away!"

The door opened again, and Lake Johnson and the pastor returned. Lake had a wide smile on his face as he said, "The pastor's got somethin' to tell you folks."

Pastor Walker moved up close to the bed. "Last night, Phyllis and I prayed for you two. We asked God to provide for your needs in a very special way. This morning when I woke up, I told Phyllis I felt I should talk to the members of the church and see if they would agree to give you the money in the building fund. I've talked to all the members except for you two. So, Lawton . . . Jenny . . . the church has agreed unanimously to give you the $1,112. The new building can wait."

Jenny flicked a glance at the sheriff, who grinned and said, "When Pastor Walker talked to me outside just now, I didn't tell him, Jenny. I wanted you to hear what our dear pastor and friends in the church family were willing to do for you."

Walker looked back and forth in confusion between Jenny and the sheriff. "Tell me what?"

"How the Lord just blessed Lawton and me in a wonderful way," Jenny said.

Lawton spoke up. "Pastor, Jenny has a bank deposit receipt she'd like to show you. Our friend John, here, deposited a gift to our personal account this morning. Show it to him, honey."

Jenny handed the receipt to Walker, whose eyes bulged. He looked at John for an explanation.

"That should tide them over till they start their new jobs and sell the blacksmith shop."

"New jobs?"

When the preacher learned the news, he wept with joy, and everyone joined him in a praise service right there in the clinic.

Lawton's voice was choked with emotion as he said, "Pastor, please tell everyone in the church how much we appreciate their kindness, but we want the money to stay in the building fund. And thank you for being such a wonderful and generous pastor."

Walker smiled and said, "God has given our church so many precious people."

"Pastor," John said, "how much money does the church lack to build as you have planned?"

"We still need about forty-two hundred dollars."

John gave him a slight smile and said, "Remind me to talk with you about that later."

Lawton Haymes turned his head toward Stranger and said, "John, before you came in, Doc was telling us about the letter you put on the front page of the *Sentinel* this morning. I hope you're going to have Sheriff Johnson and Deputy Dixon with you when you meet him."

"No, I'm going to meet this guy alone."

"But can't you hide some help nearby? I saw his face quite clearly before I pulled the trigger. He looks exactly like Payton. I'd swear it's him, but I know the Bible says it can't be."

"I have to keep my word, even to him, Lawton. If I hadn't told him I would be at the Cogan barn alone, he would never show up."

"Tell you what," Pastor Walker said. "Let's pray right now. I want to ask the Lord to keep John in the hollow of His mighty hand when he goes up against that killer tonight. And John . . ."

"Yes, Preacher?"

"Everyone in our church will be praying for you at nine o'clock."

As John Stranger and Lake Johnson headed for the sheriff's office, they met several people who stopped to comment on the letter in the *Sentinel*.

They had almost reached the office when they saw Deputy Monte Dixon standing in front of the door, talking to Jessie Westbrook and her father. Ivan Charles and his assistant, Bill Pollard, were there too.

The two men could see the lovelight evident in the young people's eyes as they looked at each other. Mark Westbrook assured Monte that he and Frances, not just Jessie, were inviting him for supper. They had enjoyed the last time he'd come to their home.

"Well, okay," Monte said. "I just don't want to become a bother."

"You could never become a bother, Monte," Jessie said.

Stranger winked at Jessie. "That depends on who's having you for supper, Monte. Now, for your boss and me, it would be a bother to have to feed you every night."

"Amen," Johnson said.

"I'd feel the same way, too," Ivan said with a grin. "I'm just glad Bill, here, has his own room at Mrs. Fillmore's boarding house. He eats like a grizzly."

"How do you know?" Pollard asked. "You've never seen me eat."

"No, but people who have tell me it's awful to watch."

Everyone laughed, then Mark's voice turned serious. "John, I read that letter on the front page of the paper. I've got a feeling the killer will take you up on your challenge."

"I hope so," Stranger said. "It's his pride that will lead to his capture. He most certainly doesn't want the newspaper labeling him a coward because he didn't show up to face me."

Ivan Charles looked concerned. "John, you'd best take an army with you. I'm convinced you're facing Payton himself."

"Ivan, if this is Payton's ghost, even an army couldn't handle him."

"All I know is, I'll be glad when it's over," Jessie said.

"Well, sweetie," Mark Westbrook said to his daughter, "we'd best be going."

"Okay, Papa." She smiled at Monte and said, "You know that some of the girls in our church take turns caring for Effie Thomas, the little widow who lives in the white house with the red shutters. It's just four doors down from us."

"Yes. You told me about it last Sunday."

"Well, today it's my turn. So if you get to my house before I do, you'll know I'm on my way."

"Okay. I'll see if I can entertain your parents until then."

Jessie laughed. "See you as close to seven o'clock as I can."

"I'll look forward to it," Monte said.

"John, you be careful," Mark said, walking away with his daughter.

Stranger nodded.

"We need to get going too, Bill," Ivan said. "Plenty of work at the shop."

At five minutes to seven that evening, Monte Dixon turned into the Westbrook yard. He couldn't wait to be with Jessie again. A lantern burned on the front porch as he bounded up the steps and knocked on the door. Mark Westbrook opened the door and smiled.

"Frances, Monte's here!" he called toward the kitchen. "Come on in, Monte. Jessie isn't home yet."

Frances appeared, wearing an apron over her ankle-length dress. "Hello, Monte. Supper's almost ready. Jessie will be here any minute. You men can sit down and chat here in the parlor, or come on out to the kitchen, if you like."

"Let's go to the kitchen," Mark said. "We can get the aroma of that fried chicken better in there."

"I'll vote for that," Monte said, and chuckled.

The men sat down at the kitchen table and talked about John Stranger's challenge to the killer while Frances dished up food and placed it on the table. She looked at the clock on the wall. It was 7:12.

Mark sensed her quietness and said, "Shall we go ahead, honey?"

"I can't understand what's keeping her," Frances said in reply, worry etching her features. "It isn't like her to be late."

"She probably had something unexpected to handle for Effie. Let's give her a couple more minutes."

"I'll go see if she's coming," Frances said, heading toward the hall.

Mark jumped up. "I'll do it, sweetheart."

When Mark was gone, Monte said, "Mrs. Westbrook, if he doesn't see Jessie coming, I'll run over to Mrs. Thomas's house and see what's keeping her."

When Jessie's father came back and said, "No sign of her

. . . I'm going over there," Monte jumped to his feet and said, "I'll go with you."

"Hurry, will you?" Frances said. "I'll do what I can to keep this food hot, but it'll cool down pretty fast."

The two men crossed the front yards between the Westbrook house and Effie Thomas's. Lantern light showed through the windows as they stepped onto Effie's porch.

Mark knocked, and turned to Monte. "Effie's getting pretty old. Anything could have happened."

When there was no response after a few seconds, Mark knocked louder.

"I don't like this, Monte." As he spoke, Mark tried the knob, and the door came open. He stuck his head inside and called, "Jessie! It's Papa!"

Silence. They moved inside and Mark closed the door.

"Jessie! Where are you? It's Papa!"

Silence.

"You check this floor, Monte," Mark said. "I'll check upstairs."

While Mark bounded up the stairs, calling his daughter's name, Monte did a quick check of the parlor, dining room, and sewing room. Near the kitchen he heard a sound like a muffled whine. He darted into the kitchen and found Effie Thomas lying on the floor, bound and gagged. Her eyes bulged with fear.

"Mr. Westbrook!" Monte called toward the staircase. "Down here! The kitchen!"

Monte knelt beside Effie and removed the gag. "He took her!" she gasped. "Payton Sturgis took Jessie!"

Mark bounded into the room, having heard Effie's words. "Effie," he said, "are you sure it was Payton?"

"Of course! I know what Payton looks like!"

Monte untied Effie's wrists. "Did he say anything, ma'am?"

"Only that he was going to fix that John Stranger real good. There's a note over on the cupboard."

Mark Westbrook's heart hammered against his ribs as he held the note so that he and Monte could both read it:

Westbrook—

I have your daughter. Tell Stranger I will be at the Cogan barn at nine. Jessie will be with me. I will have a lantern on inside the barn. Stranger is to come in unarmed and stand by the lantern. If he does what I tell him, I promise I will let Jessie go unharmed. If Stranger doesn't do exactly as I say—or if he brings anybody else with him—I will kill Jessie. Shooting me will not help. I cannot die twice.

Payton Sturgis, alias Snow Ghost

John Stranger was in his hotel room, praying for God's help in bringing the killer to justice, when there was a knock at the door. "Yes?" he called.

"It's Monte Dixon. I have Mr. and Mrs. Westbrook with me."

Stranger crossed to the door, swung it open, and stepped back. "What's wrong?"

"The killer's got Jessie!" Frances blurted. "He took her from Effie Thomas's house!"

Stranger felt his heart sink at the news.

"Here's the note he left, John," Mark said, handing it to him.

"What about Effie?" Stranger asked.

"She's fine. He bound and gagged her. She's with neighbors now. Effie swears the man is Payton Sturgis."

"Like so many others," John said. "It's a miracle he didn't kill Effie." He turned his attention to the note. While he read, he nodded as if he had just perceived something for the first time. "Okay. Monte, I'm going to write a note to the sheriff, giving him instructions on what to do at precisely nine o'clock."

Stranger moved to a small desk near the front window and pulled a sheet of paper and the stub of a pencil from the top drawer. He wrote hastily, then folded the paper and placed the killer's note with it. "Get these to the sheriff right away, okay?"

"Will do," Monte said.

John turned to the Westbrooks. "You two go with Monte and stay with Sheriff Johnson. We're going to get Jessie back safe and sound."

"But how can you be sure?" Frances pressed him, the panic rising in her voice. "The man's a heartless killer!"

"Trust me in this, ma'am. Jessie will be all right. The Lord's not going to let anything happen to her."

As the Westbrooks headed out the door, Monte said, "Mr. Stranger, what are you going to do between now and nine?"

"No time to explain. Just get those notes to the sheriff."

"We'll be praying, John," Mark said.

"So will I. This whole thing is just about over. Jessie will be back with you safe and sound before 9:30."

"God bless you, John," Frances said, wiping tears from her cheeks.

The night sky was alive with twinkling stars as John Stranger cautiously opened the door of the Cogan barn. A lighted lantern sat in the middle of the floor, just as the killer had said it would.

John left the door open behind him and took a few steps forward, barely putting himself within the ring of light.

Suddenly a harsh voice from the hayloft said, "All the way in, Stranger! Stand beside the lantern."

John stayed where he was and said, "Jessie, are you all right?"

He could barely hear Jessie say, "Yes, I'm all right."

John tried to see through the shadows in the dark loft as he said, "Give it up, Layton! Let Jessie come down. You can't win."

There was dead silence for several seconds, then the harsh voice said, "How did you find out?"

Stranger turned slightly and motioned for someone who stood just outside the door to come in.

"Layton, I know your note said for me not to bring anyone, but I want you to see this man."

When the tall, slender man with his hands cuffed behind his back stepped inside the barn, the killer gasped. "Ivan! What are you doing here?"

"Do as Stranger says, Layton. Let Jessie come down, and give it up."

Layton Sturgis screamed wildly. "No! I'm gonna kill that dirty Stranger! He's the one who caught my brother and got him hanged!"

Ivan Charles kept his voice level as he said, "Layton, you'll end up dead if you don't do as John tells you. Now let go of Jessie so she can climb down. Then you come down behind her."

"I'm not letting Jessie come down till I kill Stranger!"

"Layton," Stranger shouted, "I guess I was wrong about you! I really thought you'd meet me man-to-man, but now I see that you hide behind a helpless girl."

Stranger's words made Layton Sturgis choke with anger. Finally he said, "I'll let Jessie climb down if you'll step over beside the lantern so I can see you clearly! If you're not armed, and you stay beside the lantern, I'll let her go!"

"Don't do it, Mr. Stranger!" Jessie called. "He's got a gun! He'll shoot you!"

"You shut up, girl!" Layton hissed. "Stranger, how about it? You gonna step over beside the lantern? If you don't, I'll shoot Jessie and throw her body down!"

"Layton, don't you hurt that girl!" Ivan shouted. "She's done nothing to you! Let her go!"

"No! Not unless Stranger does as I've told him!"

"Layton, do you want to die?" the undertaker asked.

"Of course not!"

"Then give it up! John knows you're Payton's twin brother, and he told the sheriff. This place is surrounded by armed men. Sheriff Johnson and Deputy Dixon are leading them. If you harm a hair on that girl's head, you're a dead man! She's innocent, and doesn't deserve to die. Do something decent for a change. Let her go now and give it up!"

There was a long silence.

"Stranger," Layton said, "if you're so brave, step out by the lantern, and I'll let Jessie come down! I promise!"

Stranger held his ground, his mind racing.

Layton's voice sounded insane as he cried shrilly, "Stranger, if you're not out there by the lantern in ten seconds, I'll kill this girl!"

"He means it, John," Ivan whispered.

"Okay, Layton, I'm coming out! But when I'm by the lantern, I want Jessie coming down that ladder!"

"You better be unarmed or I'll shoot her!"

Stranger moved toward the lantern, his mind going to Breanna, telling her in his heart that he loved her.

CHAPTER

TWENTY-TWO

As John Stranger stepped closer to the flickering lantern, he was able to see Layton Sturgis and Jessie Westbrook in the shadows at the edge of the loft. By their position, he realized Layton didn't have a clear shot at him.

The crazed killer had Jessie locked in his left arm, and a revolver in his right hand.

"Okay, Layton," John said. "I'm here. Let Jessie go."

Layton sprayed saliva as he shouted, "Take your coat off and drop it on the floor, Stranger! I want to make sure you're not carrying a weapon!"

Stranger quickly removed his coat and tossed it over the curved handle of a nearby plow leaning against a barrel. He had removed his gunbelt before entering the barn. Now he held his arms away from his body and turned a complete circle, then looked up and said, "Let her go."

Layton's laugh sounded demonic. "Oh, am I gonna enjoy this!"

"You promised you'd let Jessie go when I came to the lantern unarmed, Layton! I thought you were a man of your word."

"I am!"

"Then let her go!"

Layton was breathing heavily with the excitement of having John Stranger right where he wanted him—unarmed and vulnerable. He would toy with Stranger for a while and enjoy watching him squirm.

"Layton!" Ivan Charles said, "Stop stalling! Release Jessie this instant! She shouldn't have to watch Stranger die!"

"Okay," Layton said, his voice tense with excitement. "Here she comes."

Jessie made a tiny mewing sound when the strong arm that held her released her. She hurried to the ladder a few feet away and started down.

Stranger kept one eye on Layton and the other on a terrified Jessie as she quickly descended the ladder. When her feet touched the floor, John said in a low tone, "Go outside, Jessie."

Layton Sturgis moved out into the light, standing at the very edge of the loft. He watched as the girl moved past Ivan and stepped out into the black void beyond the door.

Outside, Jessie found herself in the strong arms of her father. Her mother burst into tears and embraced her.

Monte Dixon gave a cry of relief at the sight of her. He and the sheriff stood with a crowd of men in the barnyard, guns in hand.

Jessie's mother had unwittingly helped John Stranger with her crying. For an instant, it drew Layton's attention toward the open door.

In a flash, Stranger leaped into the shadows behind the barrel. When he hit the floor, he pulled up his pantleg and whipped out a .36 caliber Navy Colt from his boot.

He could hear the madman swear at him and fire a shot. The bullet hit the barrel. John rolled on the straw-matted floor and took quick aim, firing the Navy Colt. The bullet struck Layton in the chest, and the breath gushed out of him as he cursed Stranger again, his knees buckling.

Layton staggered, trying to stay on his feet, and aimed his

gun toward Stranger below. Before he could squeeze the trigger, Stranger fired again, putting the slug into Layton's heart. The killer peeled headfirst from his perch and hit the floor with a loud *whump*.

Ivan Charles watched more than two dozen men charge through the door. They quickly gathered around John Stranger, who was kneeling beside the man who looked exactly like Payton Sturgis.

John looked up at the circle of men and said, "He's dead. Praise the Lord, the horror is over."

Lake Johnson glanced toward the open door, and said, "It's all right, Mark . . . Frances. You can bring Jessie in. The so-called snow ghost is dead."

The men made an opening for the Westbrooks. Jessie's face contorted as she looked down at Layton's body. "It's really over, isn't it?" she said in a half-whisper.

"Yes, honey," Stranger said. "It's over."

As Stranger stood up, Sheriff Johnson said, "All right, John. What do you know about this snow ghost? We're all dying to know who he is."

Stranger glanced back at the undertaker, who looked quite ill, then said, "Well, too many people who had actually seen this snow ghost said it was Payton. Ivan told me Payton had no siblings. Tonight, I finally decided the killer had to be his identical twin and that Ivan had lied to me about Payton having no siblings."

All faces turned toward Ivan, who looked at the ground.

"Ivan was in on the whole thing. He was the accomplice I said had to be involved in this. He fed the killer information about everything going on in this town.

"When I went to Ivan's apartment about an hour and a half ago, I confronted him and told him I knew he had lied to me. He tried to overpower me, and I had to knock him out.

When he came to, he was scared. He admitted his part in it, and asked if I would put in a good word for him if he tried to help save Jessie's life. I told him I couldn't guarantee how the new judge might look at it, but I promised to try to save him from the noose."

"Well, we're not going to try him here and now, much as some of us might like to," Lake Johnson said. "Let's break this up, and all of you go home and get a good night's sleep . . . maybe the best night's sleep you've had in a long time."

"We want to hear the whole story, Sheriff," someone said.

"You can read it in my paper tomorrow," Cliff Morgan said.

At the sheriff's office, Ivan Charles sat on a chair, still handcuffed. John Stranger, Lake Johnson, Monte Dixon, and Cliff Morgan sat down in front of him.

"Okay, Ivan," Lake said. "Come clean."

Ivan's face was pale and drawn as he began speaking. "My real name is Ivan Charles Kostinov."

Lake's eyes fluttered. "Kostinov! Kostin—Turk Kostin! You're related to Turk Kostin?"

"Yes," Ivan said. "Turk was my brother. We came from Russia as boys, and we Americanized our name. I had a carpenter shop in a small Kansas town, but I was unhappy with it and was looking to relocate. Turk had moved to Butte City. He saw the potential for me here, so he wrote me, saying I should come and open up a carpentry shop."

Cliff Morgan wrote furiously to capture the man's story.

"I arrived here just after the people of this town hanged my brother for a crime he didn't commit." Ivan's eyes flashed with anger. "Of course, you all know that now. The whole town was in an uproar when I arrived here. They had just found out they'd hanged an innocent man. But Turk is dead, and he can't come back! My brother was a gentle soul who wouldn't hardly swat a fly."

"So you decided to get even," Lake said.

"I vowed to stay in Butte City and find a way to get revenge. When I hired Payton, I had no idea he had a quirk in his mind and was a psychopathic killer. As time passed, and people were being murdered, I never dreamed my assistant was the killer. Right after the ninth victim had been murdered, I found evidence in Payton's room, proving he was the killer."

"So you used him to get your revenge on the town," Stranger said.

"I let Payton know that I had found him out, then explained who I really was. I offered him money to kill the sheriff, the judge, and the jurymen who had wrongfully put Turk to death. As it turned out, these were the same fourteen men, plus you, John, who would put Payton to death."

Ivan adjusted his position on the chair. "Well, Payton agreed to murder anyone I told him to, for the money. He then told me he had an identical twin brother named Layton. Both of them had been professional killers in New York City. They had almost been caught, and fled west from the law. They were separated during a gun battle with police in Kansas City. Payton had no choice but to keep running. He headed further west, not knowing whether his twin was dead or alive, and ended up in Butte City."

"How fortunate for us," Lake said.

Ivan's expression didn't change. "When John tracked down Payton and he was hanged, I still wanted revenge for my brother. I contacted a friend of mine who ran a detective agency in Chicago. Met him when I first came to this country. I asked him if he could find out if Layton Sturgis had been killed by police in Kansas City. When my detective friend wrote back that Layton was alive and at large, I offered him a substantial amount of money to find Layton and put me in contact with him."

"You didn't have the stomach to do these killings yourself," Lake said.

Ivan looked down and shook his head no.

"You must've felt pretty sure of getting this contact with Layton and hiring him to do the killing," John said.

"Well, yes, but why do you say that?"

"Because it had to have been along there somewhere that you exhumed Payton's body from the grave so the coffin would be empty when your snow ghost started his killing spree. I'd say you dug it up some dark night before the mound was settled, so no one would notice it."

Charles nodded that Stranger was right.

"So what did you do with the body?" Monte asked.

"Buried it in the forest north of here, in a spot where it would never be found."

"So why the snow ghost thing?" Stranger asked.

"Well, since Payton always did his killing during a snowstorm, and I knew about the Crows' snow ghost legend, I figured such an approach would frighten the town."

"How long did it take to find Layton?" Dixon asked.

"About two years. Layton came to Butte City by night and knocked on the door of my apartment. My detective friend in Chicago had given him my address. I kept him in my apartment. Little by little I was able to acquaint him with the faces of every man on my list. He could see them from the upstairs windows when they were on the street in front of the shop. I worked hard at getting every one of them positioned where Layton could see their faces."

Lake Johnson shook his head in amazement. "You sure

went to a lot of trouble to get your revenge, Ivan."

Ivan didn't reply.

"The work orders you showed the sheriff," Stranger said. "I suppose you had Layton write those up so that when we compared the note he left at Dan Cogan's, the handwriting and signature would match."

"Yes. They were faked to make our ruse look perfect. Layton also did the inscribing of the grave markers at the cemetery."

Cliff Morgan's hand was getting tired, but he continued to scribble fast to get it all down. Now he looked up and ran his gaze to the sheriff, then to the undertaker. "Anything else?"

"Guess not," Ivan said.

"All right. My staff and I will work on this all night if we have to, but we'll have it in tomorrow's paper. The people of this town deserve to know all the facts."

The courtroom was packed three days later as Ivan Charles sat behind the defendant's table without counsel. Judge Wilbur P. Coggins presided over the trial, which took little more than an hour.

Charles had pleaded guilty of conspiracy to commit murder, and the jury pronounced him guilty as charged. Every eye in the courtroom stayed fixed on Judge Coggins waiting for him to pronounce the sentence.

"Will the defendant please rise?" Coggins said.

Sheriff Johnson stood next to Charles when he rose to his feet.

Judge Coggins fixed the tall Russian with a penetrating glare and said, "Ivan Charles Kostinov, you have pleaded guilty of conspiracy to commit murder before this court. Seldom is this charge met with anything but a death penalty. Do you understand that?"

"Yes, your honor," Charles replied, sounding remorseful.

"However, this court has heard testimony from Mr. John Stranger that you cooperated with him to save the life of Miss Jessie Westbrook, who was held captive by Layton Sturgis in the Cogan barn. Mr. Stranger has testified that you did attempt to persuade Sturgis to set Miss Westbrook free. The young lady is in this courtroom, alive and unharmed, and Mr. Stranger has testified that you had a hand in keeping her alive."

Charles's expression was unreadable as he waited.

"Because of this cooperation, Mr. Kostinov, and because Mr. Stranger has asked for leniency based on that cooperation, I am going to bypass the death sentence."

Ivan's body slumped a little with relief.

"As temporary judge of Silver Bow County, Mr. Kostinov, I hereby sentence you to be incarcerated in the Montana Territorial Prison at Deer Lodge for the rest of your natural life. There will be no chance of parole."

Coggins banged the gavel on the desk and pronounced the court adjourned.

Early the next morning, Ivan Charles Kostinov was sitting on his cot in a jail cell when he heard the door to the office open and close. Footsteps approached, and John Stranger appeared outside the cell.

Ivan looked at Stranger through the bars and noted the Bible in his hand.

"I'm catching the stage to Billings in an hour, Ivan. I didn't want to leave without talking to you. First, I want to thank you for helping me save Jessie's life."

"You're welcome, John," Ivan said. "It saved my own life, too, thanks to you."

"Second, I—"

"I don't want to hear it, John."

"Hear what?"

"That Bible stuff. I don't believe it."

"Do you believe you will die someday?"

"Of course. Everybody has to die."

"And then what?"

"I'm dead like a dog. No heaven, no hell. Like a dog, John, and that's the end of me."

"You're wrong, Ivan. By the very fact that Jesus Christ died and came back from the dead, we know there's an afterlife. God in His Word says—"

Ivan leaped to his feet. "I don't want to hear it, John! Thanks for saving my life, but don't try to save my soul!"

"I can't save your soul, Ivan, but God's Son can, and He *will* if you'll let Him."

"Good-bye, John!" Kostinov wheeled about and returned to his cot. "This conversation is over."

Stranger looked at the man with compassion but said no more. Quietly, he turned and left the cellblock.

The stage was due to leave at 8:30. At twenty minutes after eight, John Stranger came out of the stage office, carrying his bags. The shotgunner took them from him and placed them in the boot.

The whole town had gathered to see him off. At the front of the crowd was Pastor Walker and his wife, along with Sheriff Lake Johnson. Lawton and Jenny Haymes stood close by. Jenny was describing the scene to Lawton. Next to them were Mark and Frances Westbrook, with their daughter, Jessie, and Monte Dixon.

The stage driver and the shotgunner waited patiently as Pastor Walker raised his voice so all could hear. "John," he said, "this town owes you a debt we can never repay, but one thing we can do is tell you that we love you, and thank you from the bottom of our hearts for coming here and ridding us of the snow ghost."

"God bless you, John!" Georgene Pederson called out.

Voices lifted in thanks from all areas of the crowd.

"I'm glad I could have a hand in it," John said, "but I want all of you to thank God and praise His name for our victory. May you all rest easy now, and have happy lives!"

Suddenly Jessie Westbrook and Monte Dixon approached Stranger, who smiled at them.

"Mr. Stranger," Monte said, "I want to thank you for leading me to the Lord."

"It was my privilege, Monte."

"And I want to thank you for saving my life," Jessie said, raising on tiptoe to kiss his cheek.

When Jessie stepped back, Lake Johnson moved in and wrapped his arms around Stranger, pounding him on the back. "Thanks for coming back when I needed you, John. You're a real friend."

"Anytime," Stranger said.

The tall man turned back to Jessie and Monte. "You two follow the Lord's leading in your lives, won't you?"

"We will, sir," Monte said.

"You do, and I have a feeling one day you'll meet at the marriage altar."

They smiled at him and then exchanged loving glances with each other. "You're right about that," Monte said.

Tom McVicker pressed to the front of the crowd with Nadine at his side. "John!" he said, loud enough for all to hear. "You and Pastor Walker were right. You said the killer was a mortal man—that nobody comes back from the dead!"

Stranger smiled. "The only Person who ever brought Himself back from the dead was the Lord Jesus Christ.

Nobody else has, and nobody else ever will!"

The crowd cheered as Stranger stepped into the coach and closed the door. The cheers were punctuated by voices calling out their good-byes as the driver and shotgunner climbed up into the box.

John lifted his hand as the stage pulled away and kept waving until the crowd passed from view.

CHAPTER

TWENTY-THREE

The stagecoach carrying John Stranger rumbled through the canyons of the Rockies toward Billings. John thanked the Lord for sparing his life in the Cogan barn, and even more, that Jessie Westbrook had not been harmed. It felt good to know that the people of Butte City could get their lives back to normal.

Soon John's thoughts turned to Breanna. He thanked God that she was waiting for him in Denver. The thought of marrying her thrilled him.

As the coach descended from the mountains, his eye caught movement on the wind-swept, snow-covered prairie. A small herd of wild horses stood on a rise, watching the stage. A white stallion reared, pawed the air, and whinnied.

John smiled as he beheld the animal's beauty. *So you're the leader of the pack, are you, big boy?* he thought. His mind naturally went to Chance, the black stallion who had saved his life last summer. *Where are you this morning, Chance, ol' boy?* he wondered. *Running wild and free somewhere north of here, and leading your herd in God's Big Sky country.*

The stage changed horses at Bozeman, and the fresh team quickly put miles behind them as they galloped across the rolling Montana prairie.

It was midafternoon when the stage rolled into Billings.

John took his luggage from the shotgunner's hands and headed along the east edge of town toward the railroad station. The train from Cheyenne City wouldn't arrive in Billings until almost five o'clock, and it wouldn't pull out until six-thirty. John had nearly four hours to wait.

He strolled about the town and occasionally greeted people. He was still a ways from the depot when he saw the Billings Cattle and Horse Trading Company's corrals and barns across the road to the east. There were about fifty cowboys lined up along the fence at the largest corral. They were shouting and cheering as one of their own rode a bucking horse.

John crossed the road and walked toward the corral. As he drew near, he saw a smaller corral, where some twenty mares were penned up. He blinked when he recognized one of the mares. She had run with Chance! Her markings were too unique to mistake.

John hastened toward the smaller corral and saw another mare who had followed Chance, then another, and another.

A cowboy came out of the small log cabin that served as the office and nodded a greeting. John hurried toward him and said, "Do you work for this company?"

"Sure do, pardner. You look to be afoot. You in the market for a horse?"

"Ah . . . no. I'm taking this evening's train to Cheyenne City, then going on to Denver. But I'd like to ask you something."

The roar of the cheering cowboys filled the air.

"These mares . . . I saw them last summer, running wild with a big black stallion up north of here. Fella couldn't mistake them."

"That's for sure," the cowboy said. "My boss and some of

the men were up in the north country a couple weeks ago and rounded up this herd." He paused and extended his hand. "I'm Lefty Durham."

"Just call me John." Stranger set down his bags and shook the cowboy's hand. "Lefty, your boss didn't happen to bring in their leader, did he?"

Durham grinned. "He sure did."

John's heart leaped in his chest. "Is he still here?"

"I'll say he is. All these mares have been broken to the saddle. But not their leader. That big black beast is meaner'n a snake. Nobody's been able to break him. They can't stay on his back long enough."

"Is that so?"

"Yeah. Twenty-two men have tried to ride him. In fact, number twenty-three is over there tryin' to ride him now. That's what all the hollerin' is about."

Lefty could tell by the shouts that the rider had just been thrown. He laughed. "Well, there'll be another poor sucker try here in a minute or two. He'll get throwed, too. That black devil ain't never gonna let nobody stay on his back."

Stranger grinned. "I'd say that must be some kind of horse if twenty-three men can't break him."

"That he is. In fact, the contest now is for ownership."

"What do you mean . . . contest?"

"Well, the big black has become somewhat of a legend around here. My boss, Biff Symonds, has announced that he'll flat give that horse to the first man who rides and tames him."

The cheers had subsided, but now picked up again.

"I want to see this," John said.

Lefty chuckled and motioned for John to follow him. As they drew up to the large corral, John looked over the fence and his blood warmed at the sight of the big stallion who had carried him out of the forest fire.

Chance! he thought. You big beautiful piece of God's creation!

The stallion bucked savagely as he bounded across the corral. Suddenly the rider went sailing through the air and landed hard on the ground. Chance snorted, pawed earth, and trotted away, dragging the reins on the ground.

John wondered if Chance would remember him. If he could get in on the contest . . .

Suddenly the cowboy stood to his feet as his friends kidded him from behind the fence. His face was purple with anger. He ran to Chance and picked up the reins, cursing him.

Chance laid back his ears and whinnied as the cowboy held the reins and jerked off his belt. All the other cowboys went quiet as the angry rider began striking the horse across the face with his belt.

"Hey!" Stranger shouted, dropping his bags and vaulting the fence.

Biff Symonds had opened the gate to charge in and stop the rider, but John was ahead of him. When Stranger reached the cowboy, he jerked the belt out of the man's hand and sent a hissing punch to his jaw that laid him flat on his back.

Chance backed away, wheeled, and trotted to the farthest side of the corral. He stood there pawing the ground.

Symonds drew up to Stranger and said, "I don't know who you are, mister, but thanks for knockin' his block off. He had it comin'." Then he looked toward the crowd of cowboys and said, "Couple of you boys come and drag this guy outta here!"

When Symonds turned back to John, he saw him staring at the stallion. "Some animal, eh?"

Stranger nodded. "Yes, sir. Your man Lefty Durham just

told me you've offered to give him to the man who rides and breaks him."

"That's for sure. The man who can do it deserves to own him."

"How many more are standing in line?"

"None. You want to try it?"

"Yes, I do."

"Well, it's your life and limbs. What's your name, stranger?"

"That's good enough."

"What?"

"Just call me Stranger. John Stranger."

"Okay, John Stranger, you want to be the next victim?"

"Sure."

Symonds looked toward the men at the fence. "We've got another taker, guys! This fella wants to see if he can ride the big black!"

Cheers went up.

John headed toward Chance, who was still on the far side of the corral. Symonds headed for the gate, laughing. "Well, boys, that guy says his name is John Stranger. He'll be victim number twenty-five!"

Chance was breathing hard and nickering as John drew near. The horse had not looked directly at him until that moment. Now his ears pricked up, and his whinny came out deep and low.

John smiled as Chance began bobbing his head. "Hey, big guy, you *do* remember me, don't you?"

The stallion moved toward John, and when they came together, Chance whinnied soft and low again. The cowboys watched, awestruck, as the man in black stroked the stallion's face while speaking to him in soft tones.

"Well, ol' boy," John said, patting the horse's muscular

neck, "you let me ride you once to save my life. How about a second time, so I can take you home with me?"

Chance nickered affectionately, bobbing his head.

The crowd of horsemen stood spellbound as they watched the tall stranger place his foot in the stirrup and swing aboard. The stallion remained calm and obeyed Stranger's touch as he trotted toward the gate and the bunched-up cowhands.

Stranger reined in at the gate and said to Biff Symonds, "If you'll open the gate for me and my horse, Mr. Symonds, I'll appreciate it."

A wide-eyed Symonds opened the gate and said, "Mister, you can have the bridle and saddle, too."

Stranger smiled broadly as he nudged Chance out of the corral and drew rein where he had left his two bags. As he started to dismount under the admiring gaze of the crowd, Symonds hurried to him with Lefty at his side, and said, "Stay in the saddle, Mr. John Stranger. Lefty and I will carry your bags to the depot for you."

The tall man in black was the talk of the crowd as he rode the stallion away, followed by the two men who carried his luggage. At the depot, Biff and Lefty told Stranger good-bye and headed back for the corrals.

John went to the ticket office, paid to have a stock car attached to the train, then rode Chance around town for a while.

The train arrived on schedule, and after the stock car had been coupled to it, Stranger led Chance into the car, which was equipped with a feed trough. While the big black stallion munched on hay, Stranger patted his neck and said, "Just wait, ol' pal. Breanna's wanted to meet you ever since last summer. She's going to be so excited when I give you to her for an early wedding present!"

Chance nickered and bobbed his head as if he understood.